WILD BEASTS

Photographs by Nicolas Bruant
Introduction by John Heminway

CHRONICLE BOOKS
SAN FRANCISCO

Photographs copyright ©1993 by Nicolas Bruant.

All rights reserved. No part of this book may be reproduced without written permission from the Publisher.

Printed in Hong Kong.

Translation and informational captions by Laure Oliver.
Book and cover design by Gail Grant.

Library of Congress Cataloging-in-Publication Data:
Bruant, Nicolas.
   Wild beasts / by Nicolas Bruant; with an introduction by John Heminway.
   p. cm.
   ISBN 0-8118-0490-9
   1. Wildlife photography—Africa.   I. Title
TR729.W54B78 1993
779'.32—dc20   92-37888
                     CIP

Distributed in Canada by Raincoast Books,
112 East Third Avenue, Vancouver, B.C. V5T 1C8

10 9 8 7 6 5 4 3 2 1

Chronicle Books
275 Fifth Street
San Francisco, CA 94103

A André Martin, mon bon maître.

I would like to thank Jean Pierre Van der Becke, my dear friend who has devoted his life to the gorillas in Rwanda; my thanks also go to Marie Josée Triboulet—she knows why; to Mr. and Mrs. Richard Stone; to Armand Deleuremé; and to Stratis Meimaridis, for all his invaluable and generous help in Kenya.

Contents

Preface

Introduction

Elephants & Hippopotamuses

Reptiles

Zebras, Antelopes & Gazelles

Cats

Gorillas

Buffalo & Wildebeests

Birds

Various Other Beasts

Captions

Bibliography

Preface

I was twenty years old when I discovered Africa for the first time. Working as an assistant to the French photographer André Martin, I had accompanied him to Kenya to take pictures of animals. The year was 1972, and I was far from imagining that I would spend three or four months out of each of the next twenty years in the parks and reserves of Kenya, Tanzania, and Zaire.

My first African experience was seeing before me everything I'd ever dreamed of since my earliest childhood. In my imagination, Africa had been first and foremost a landscape and an atmosphere. And so it was: vast, green expanses that pushed endlessly against the horizon; the dizzying cliffs of the Rift Valley; a silence from the beginning of time or a silence of watching and waiting; and hundreds and hundreds of miles of parks and nature reserves, all without people. On my first trips to Africa, I would go, sometimes for three weeks at a time, without seeing another human being.

Later I came to know eastern Africa better, this cradle of humanity where I would spend a quarter of my life. I'd have to write another book to relate what I've learned beyond my photographic work. In large measure, my impressions echo the concerns expressed by John Heminway in his introduction to this book: the poaching and premeditated, wholesale slaughter of Africa's animal populations. But, I would add two more issues, which are at the same time fundamental and paradoxical: the disappearance of entire *human* populations from the Sahara—nomads decimated by desertion and civil strife, such as the horrifying civil war in Somalia; and Kenya's population explosion, which threatens the country's animal species.

But in 1972, I came to Africa to photograph, and I had only one idea in mind: the animals. My work, like the trip itself, was an initiation. I was discovering a new world, and I had everything to learn. I realized how hard it is to tell a story through the photo of an animal. For example, the movie camera does a better job of capturing the slight movement of the elephant's trunk, foot, or head that bespeaks emotion or surprise. It was difficult for me to convey these movements or any others. I also discovered the challenge of

framing the subject, a factor that led me to be more selective in my shooting. Very often, watching the movement of the animal made me forget whatever aesthetic accident might be occurring. Suddenly, I had too many things to pull together: light, focus, expression, and surroundings, to say nothing of my own, almost pathological, anxiety every time I had to press the shutter. Out of this came the desire to narrow the scope, and, in some cases, to play down the background. I like the idea of zeroing in on a subject, of drawing the tightest possible line between the animal and myself, and getting directly to each animal's essence—or to my own—as the animal's intermediary. I had to trust that random chance could unite our wills, the animal's and my own.

Little by little, I understood certain things: that the most interesting way to photograph a wild cat is to emphasize its gaze rather than its body; whereas, in the case of hippopotamuses and impalas, the reverse is true.

From these considerations sprang the idea of the portrait, of seizing an instant in time. I wanted to present both the near-human gaze of the animal and an aesthetic rendering of the subject. I wanted to reveal the deadly razor stroke in the crocodile's eye and the subtly woven fabric of the elephant's skin.

The light in Africa is difficult for me. It flattens the landscape, stripping it of all nuance—not to mention how badly it affects the film. Thus, twenty years ago, I deliberately opted to work in black and white. The choice allowed me to enhance the strength of the images. Each portrait had to express a kind of contained power. I had to find a way to show how a lion, apart from its body or mane, is a lion. Above all, I had to show life! I am not a theoretician of photography. I am a traveler and a watcher.

Nicolas Bruant
Kiwayu, Kenya, 1992

INTRODUCTION

Amid these photographs I came upon an Africa I didn't at first recognize. The artist's technique, vision, and patience have elevated the humdrum into a fable, movement into disquiet, a returned stare into unfathomable wisdom. I'm not certain whether I'm altogether comfortable with the Africa I see in these pages. I do know it's timely, prescient, ominous—for me, a call to action.

Nicolas Bruant has stripped Africa of the treacly sentimentality so common to coffee-table books. His carnivores brood, his elephants stage a demonstration, and great crocodiles lie in wait. Indeed, Mr. Bruant seems to prefer animals equipped with heavy-scaled skin and Pleistocene minds. His marabou storks harken back to the Ancient Mariner's albatross, and his landscapes become an infant earth after the flood. In short, he has reduced Africa to pagan essentials.

Nicolas Bruant could not have produced this remarkable work at a more appropriate time. Africa is no longer an Eden; its national parks are no longer holy sights, but often war zones with wardens, poachers, and the occasional tourist at risk. Black rhinos—once, years ago, I saw 36 in a five-mile radius and thought nothing of it—are now down to 3,000 on the entire continent. Elephants survive by virtue of a heroic, but temporary, stay of execution. Mountain gorillas are caught in the crossfires of a deadly civil war. *Rattatat:* Africa has become a killing field where both animals and men are sacrificed on the altar of greed, power, and bloody-mindedness.

Something must be done, but what? Some may cry *aux armes,* but I feel Mr. Bruant is above such instincts. In these pictures, he says, "Wait a minute." His work urges me to resist easy answers: Kill the poachers, distribute birth control devices, amputate rhino horns, relocate people, throw the bastards in jail.

This is Africa, a continent that should keep its own counsel. As I write these words I am on a Kenyan balcony overlooking Lake Victoria—a gray, inland sea that until one hundred and twenty years ago had been seen by no more than half-a-dozen whites. Since then, a buccaneering century has taken its toll. The lake is today surrounded by intensive agriculture, adjoining cities reach for the sky. Everywhere: dams, power boats, and fishery experts.

Last night a fading sun laced by angry clouds made the lake's surface a gentle English watercolor. It was all so comprehensible and satisfying until a violent electrical storm, smelling of ionized rain, swept south. The lake turned mean. Rain spat through cracks in the cinderblock walls of my hotel room. Even with the windows closed, wind twisted the mosquito netting and thunder seemed ready to lunge across the balcony into my room.

For a moment I was certain the dams would burst and the lake would be restored to a pre-colonial past.

However, Lake Victoria may never regain its innocence. In its helter-skelter passage from a nineteenth-century geographer's trophy to the victim of good intentions, it has been despoiled far more severely than any lake in western Europe. Frankly, we outsiders have only ourselves to blame: In 1960, Nile perch, common to the north, were introduced into this lake to provide villagers with a dependable source of protein—no doubt, a worthy project. Today this exotic fish is held responsible for reducing and, in some cases, eliminating whole species of cyclads, or haplochlomines—small fish who served the lake by keeping algae in check. Currently, in bays and inlets, algae now blooms uncontrollably, robbing the lake of oxygen, shutting off life. There is talk these days that this lake, source of the Nile, demon quarry of Burton, Speke, Grant, Livingston, Baker, and Stanley, will soon fail to support even the likes of Nile perch who, we believe, were the engineers of the holocaust. In effect, Lake Victoria Nyanza is dying.

In *Wild Beasts,* I believe Mr. Bruant is imploring us to consider the consequences of well-intentioned hubris. His photographs proclaim that while Africa may have great needs, they may not always be served by our logic. Mr. Bruant ascribes a spectacular wisdom to what is so often portrayed as a dumb continent. Wildness, he demonstrates, cannot be a curiosity. It must be a solution.

I have no doubt Mr. Bruant's philanthropy in assigning a portion of his royalties to the African Wildlife Foundation is in response to our common dread—the fear that Africa will be manipulated by everyone but itself. Our Foundation's approach has always been modest—we work to make Africa realize its own solutions. For over thirty years, we have served as silent partners in enabling people of this continent to protect their threatened species and endangered landscapes. In the end, successes—and there have been many—belong not to us but, mercifully, to Africa.

Mr. Bruant, as a photographer, embraces a similar kind of anonymity. He stays out of focus in his pictures to reveal the essence of creature and place. He purposefully avoids pastels in favor of angry contrast. Africa, through his lens, becomes an electric storm threatening elegance and logic. It rattles the windows of our good intentions and makes us face the boom and brightness of a sensually new, but systematically, old land.

I am challenged by *Wild Beasts* and very grateful to Mr. Bruant's tenacity, insight, artistry, and generosity.

JOHN HEMINWAY
Chairman, African Wildlife Foundation, 1992

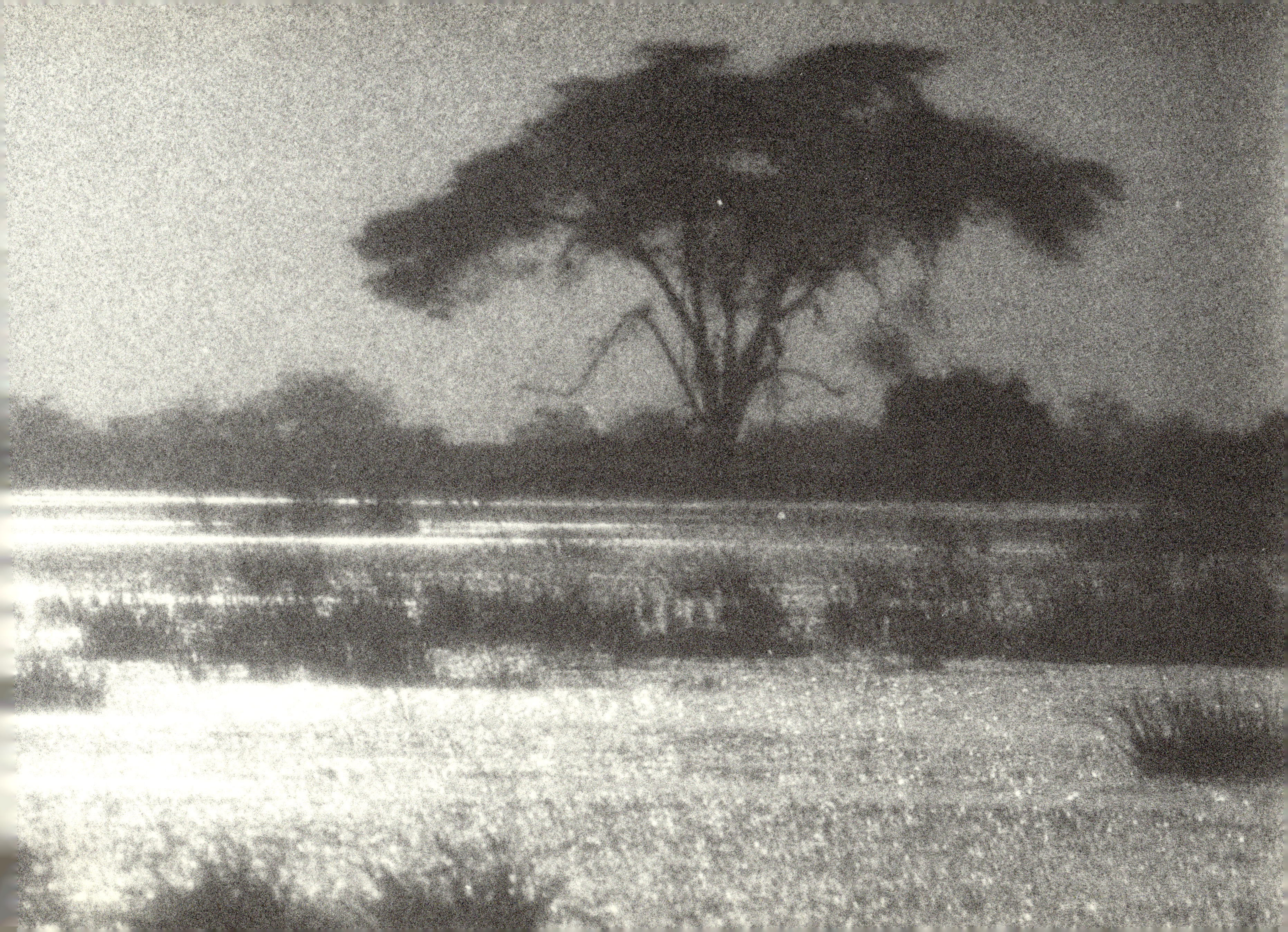

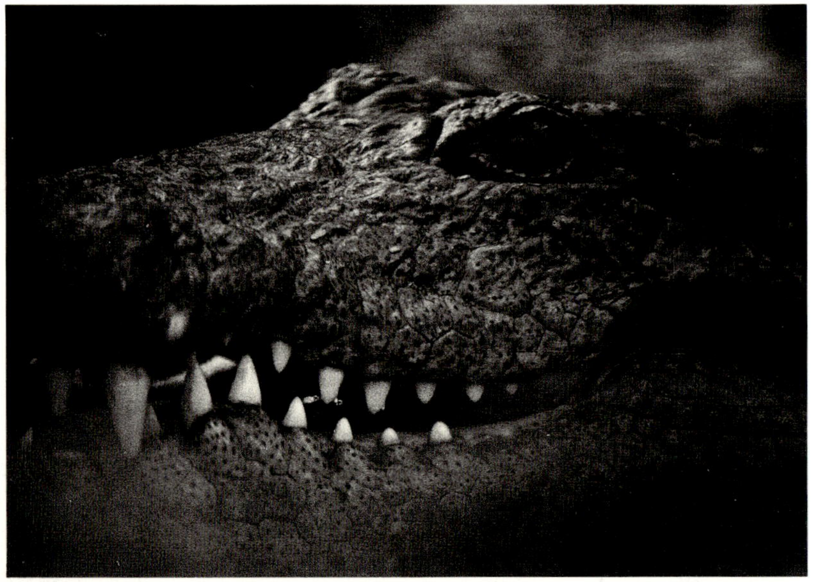

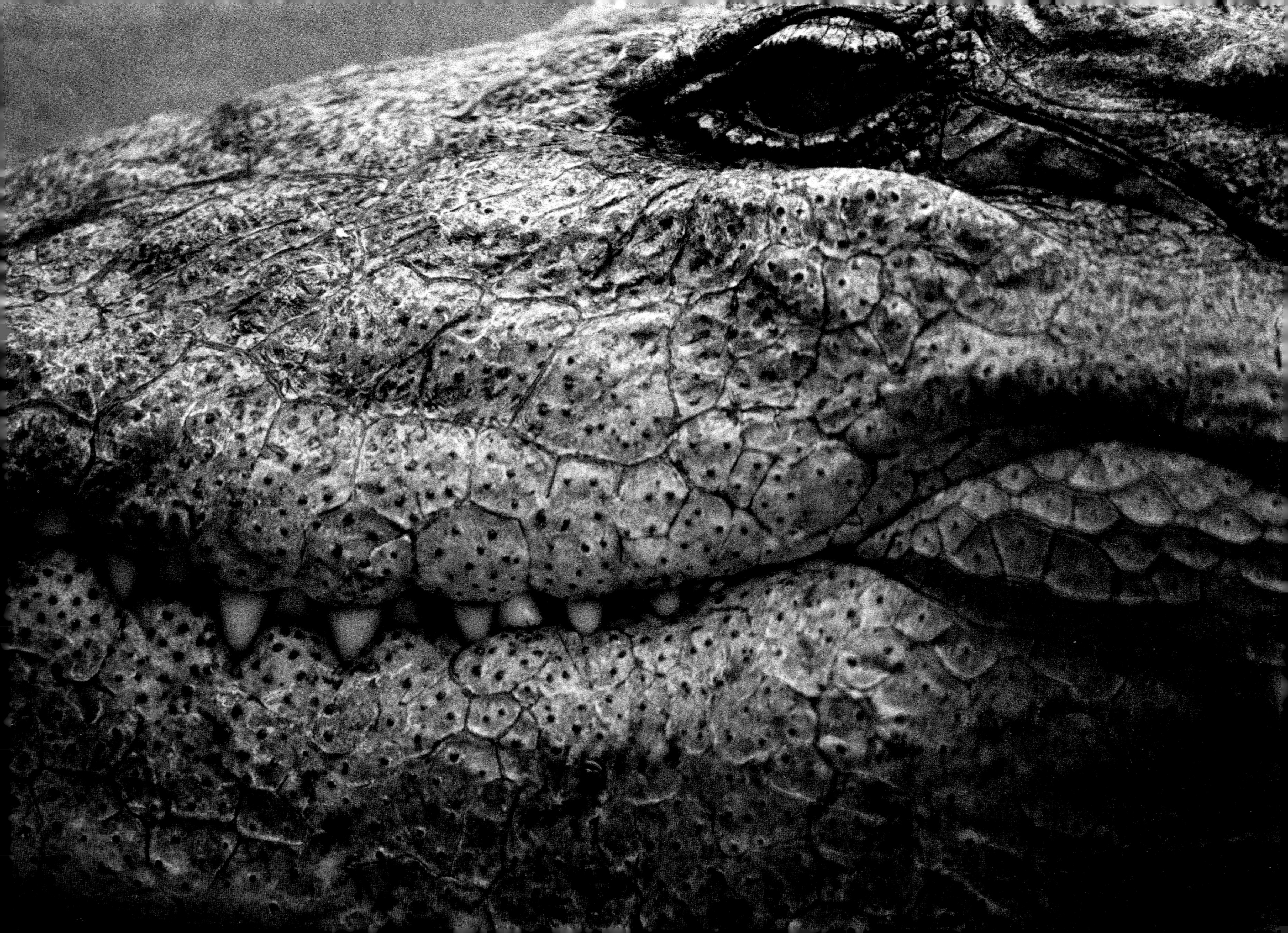

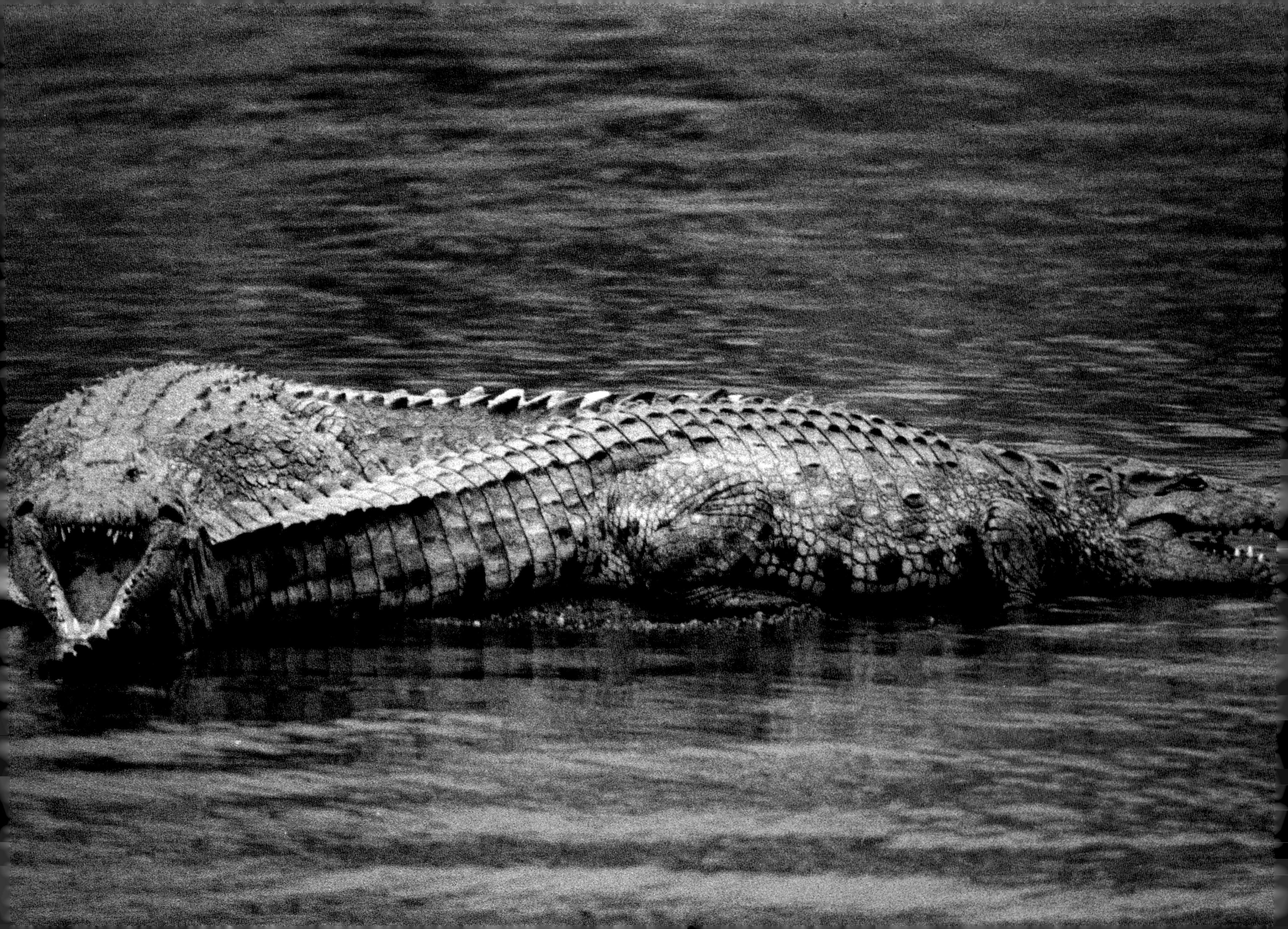

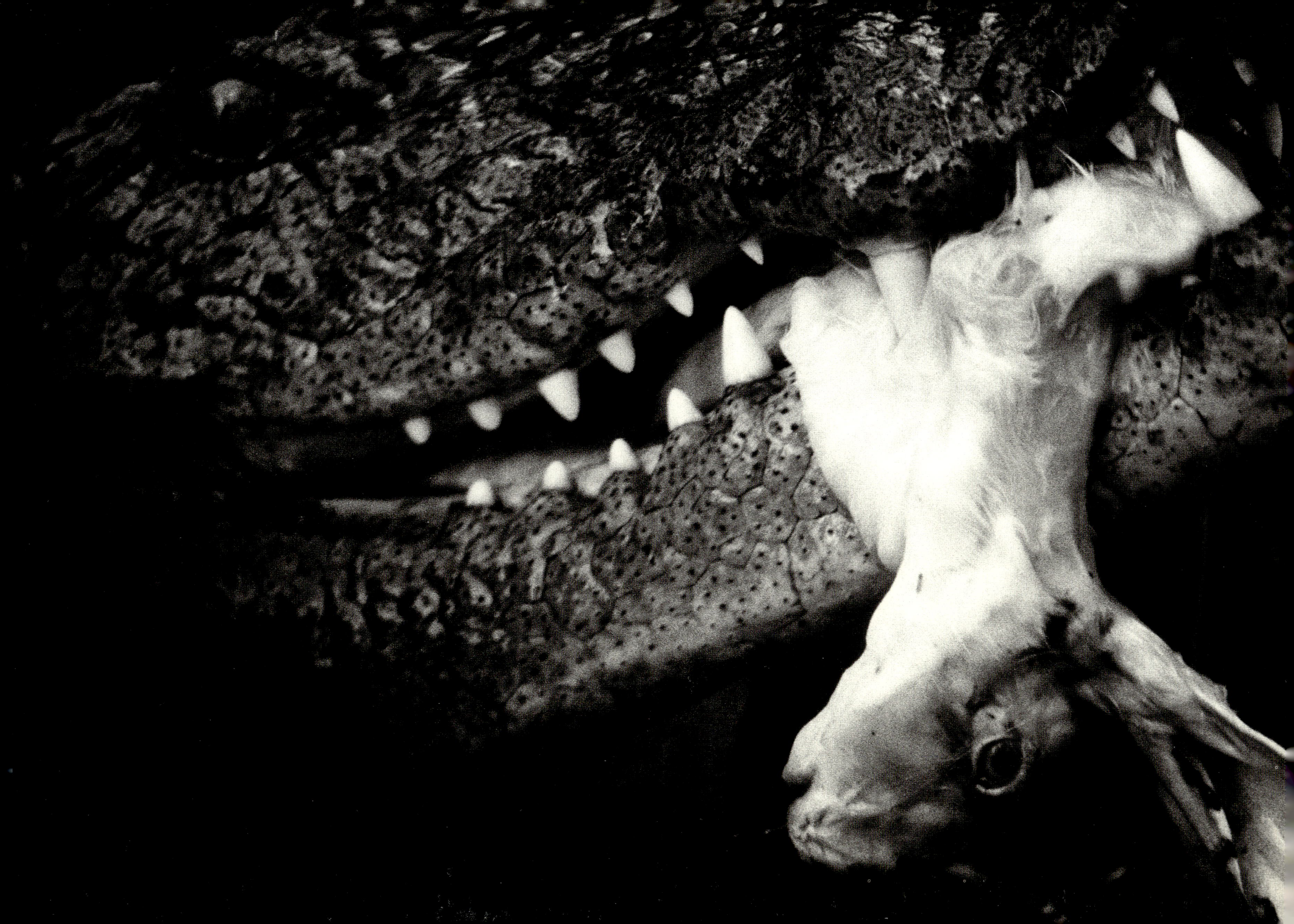

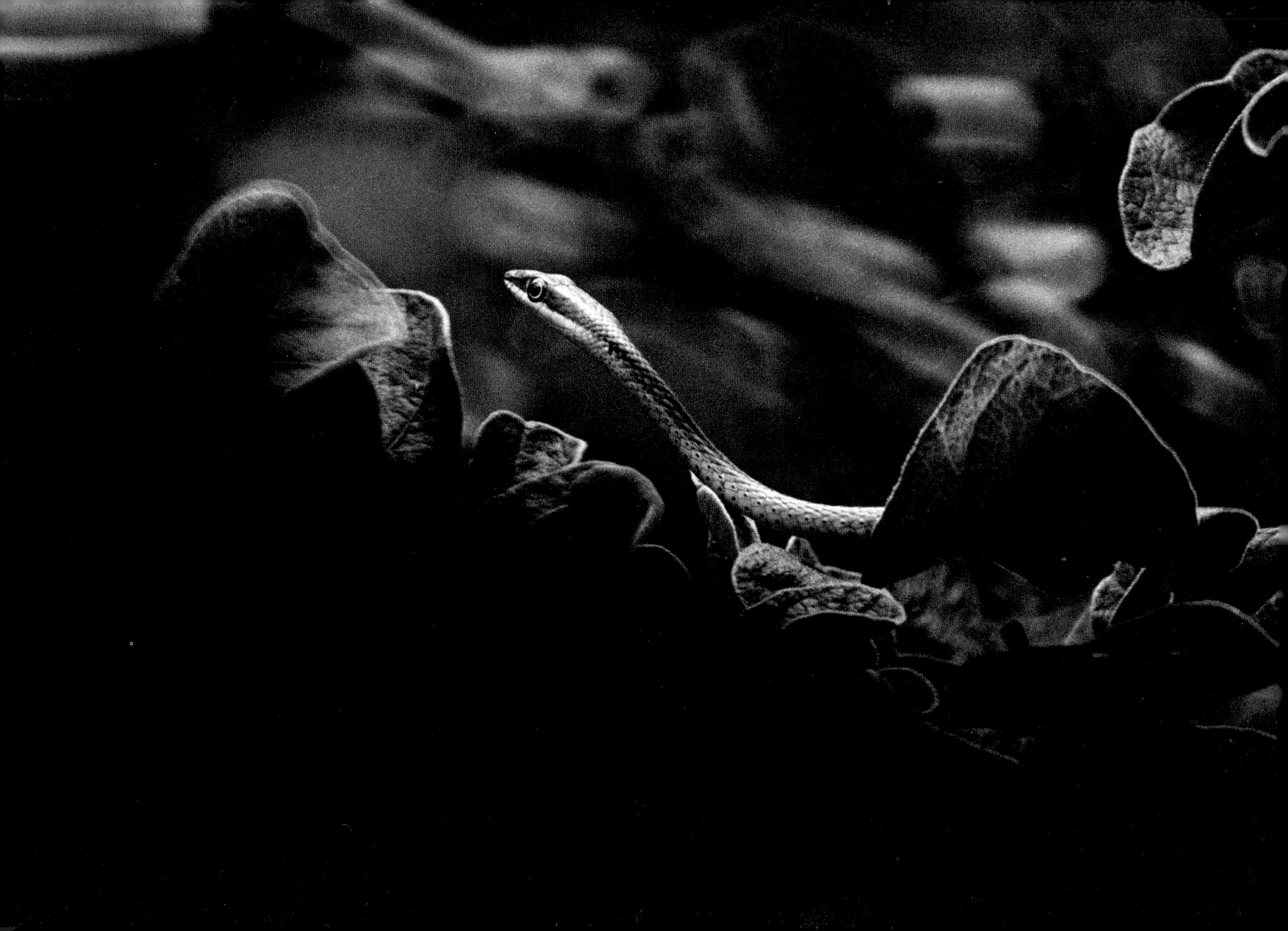

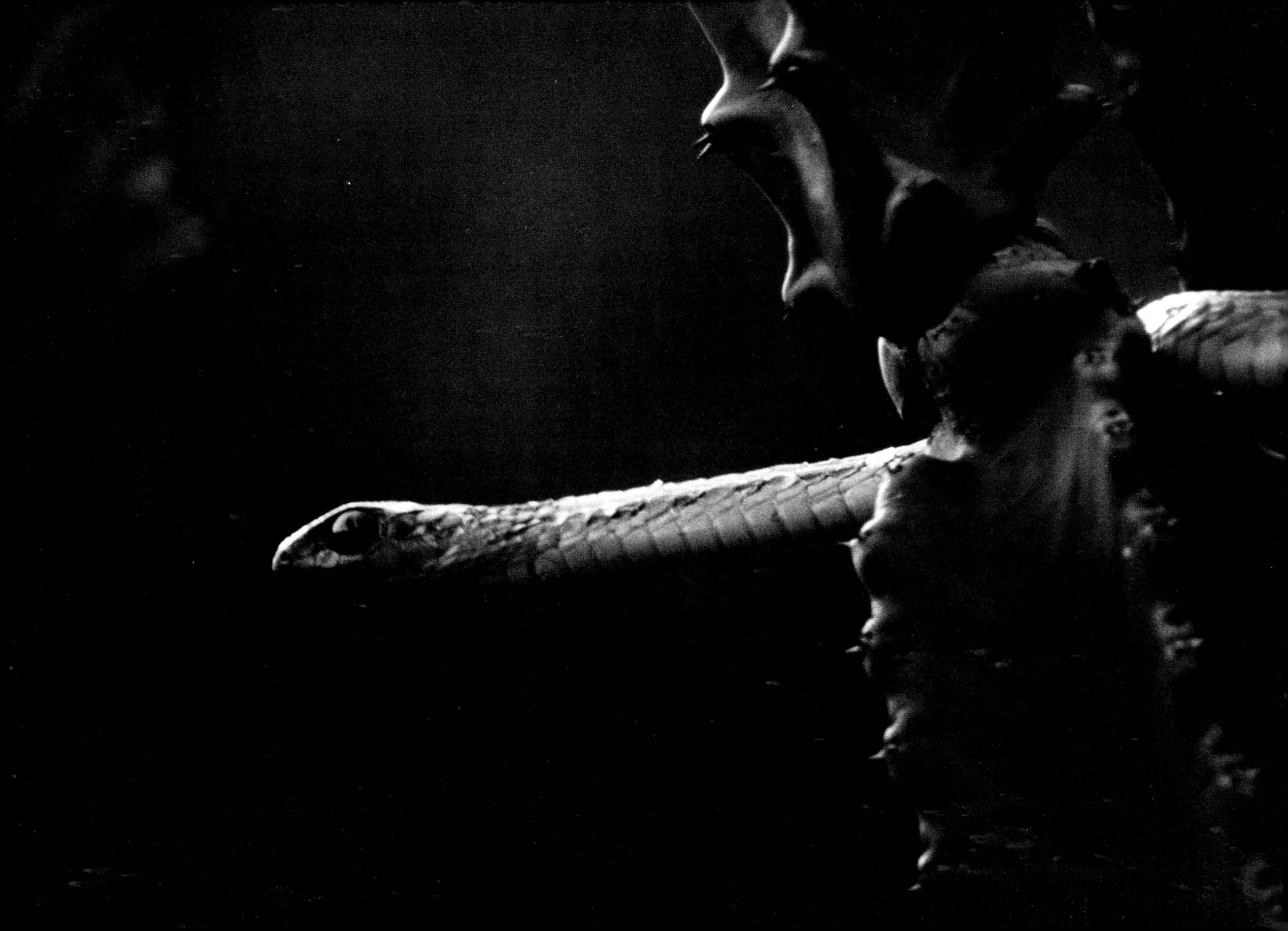

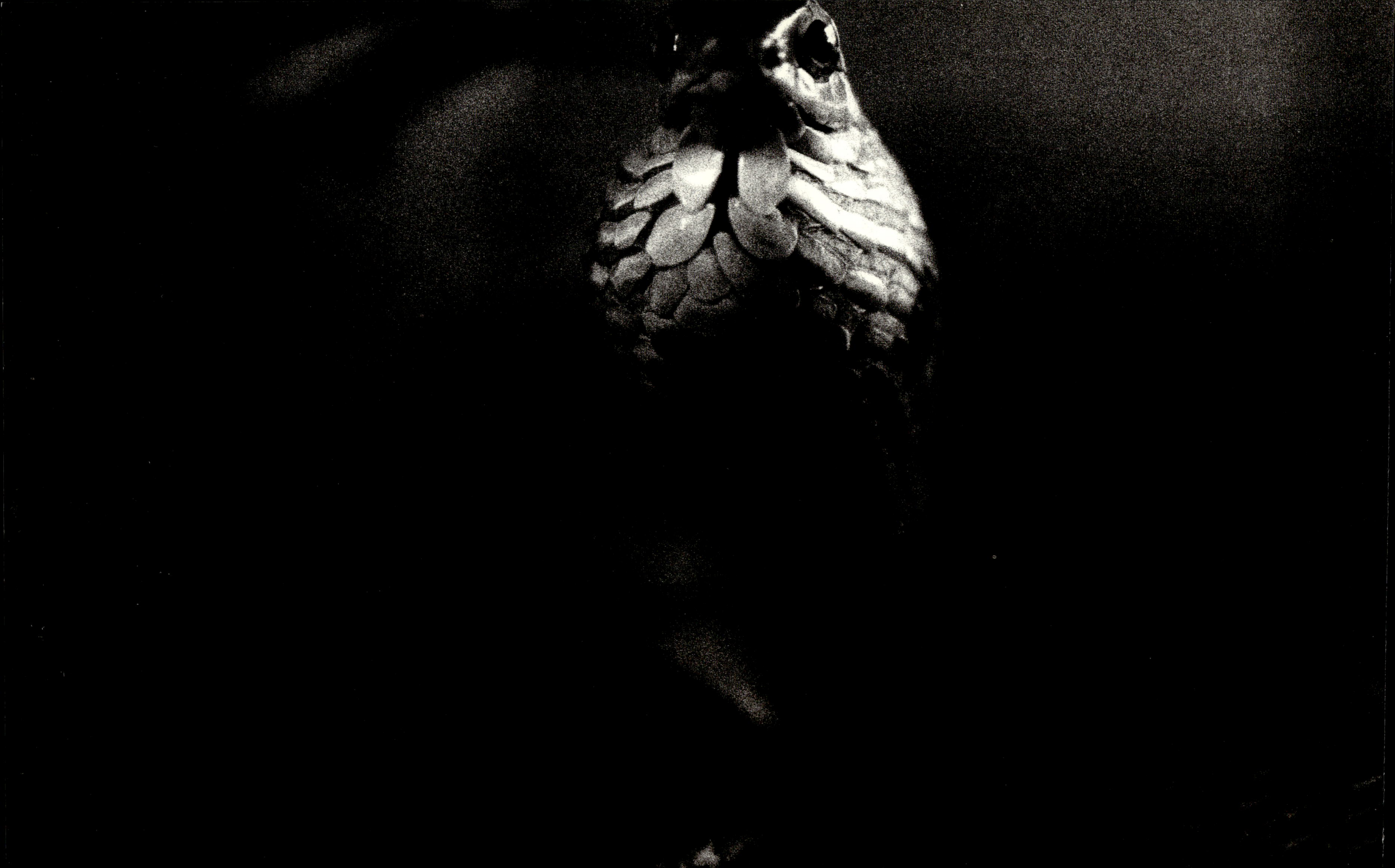

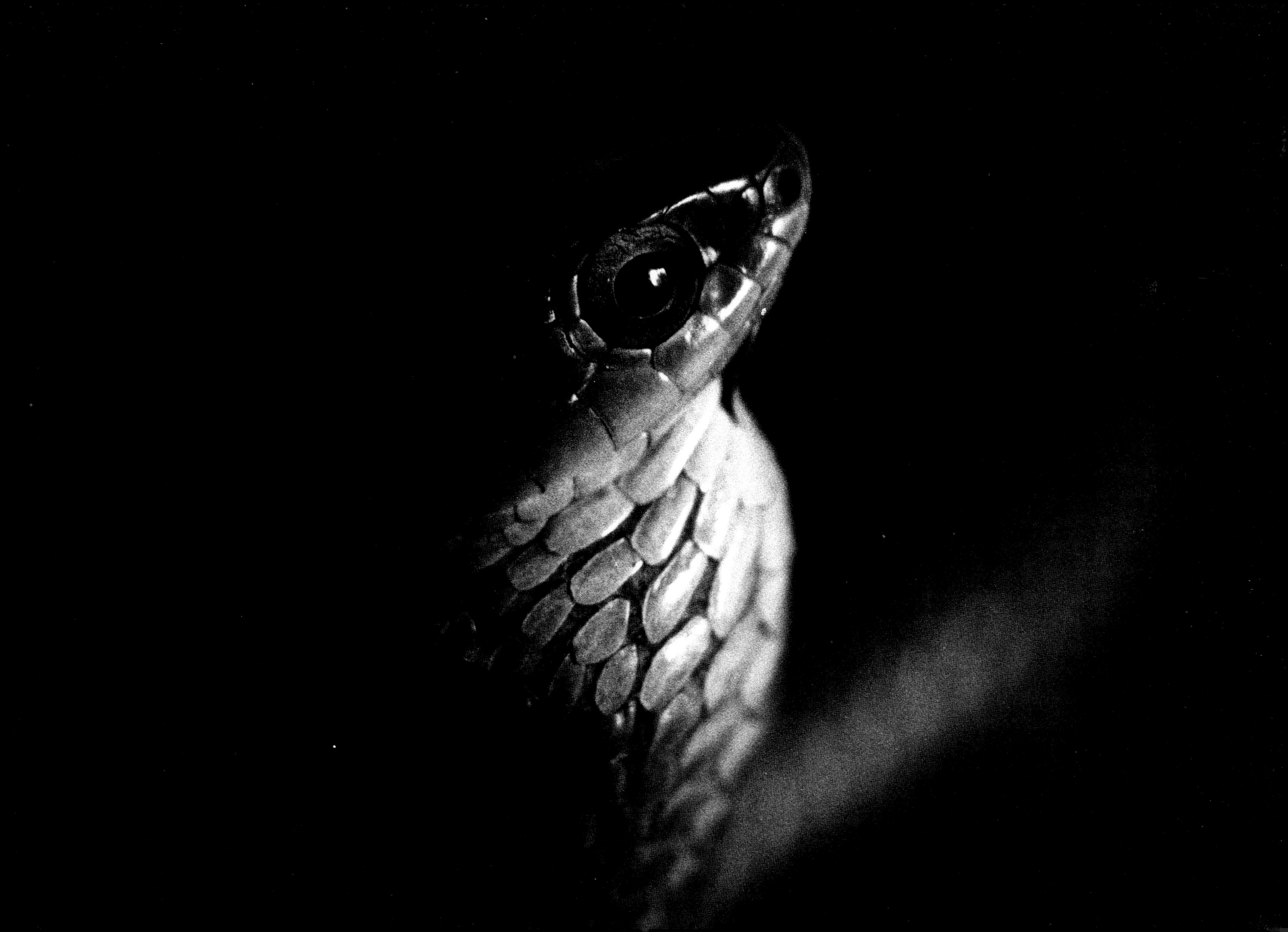

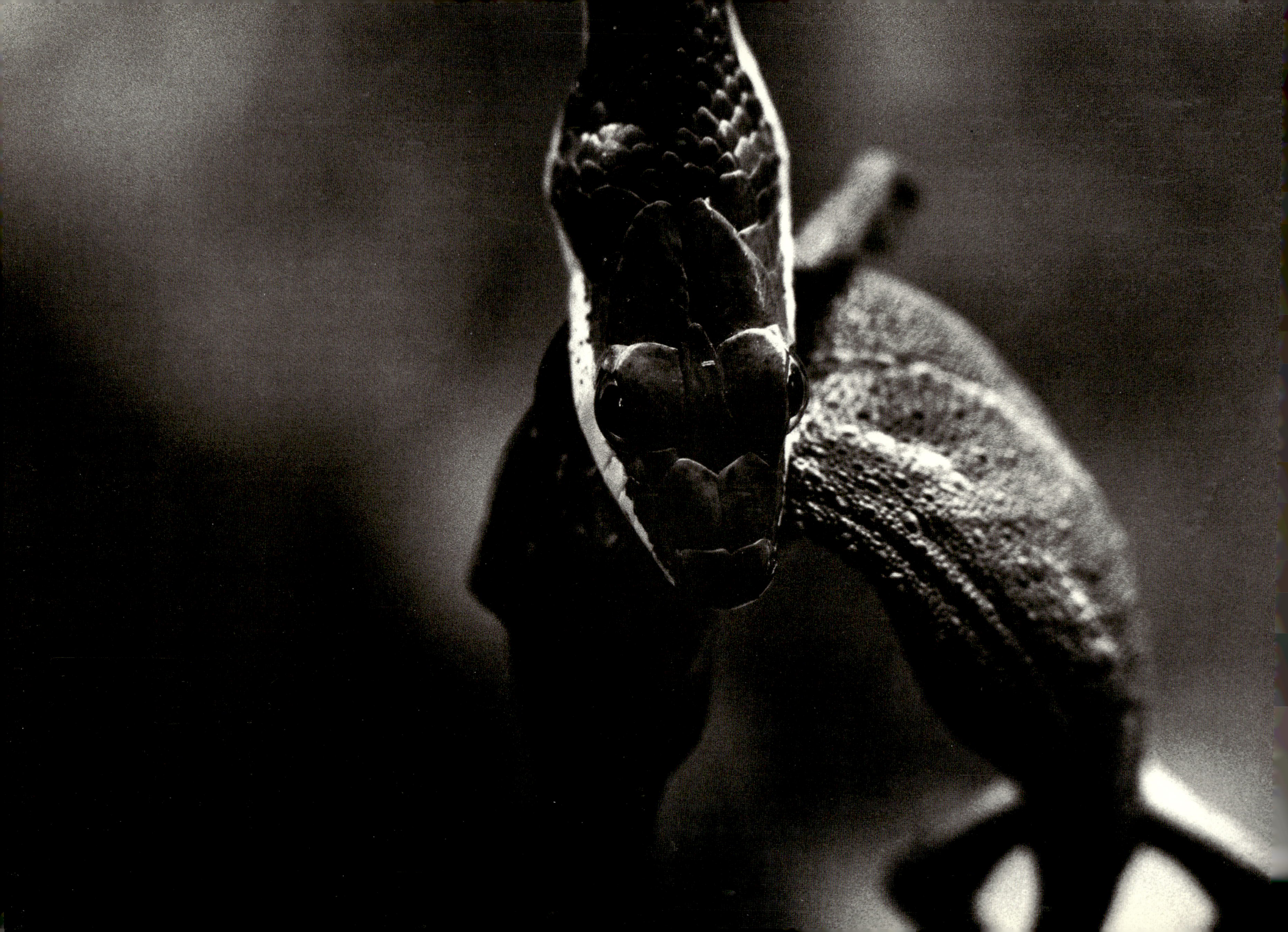

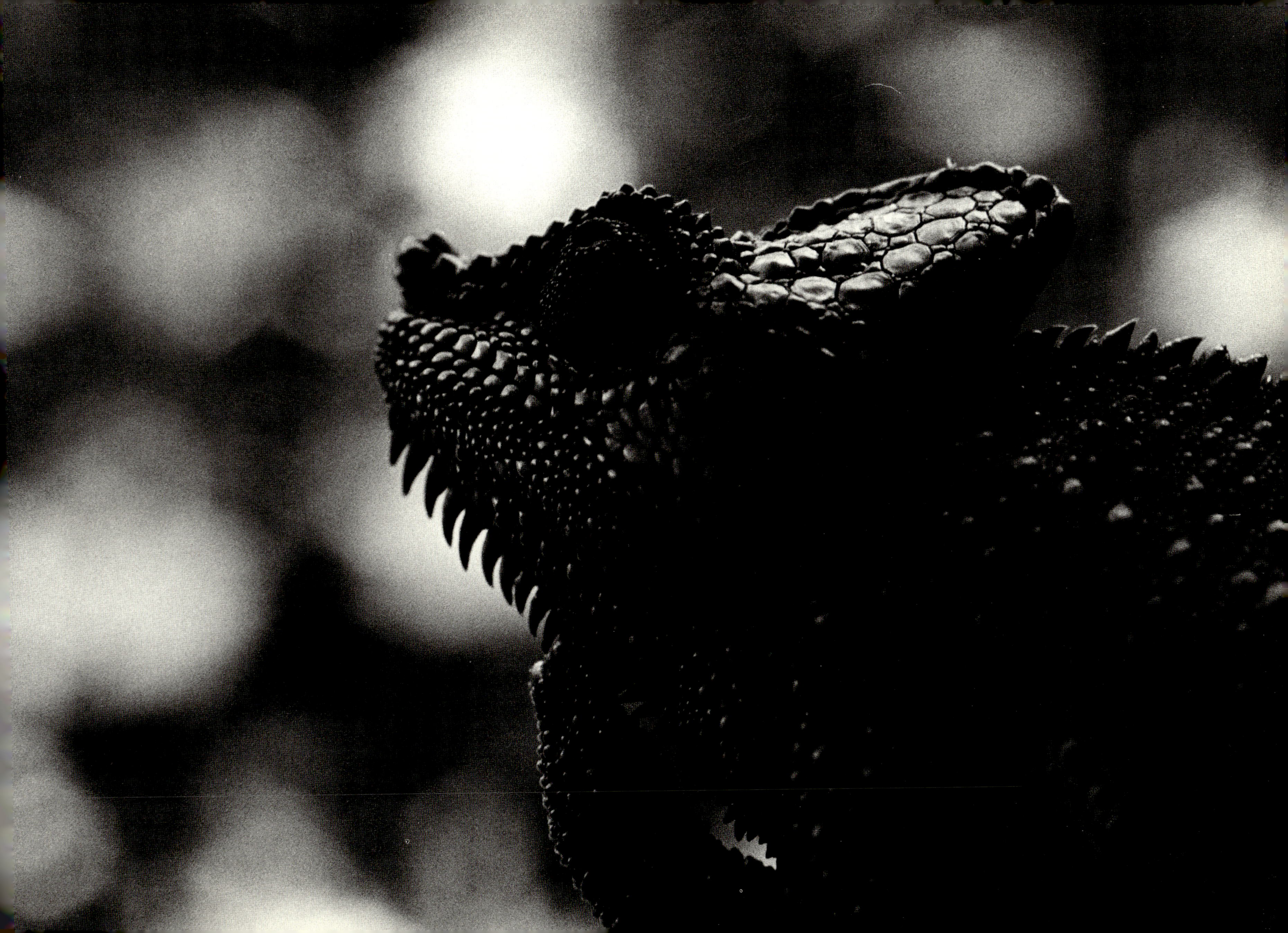

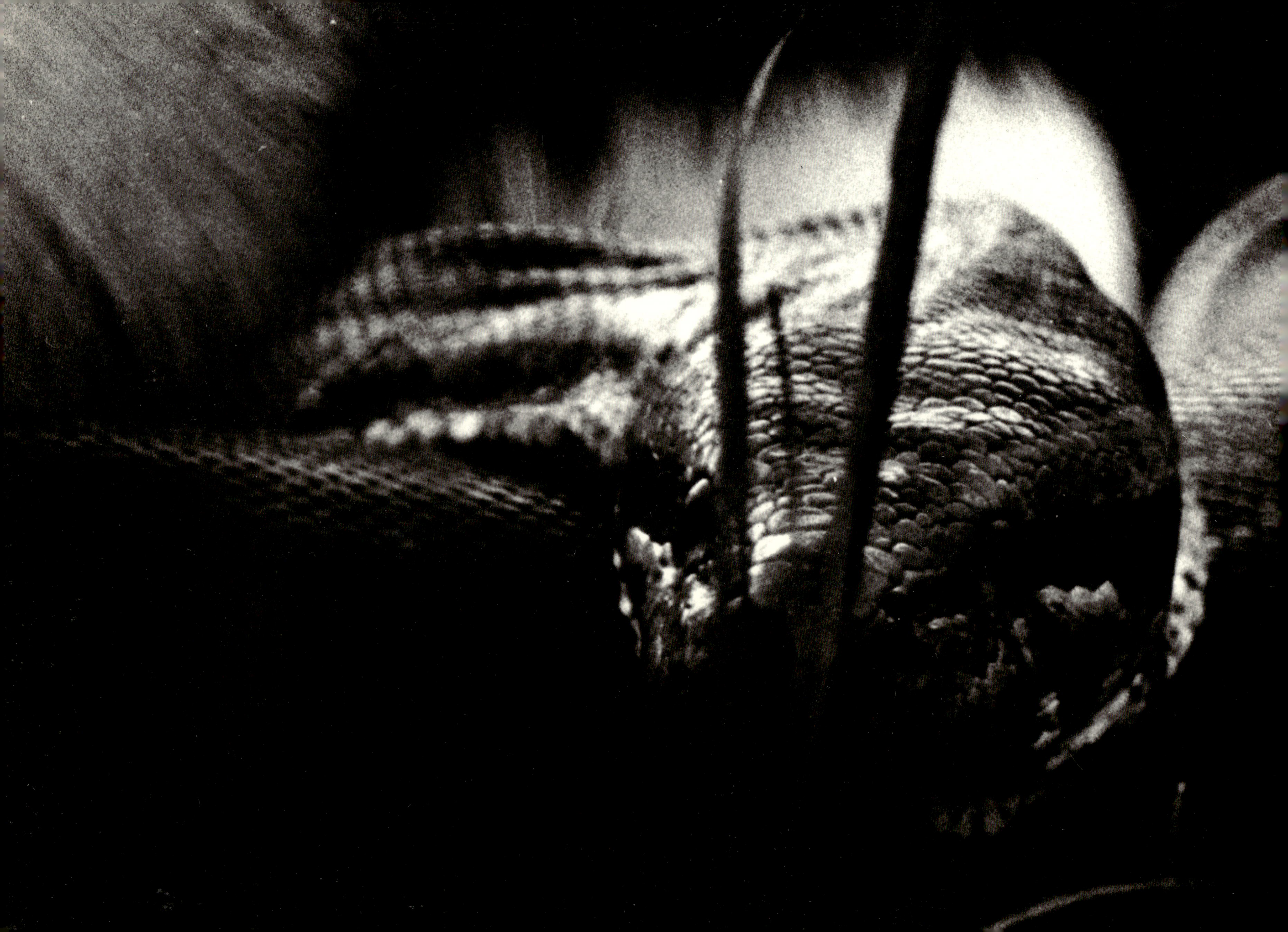

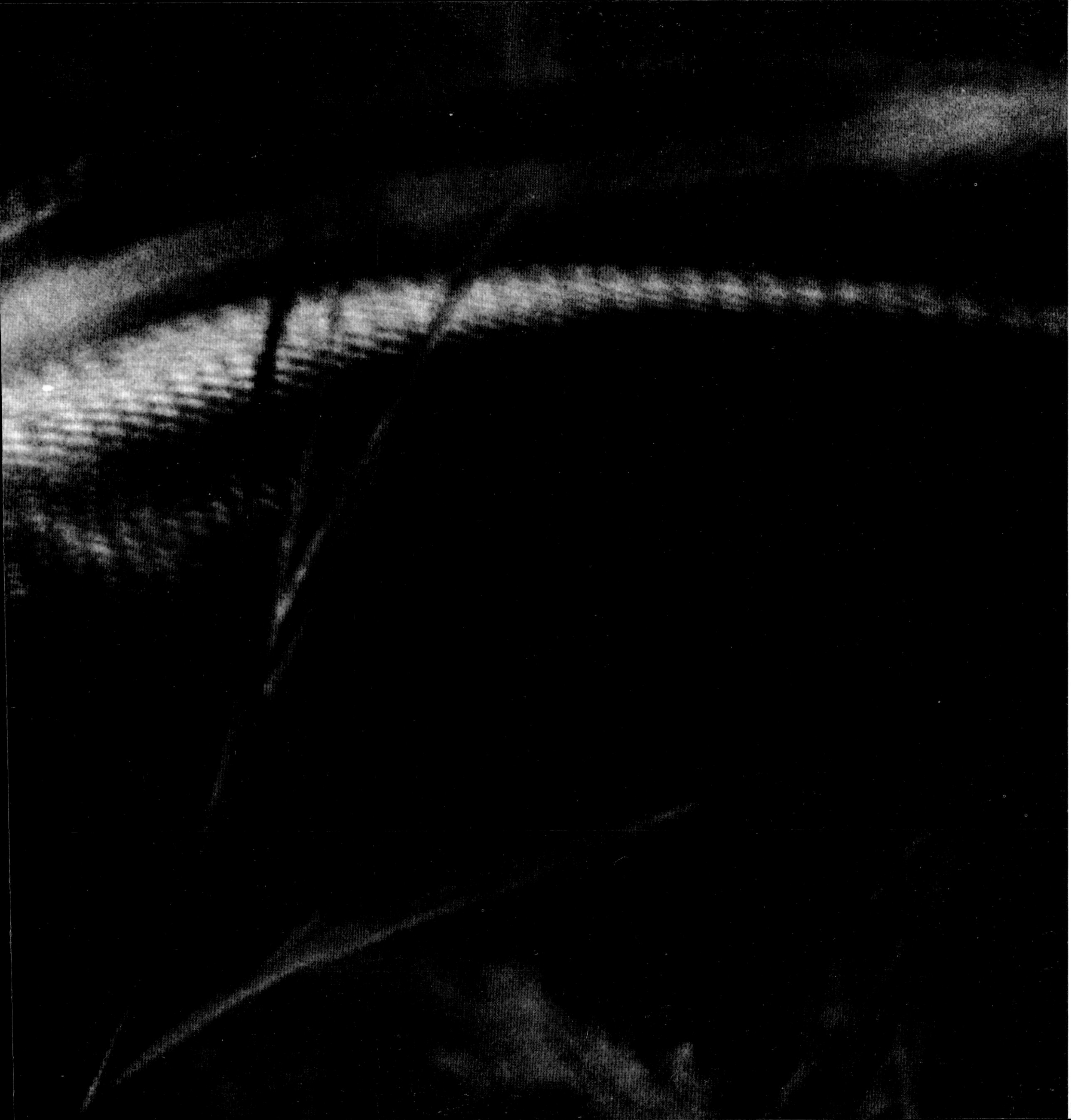

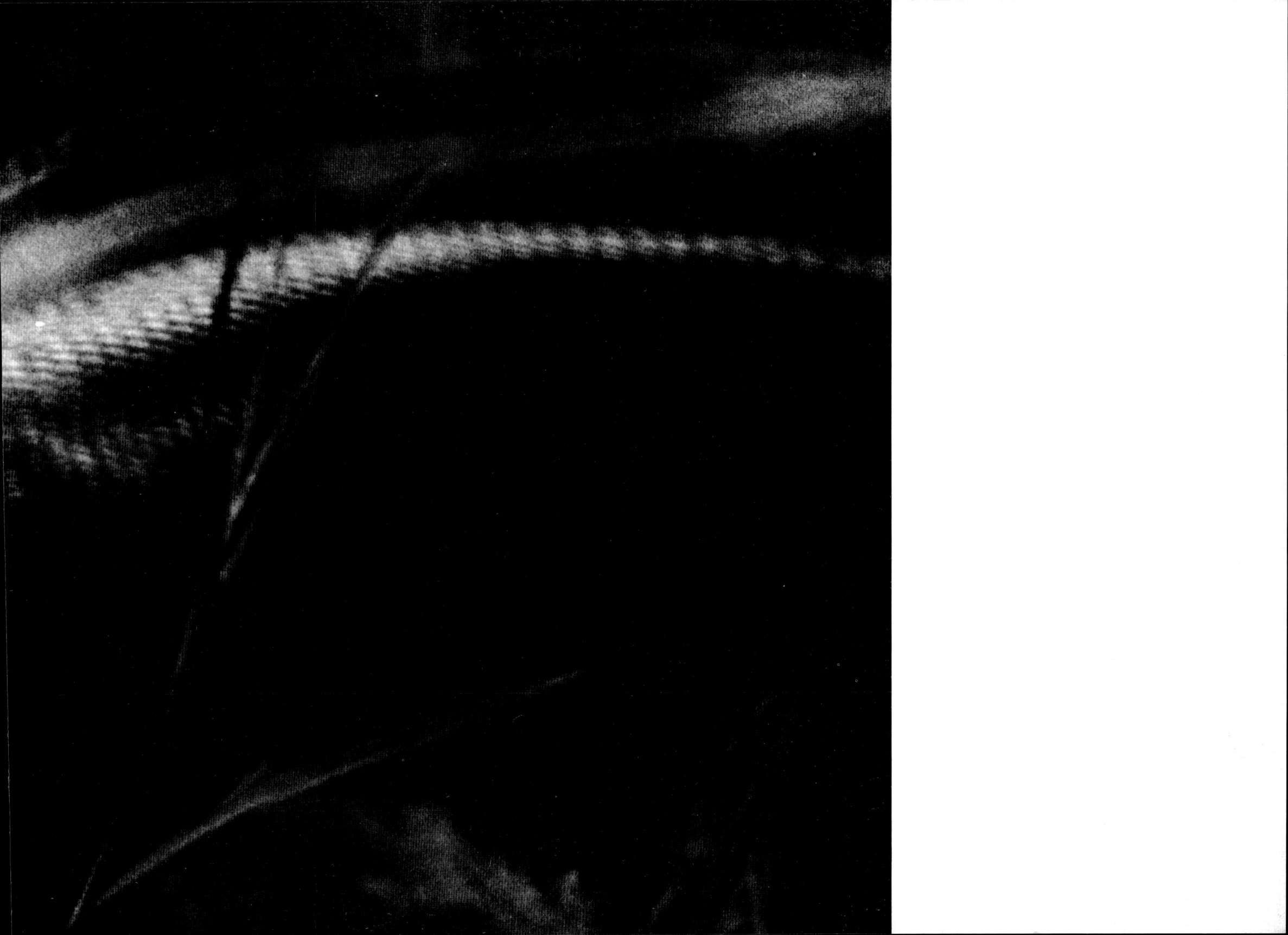

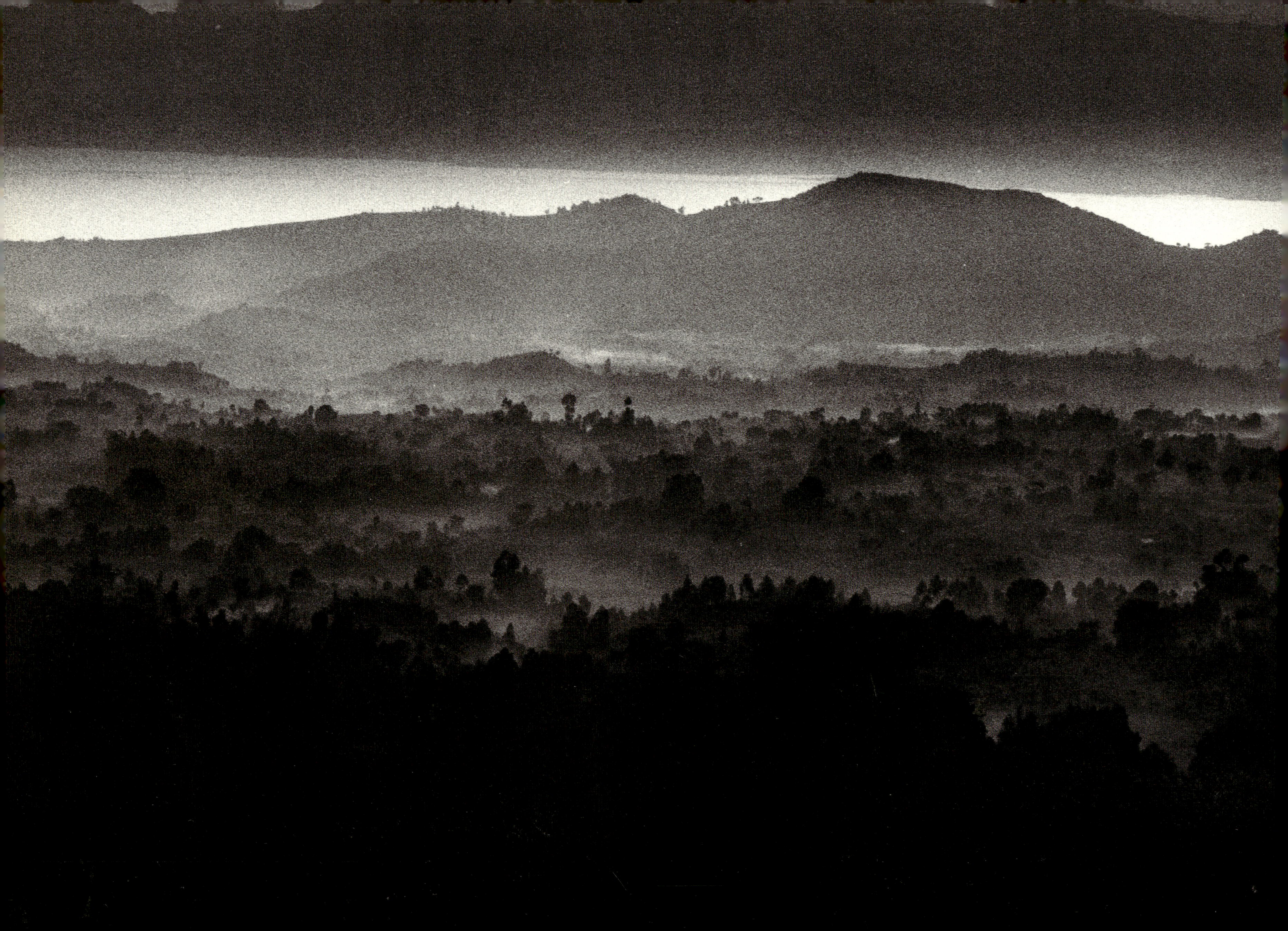

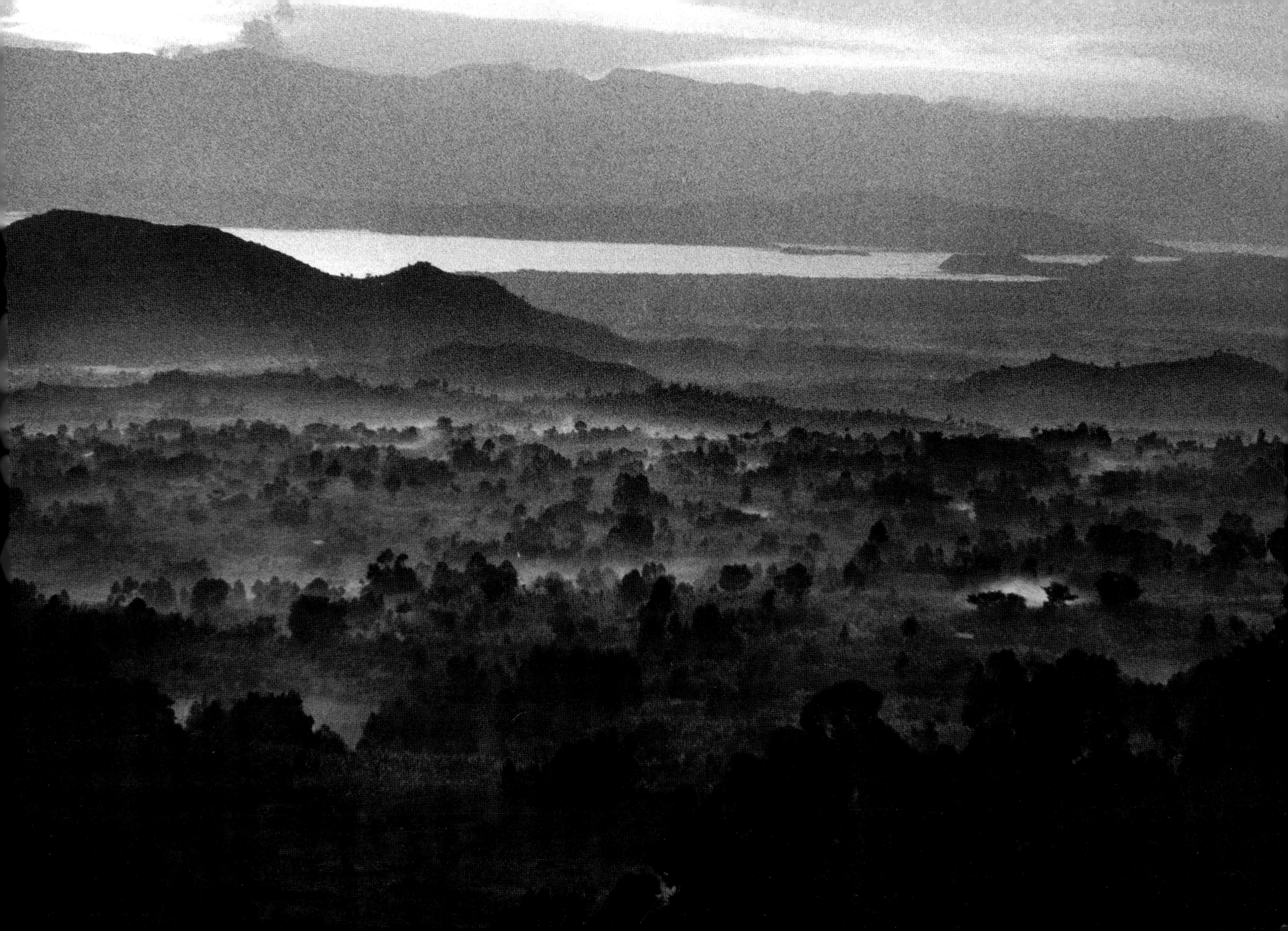

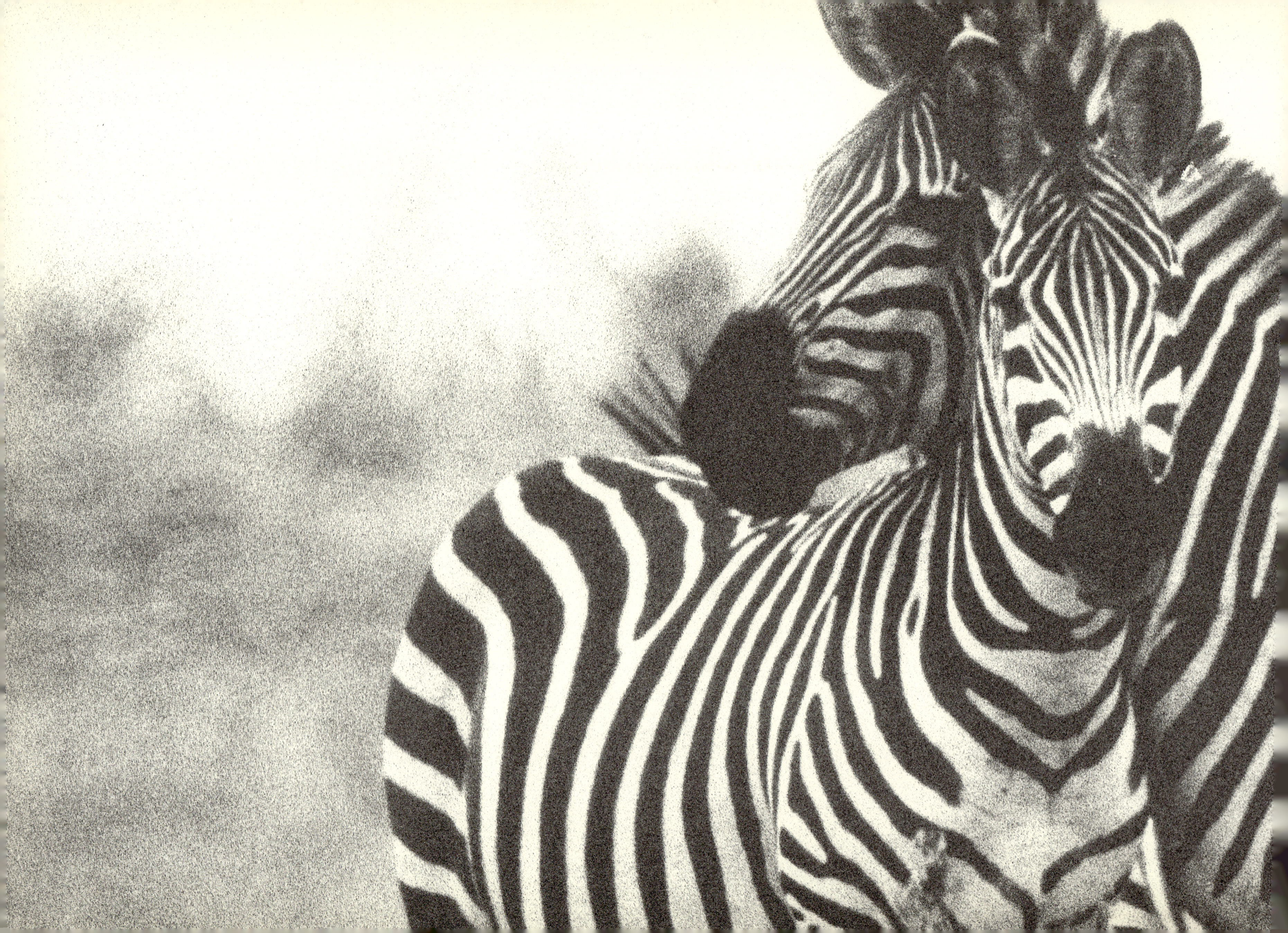

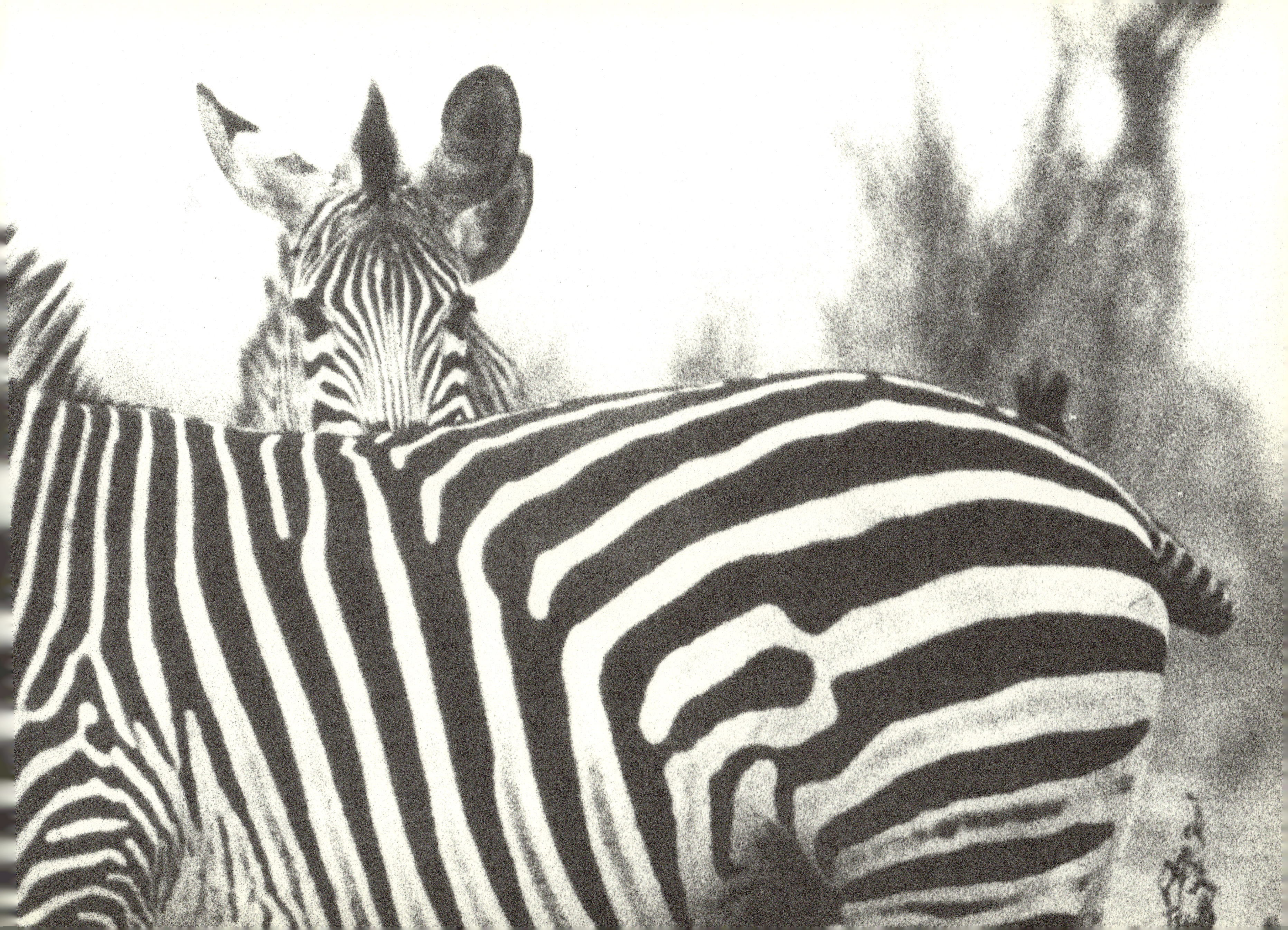

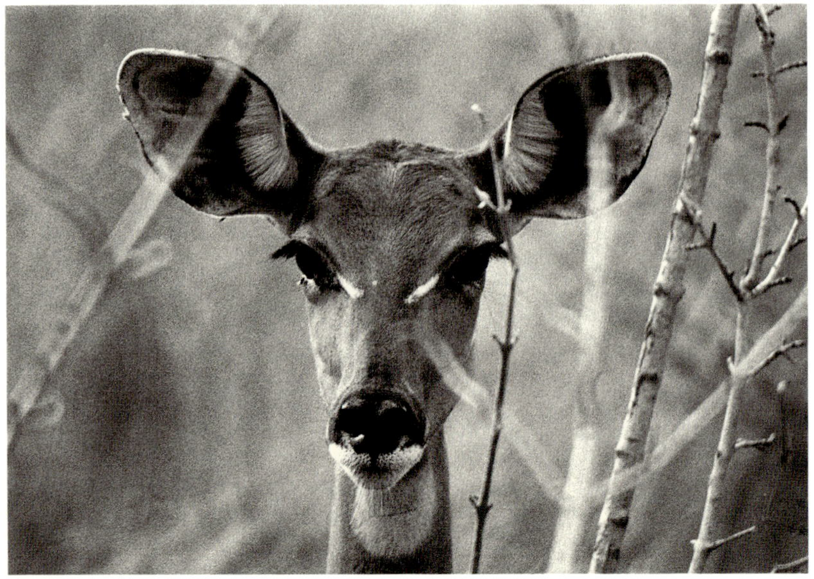

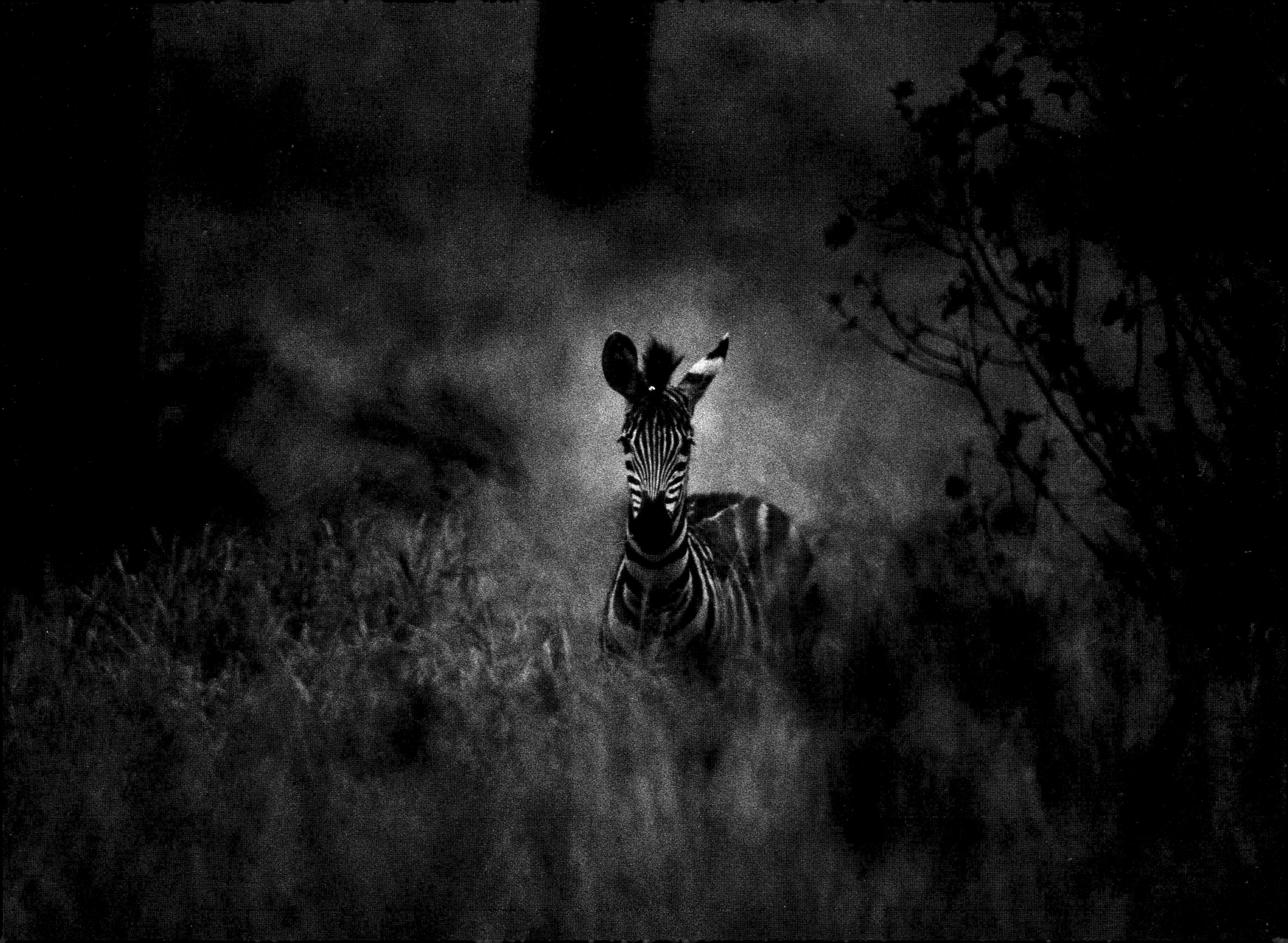

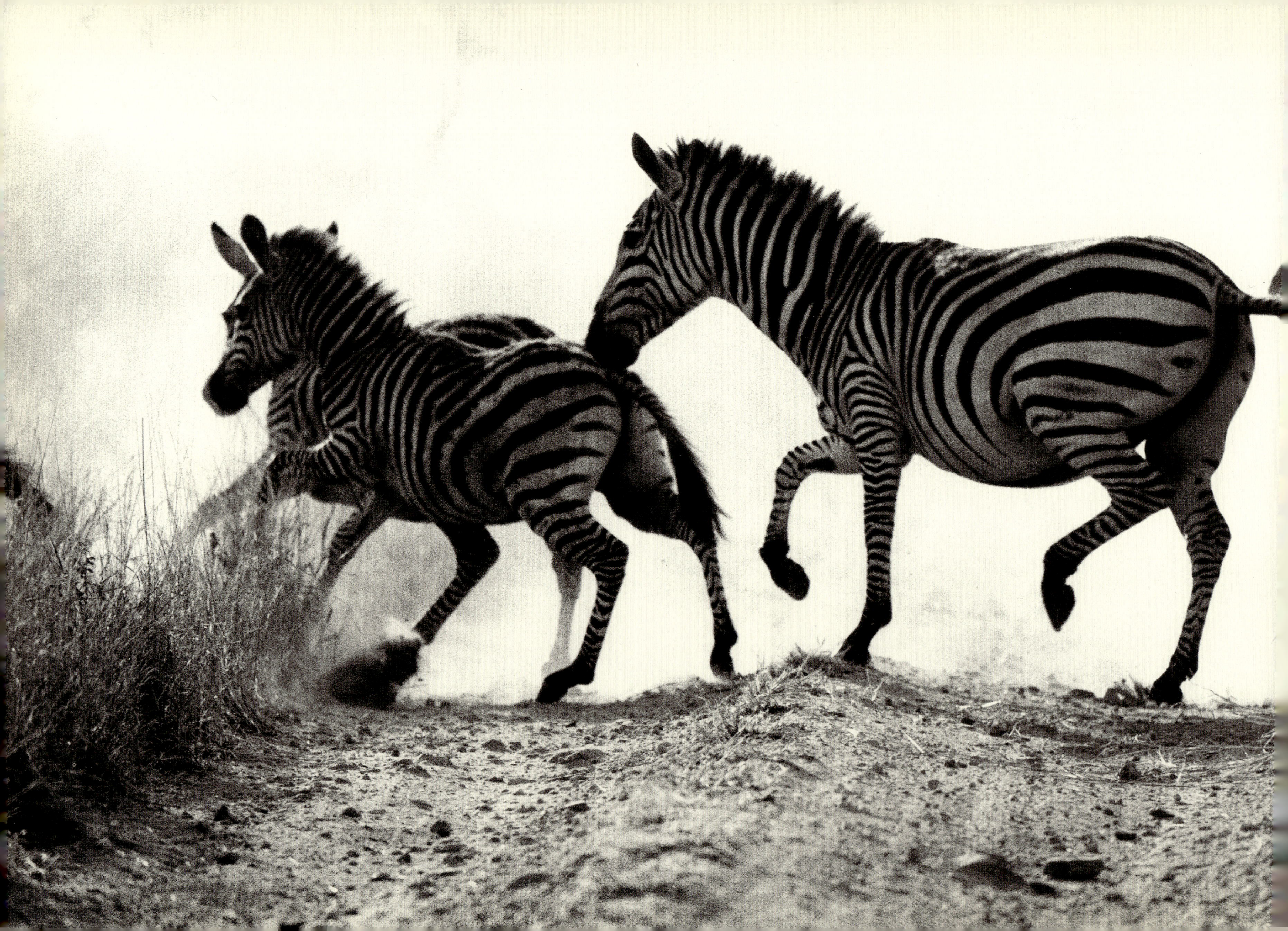

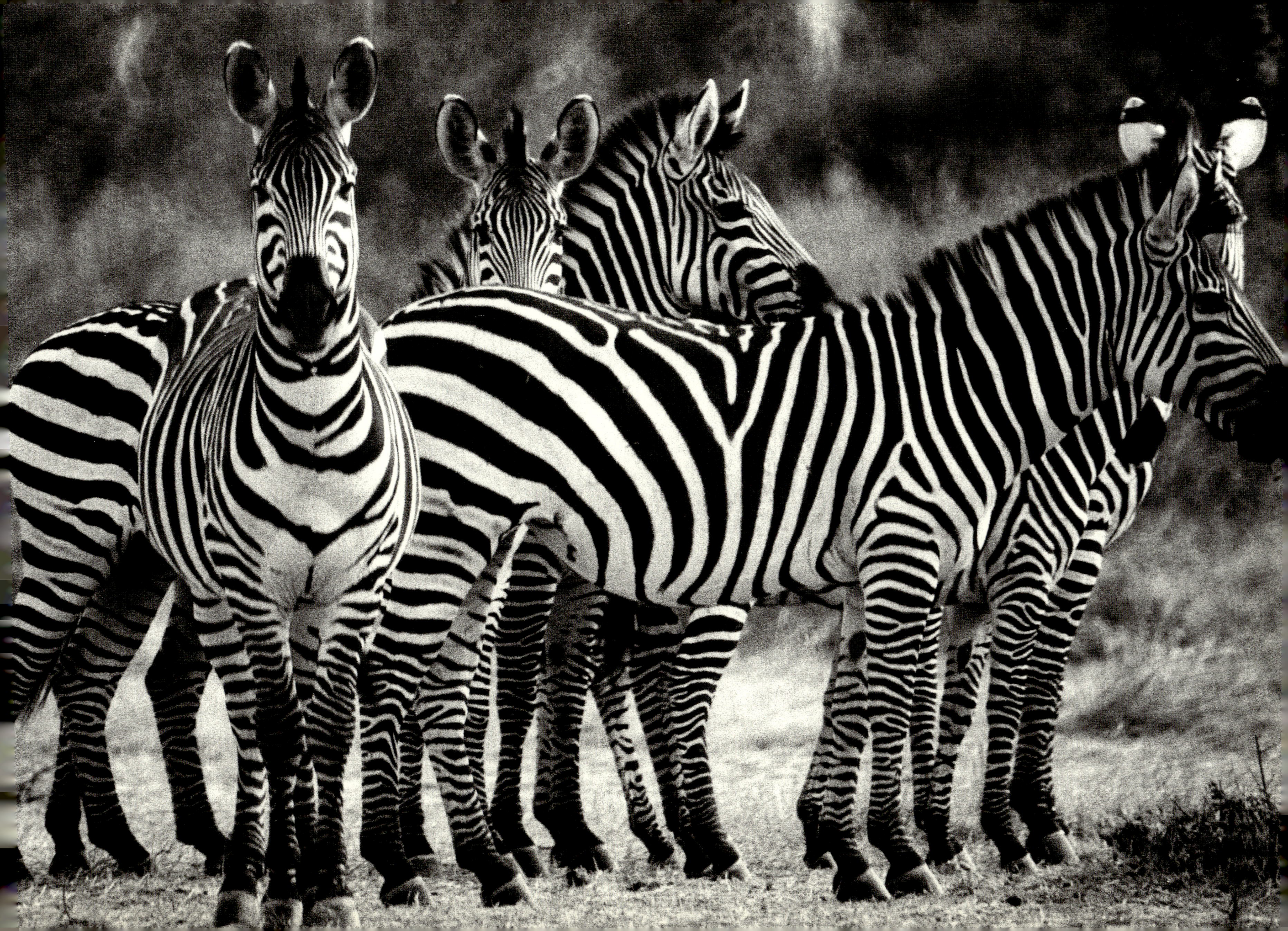

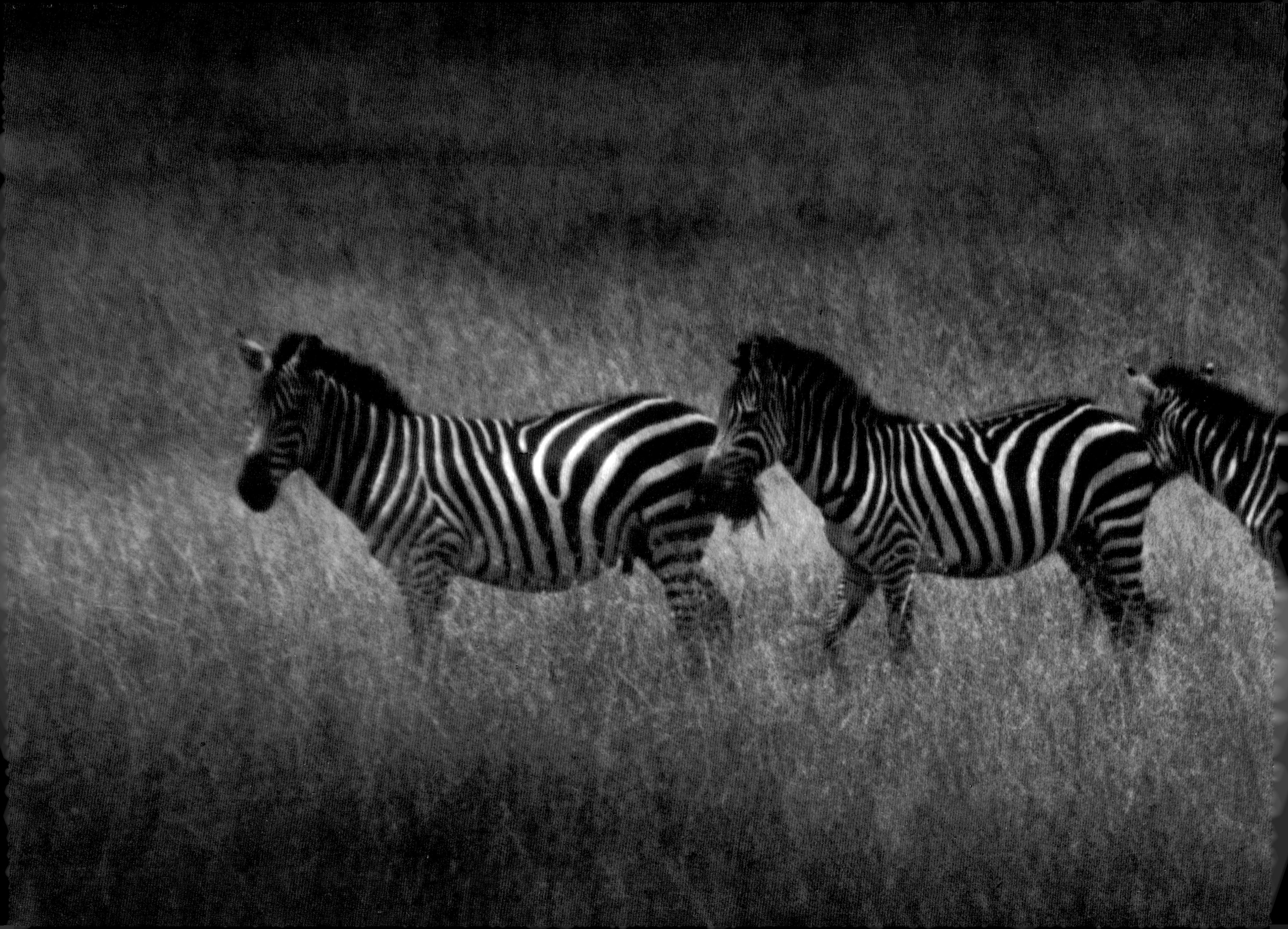

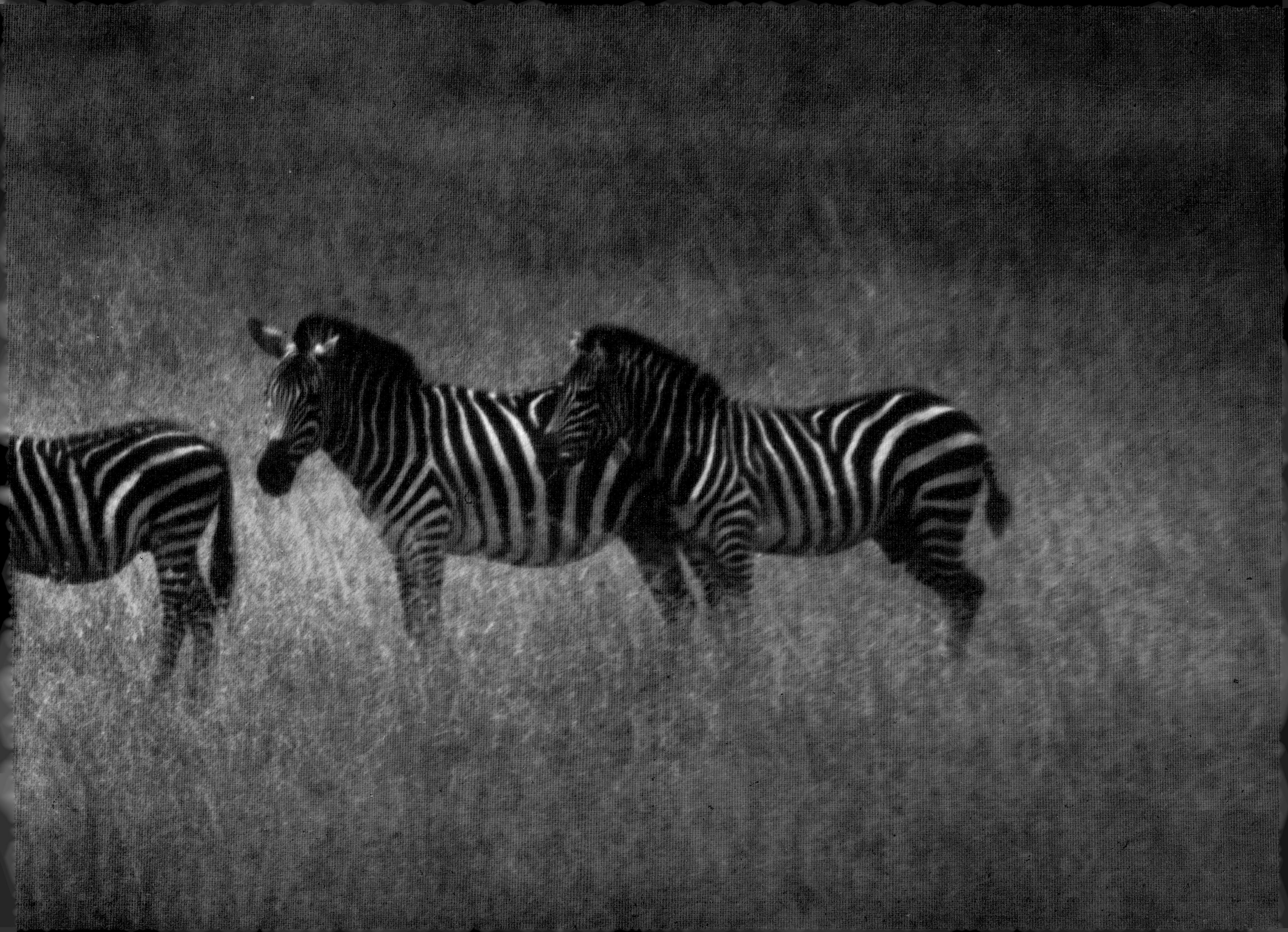

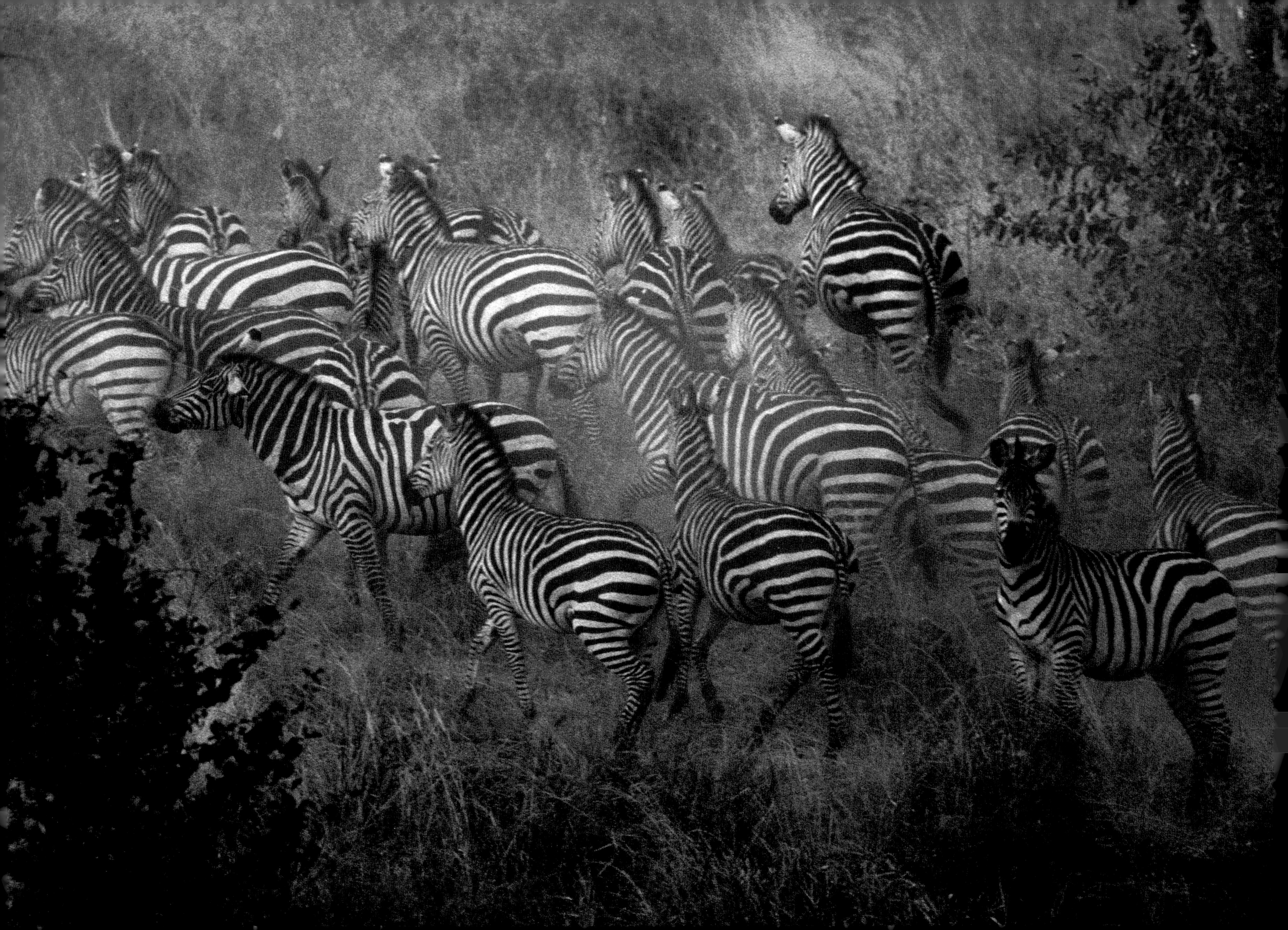

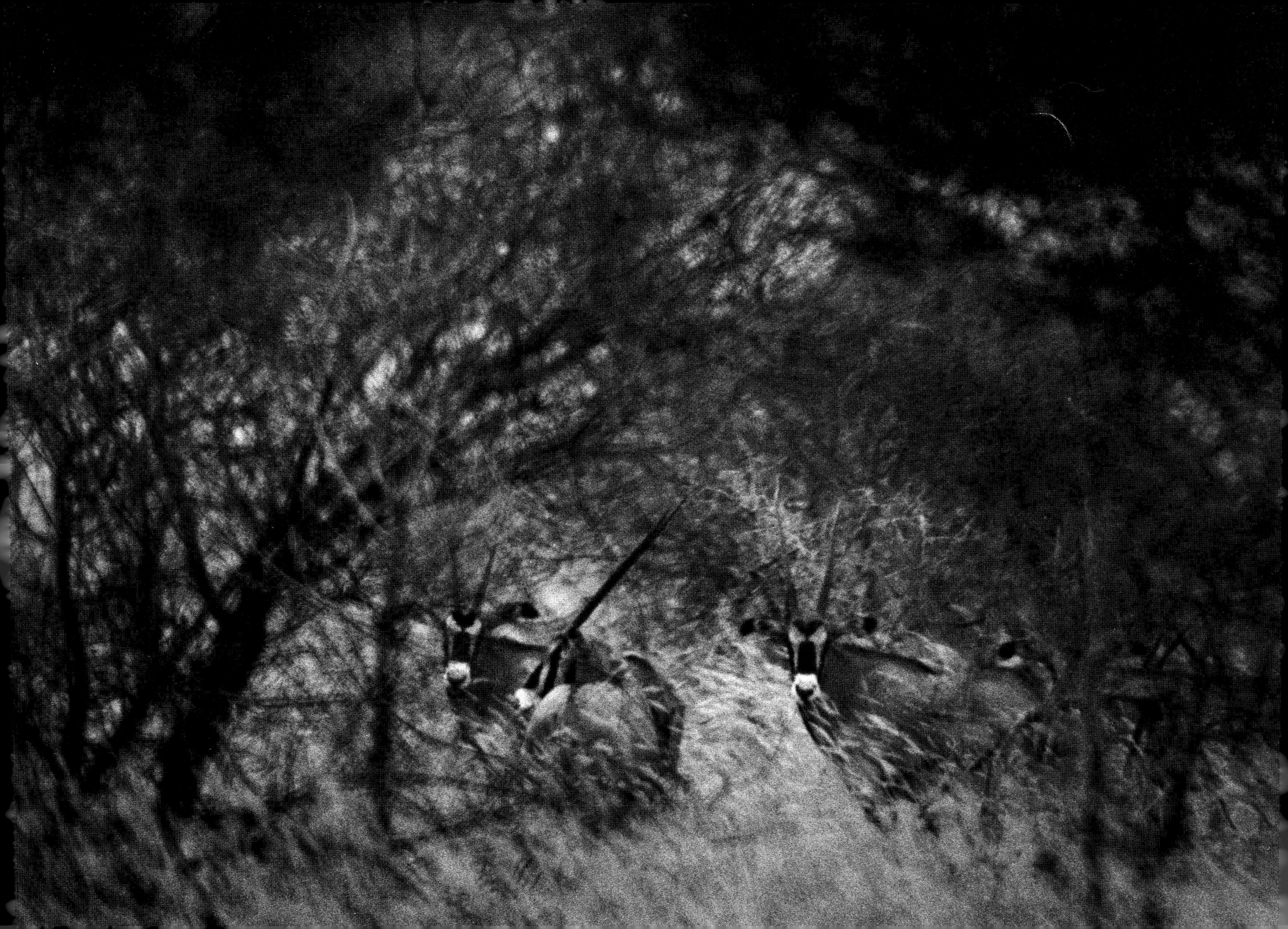

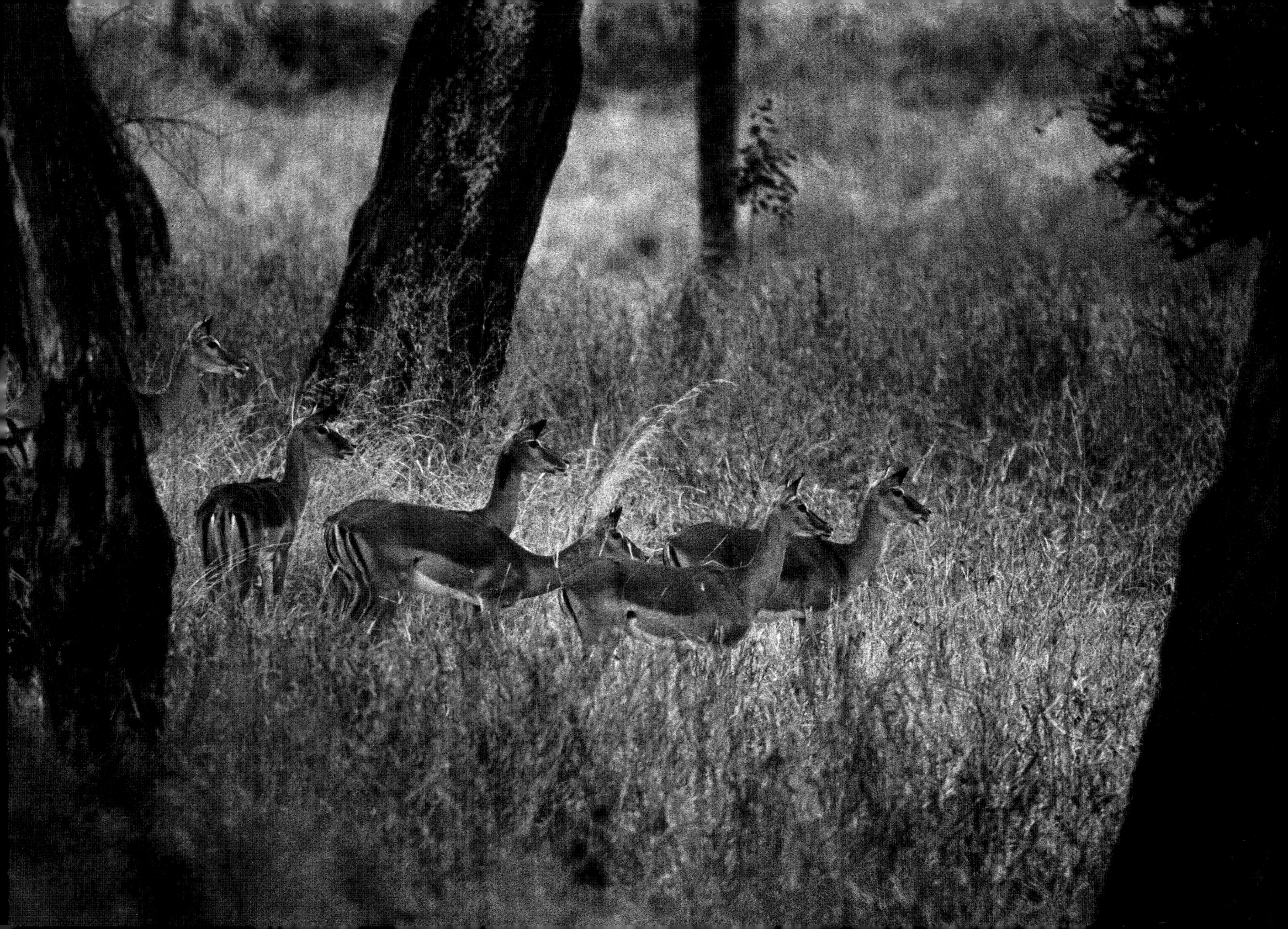

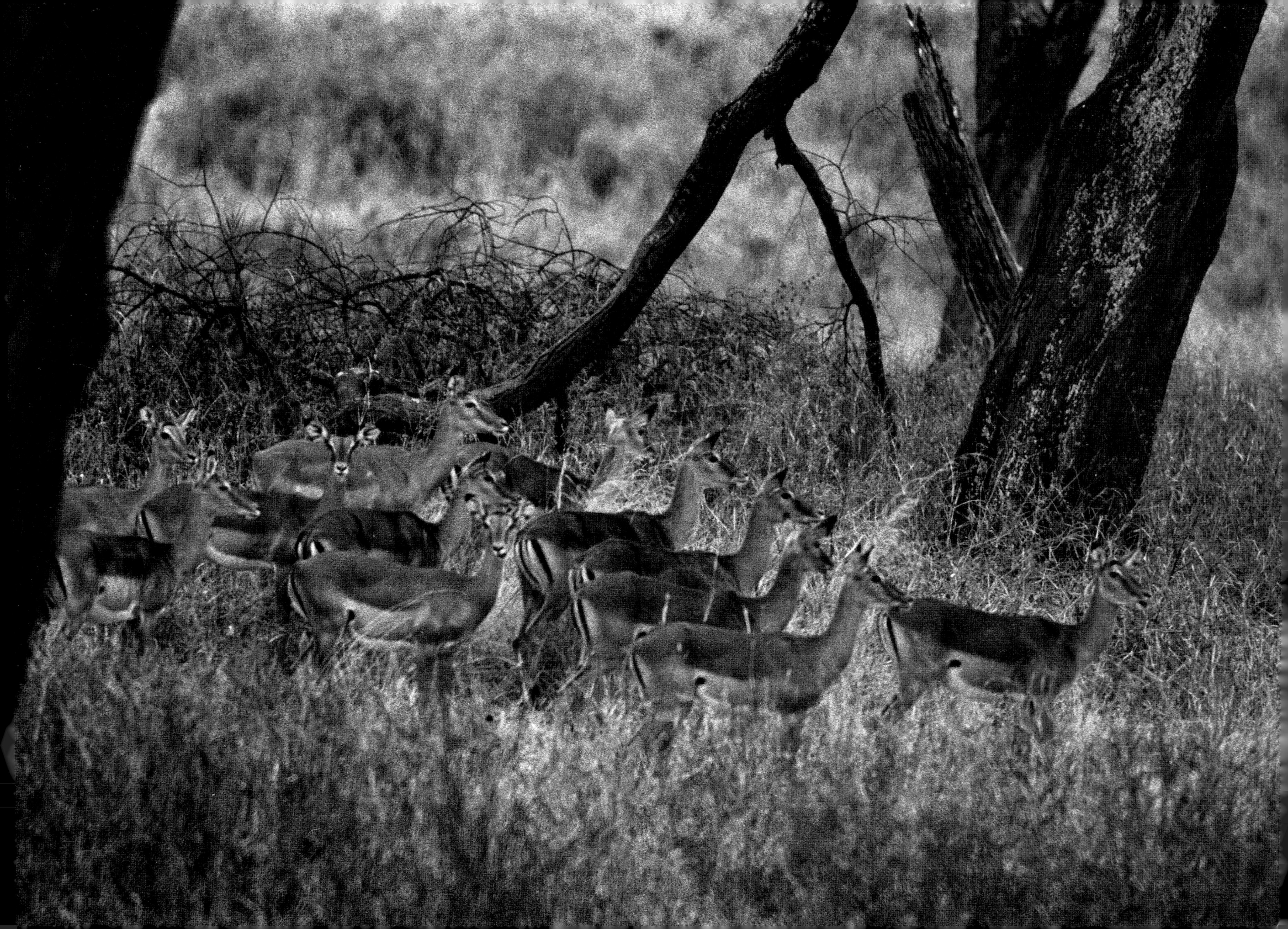

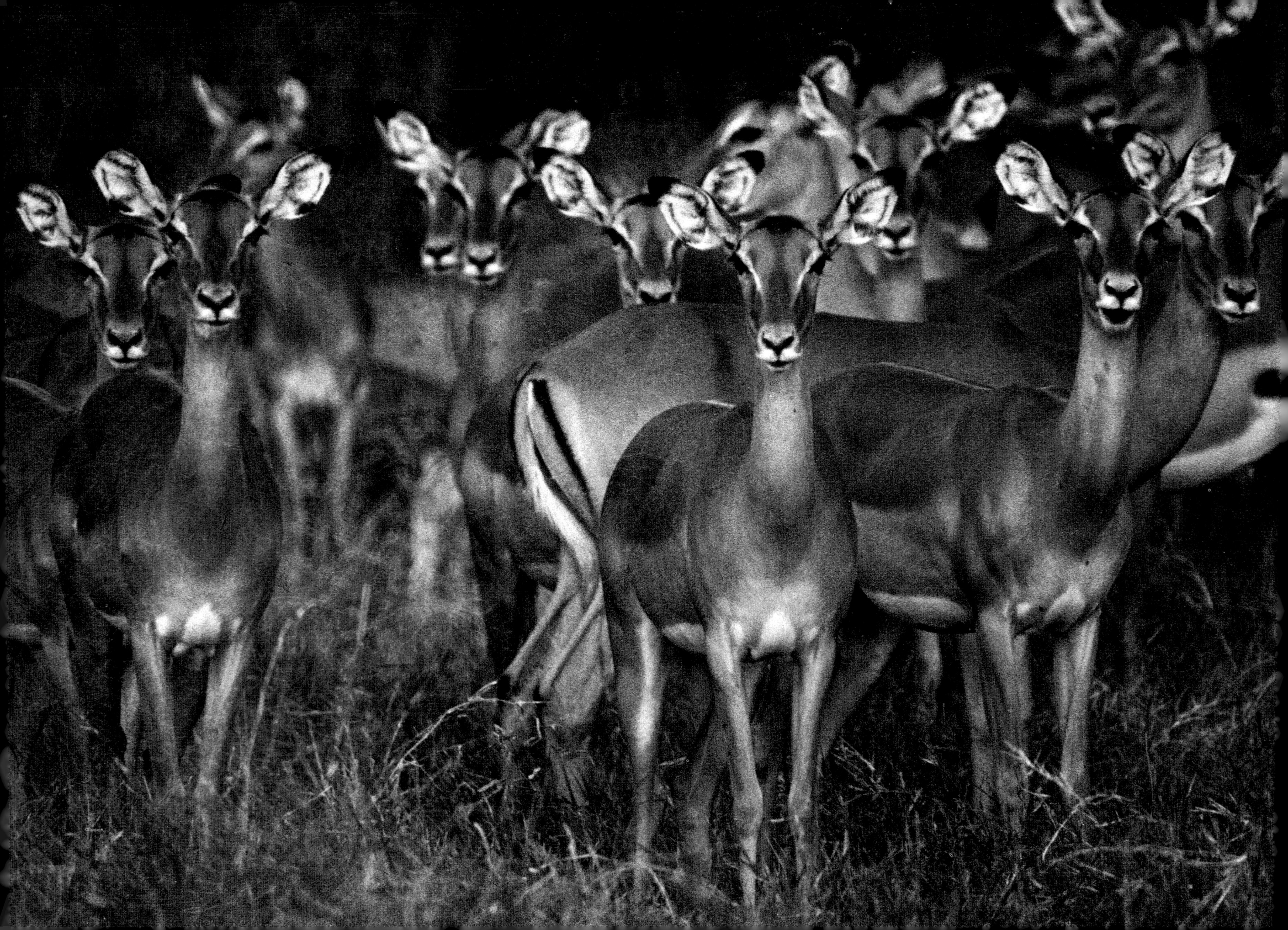

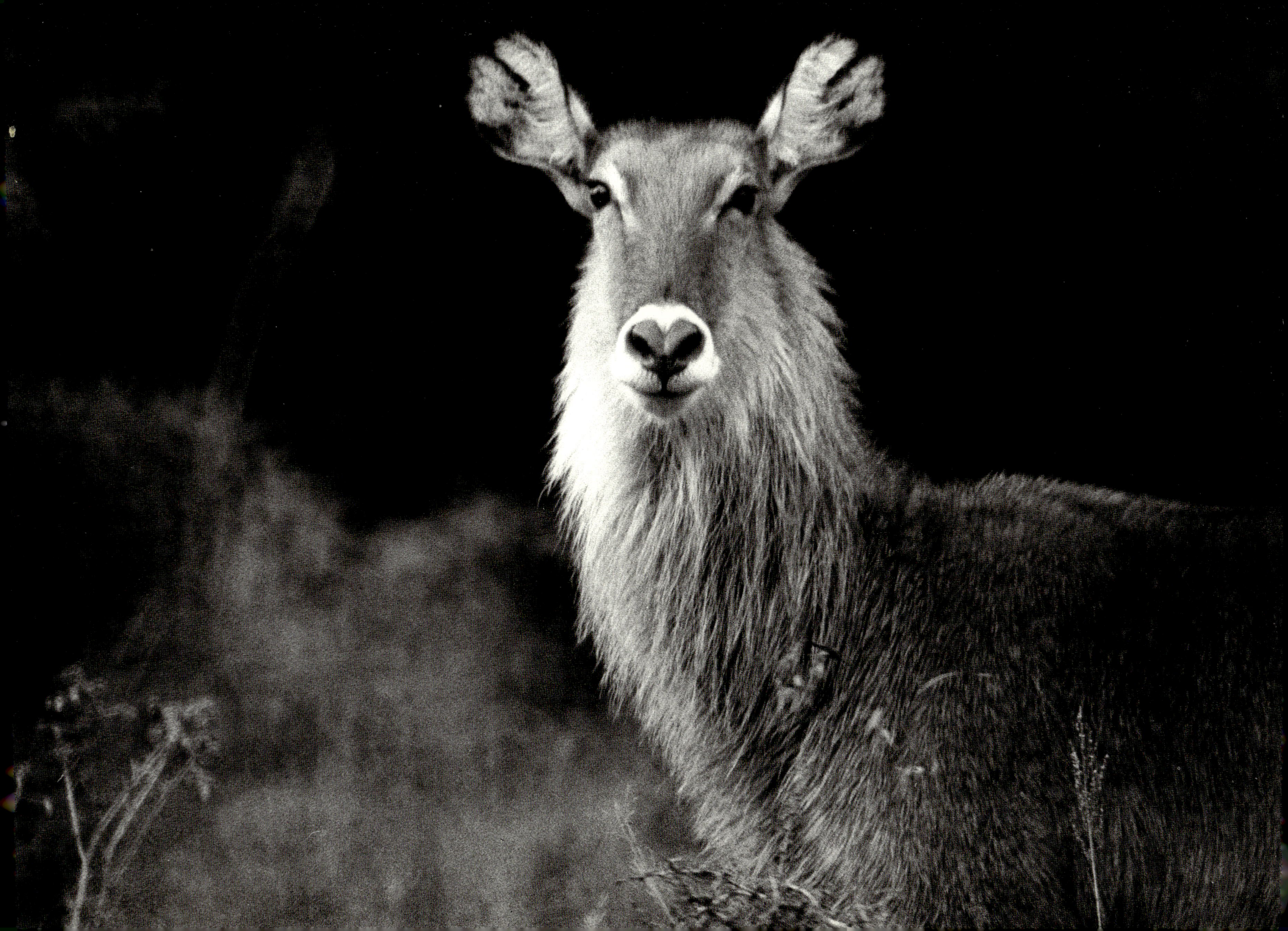

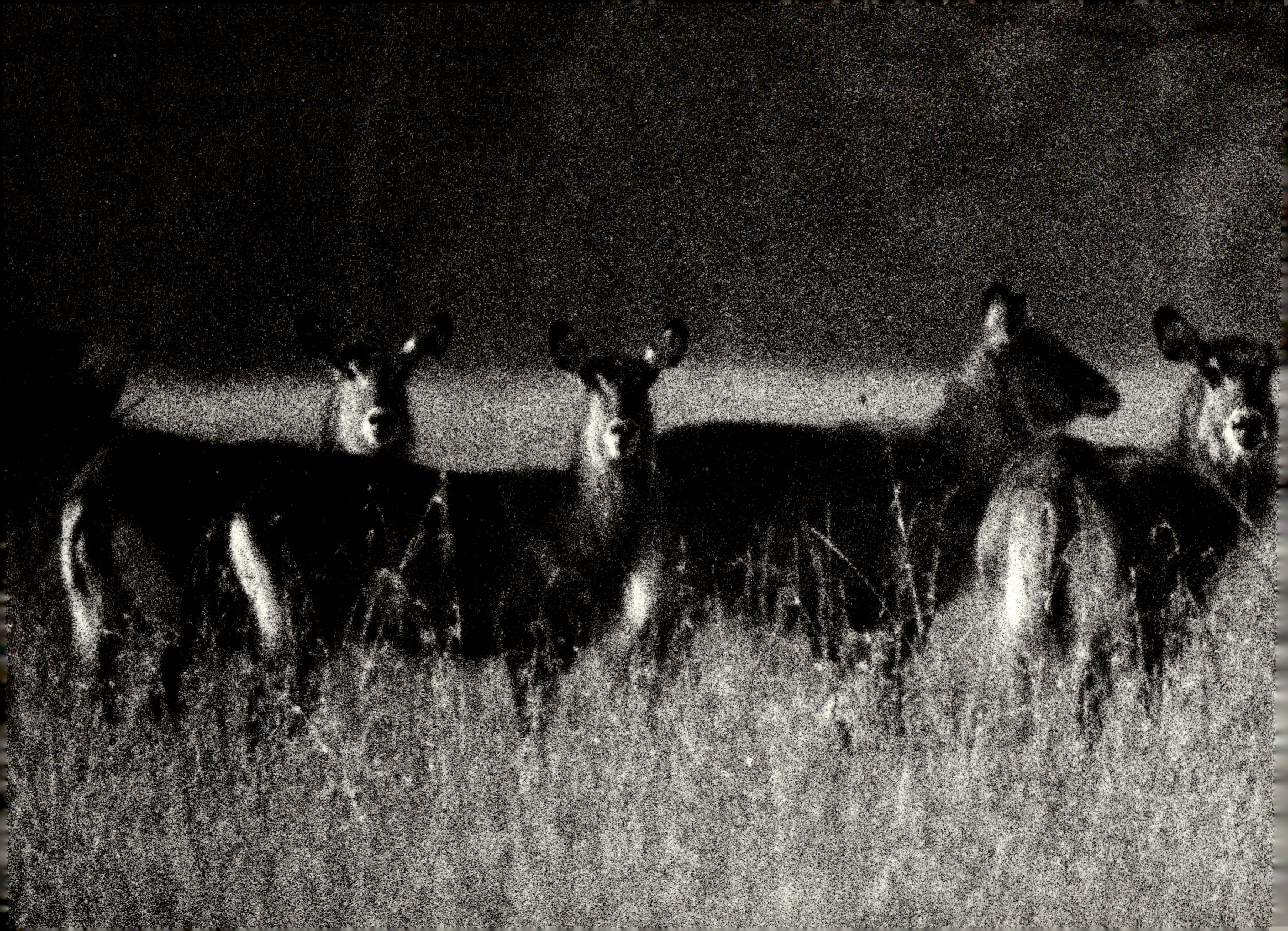

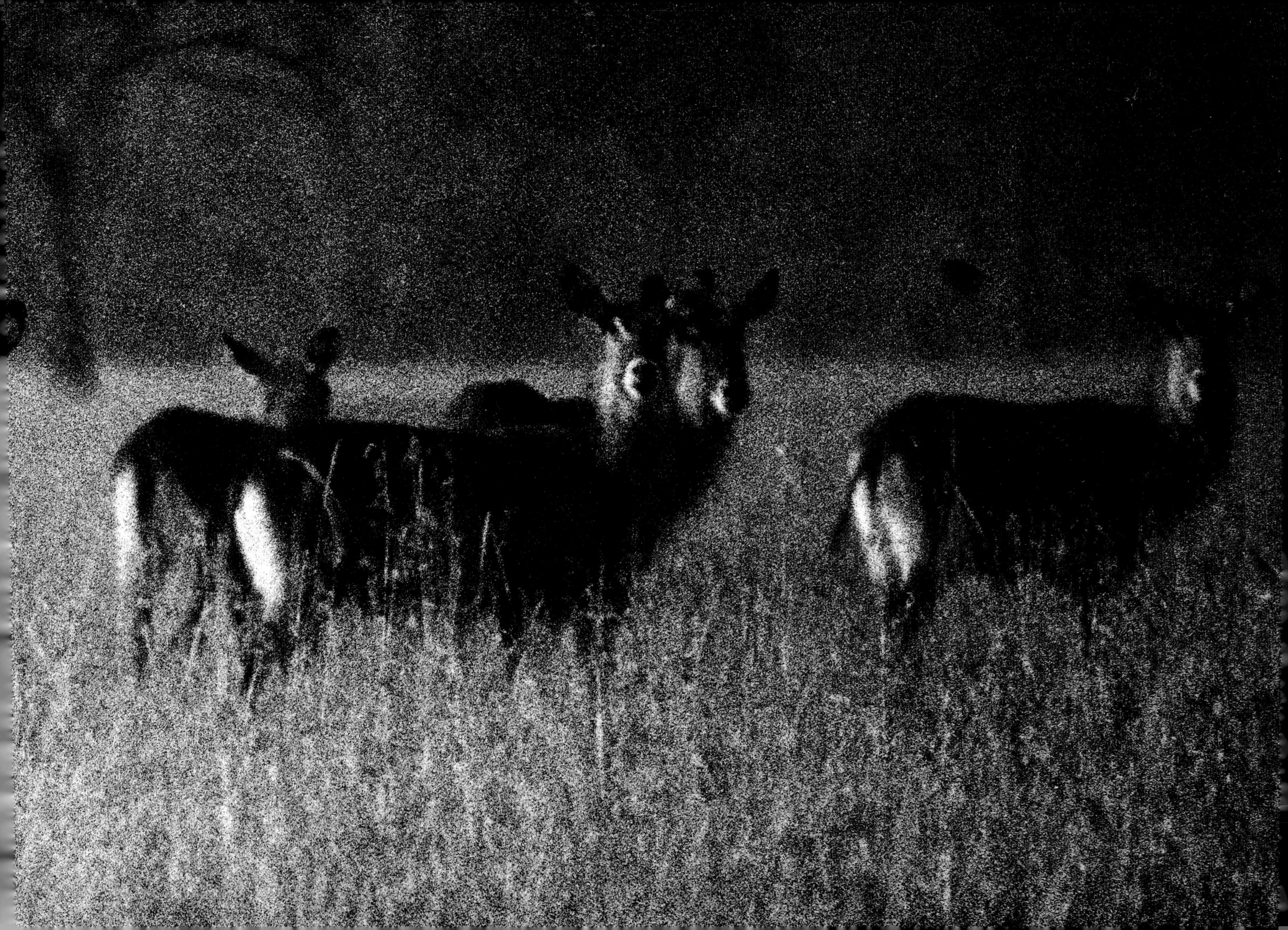

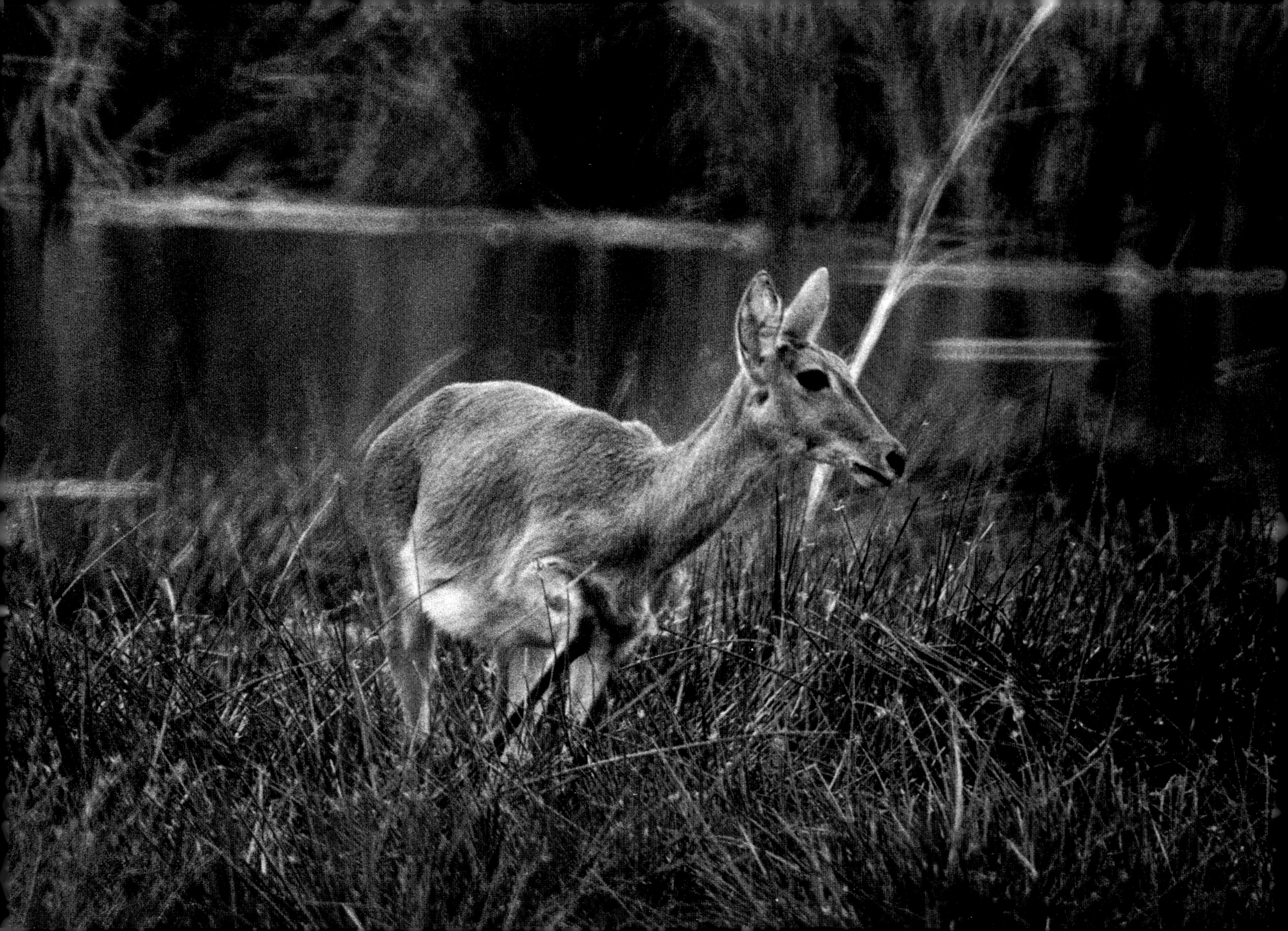

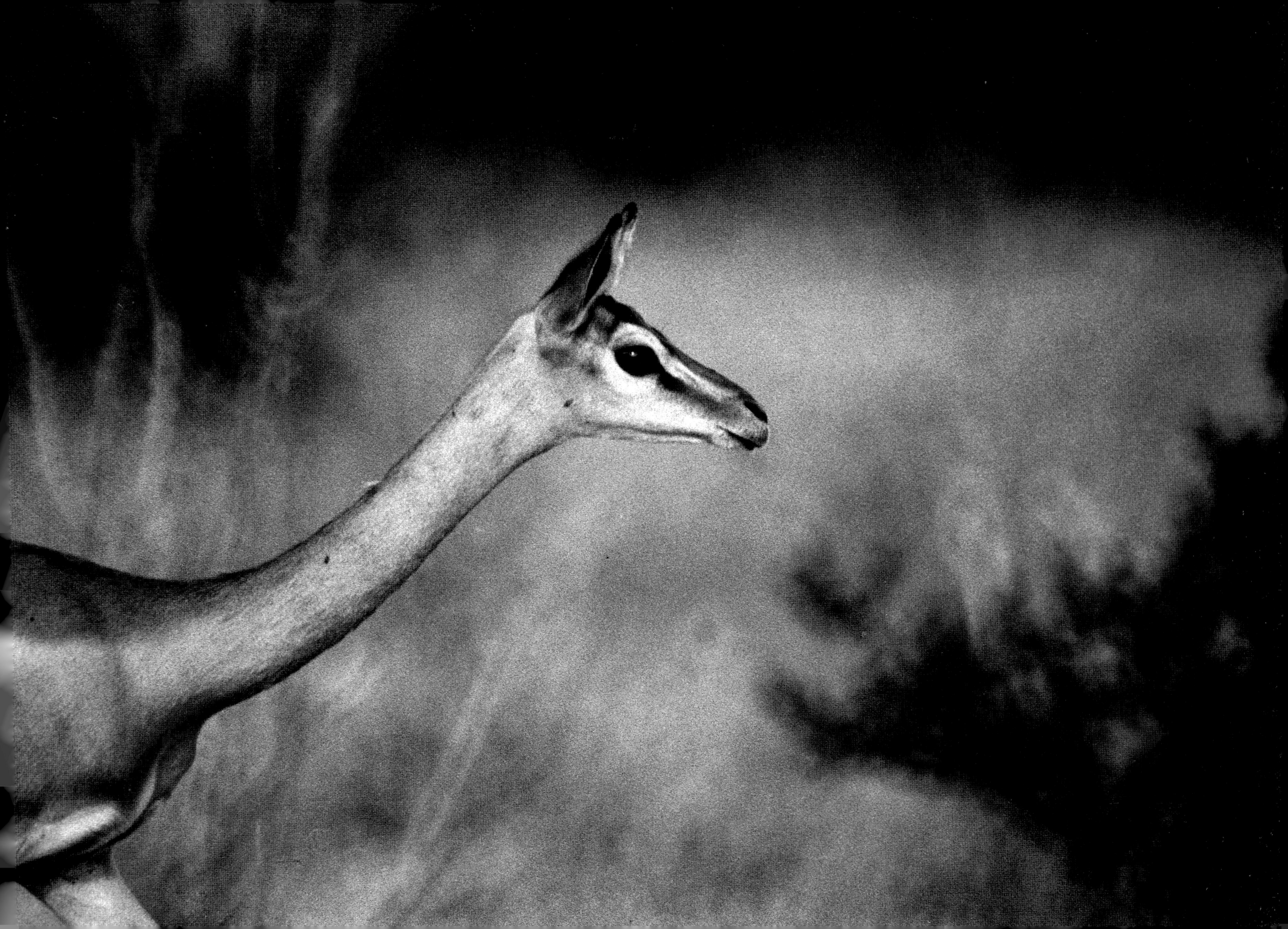

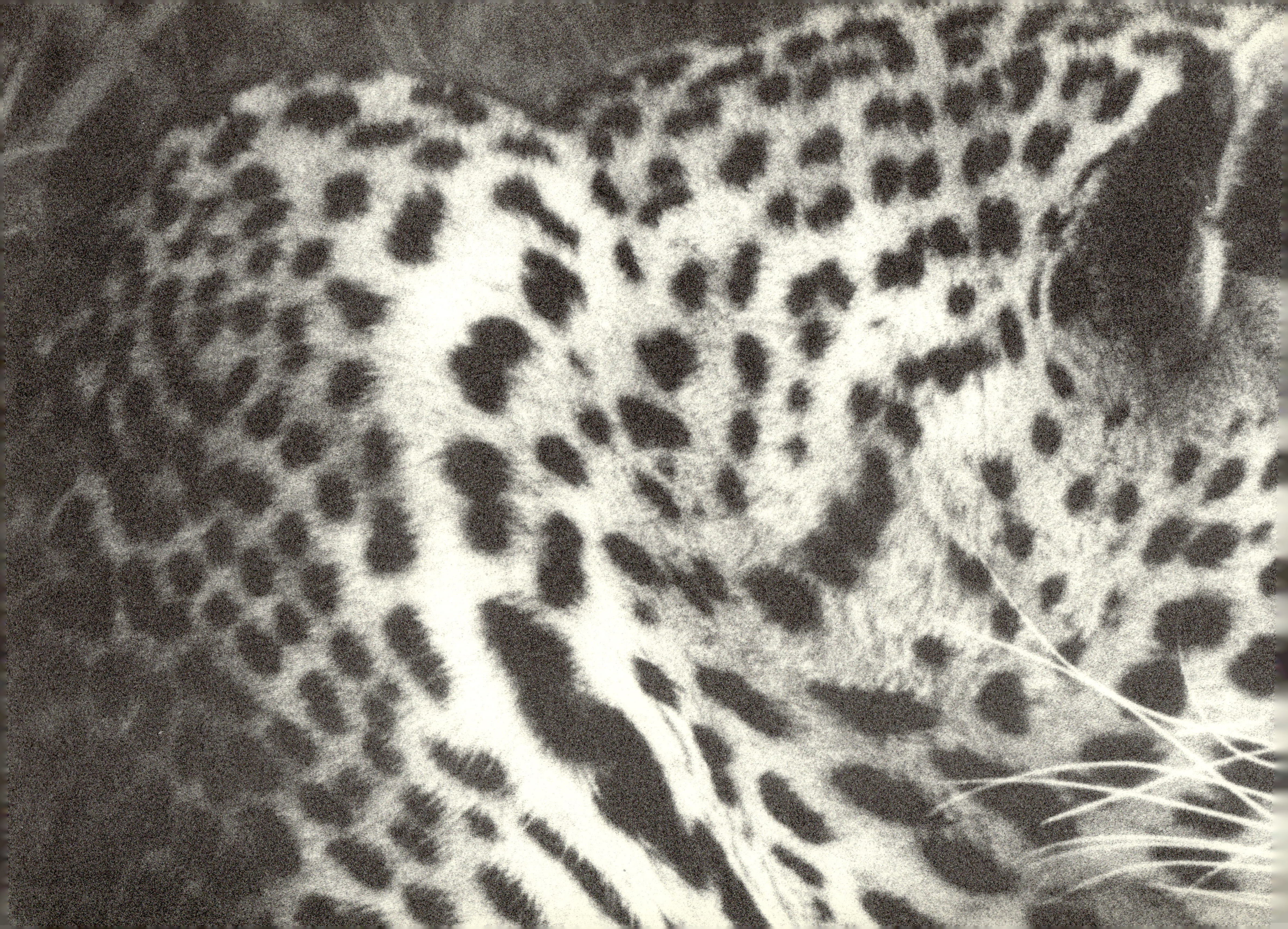

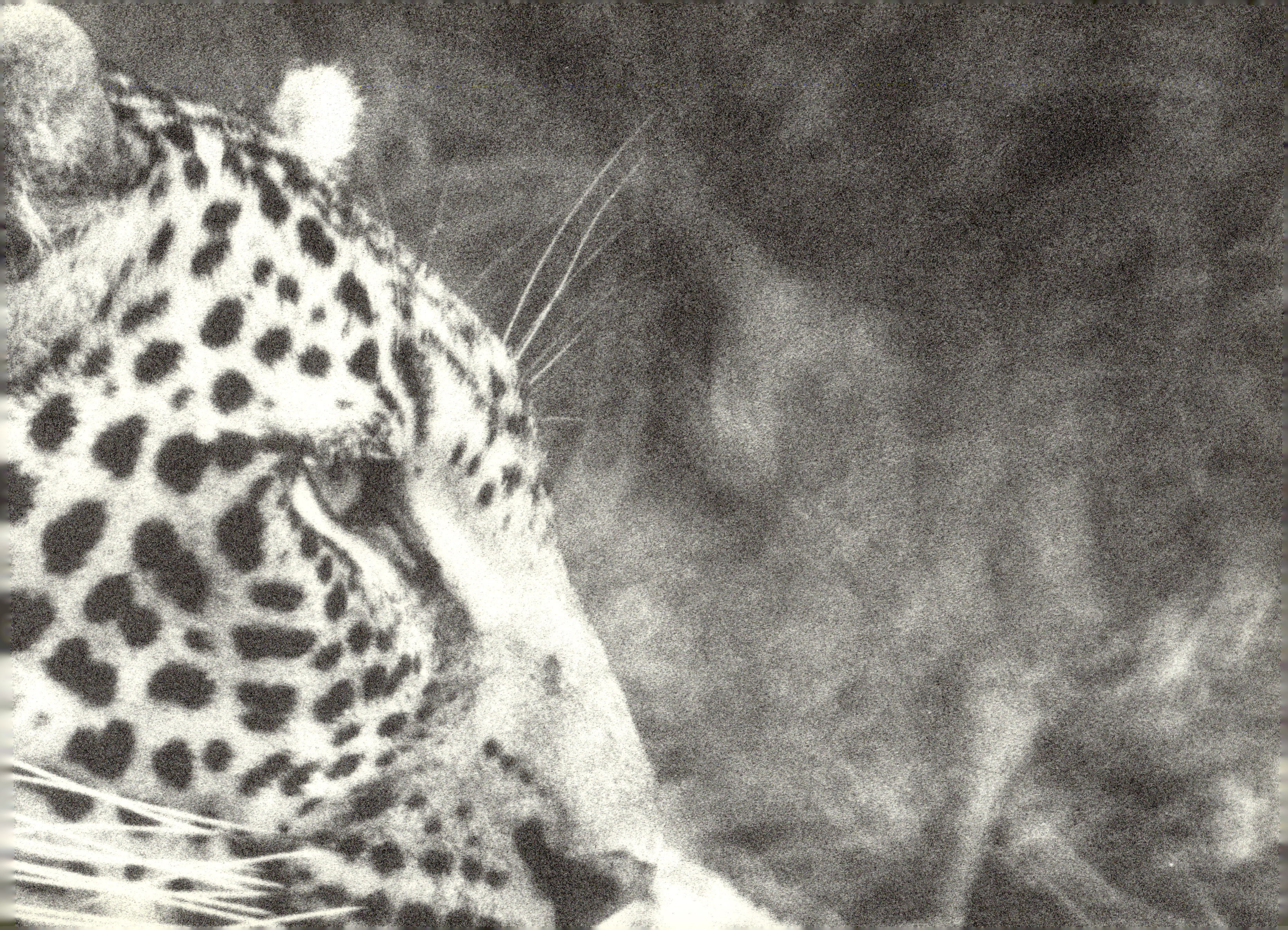

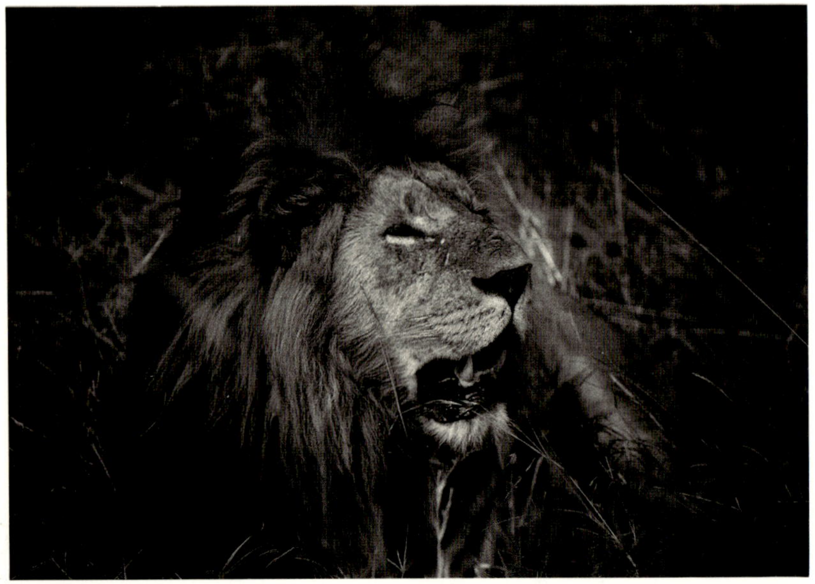

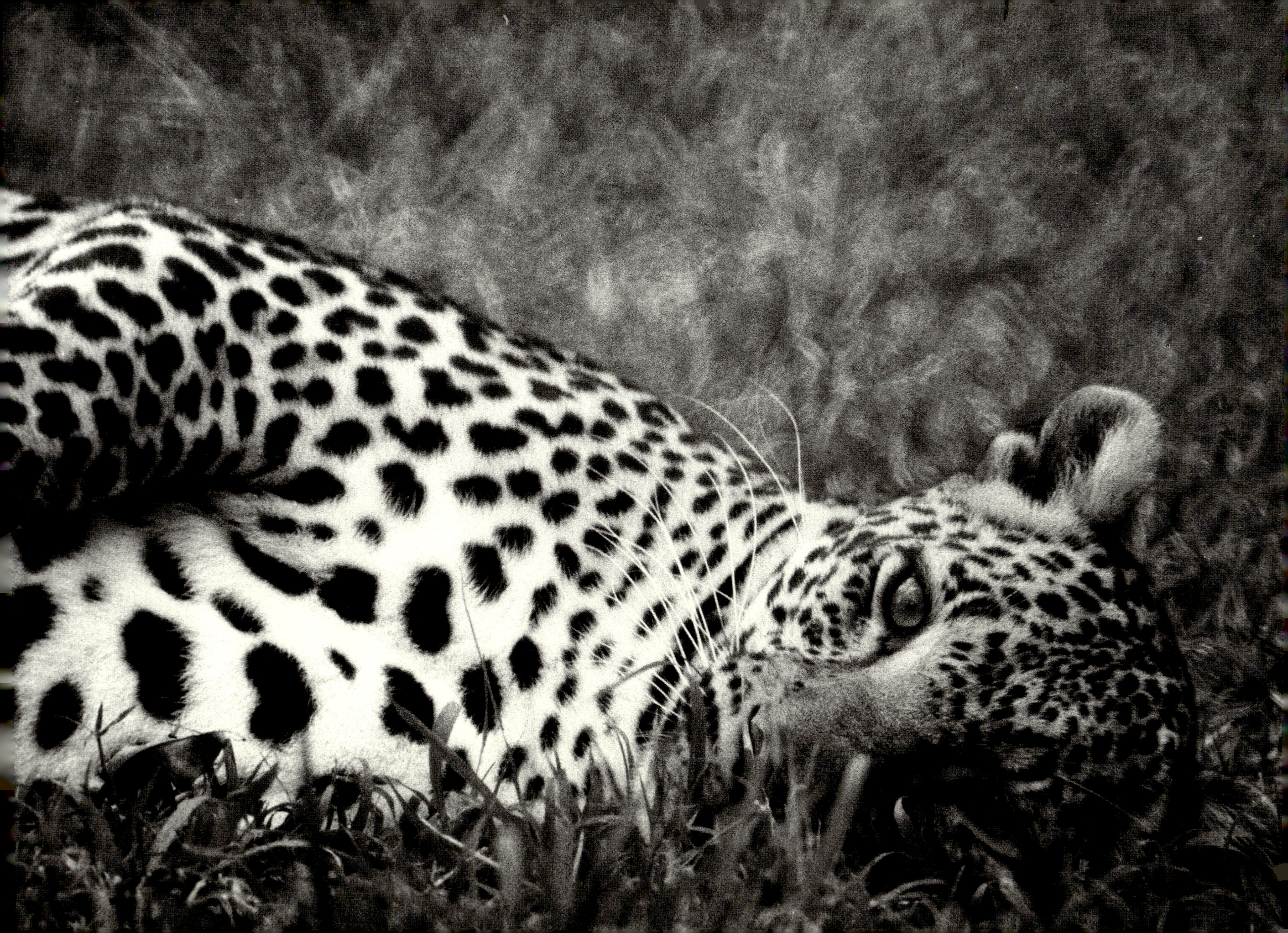

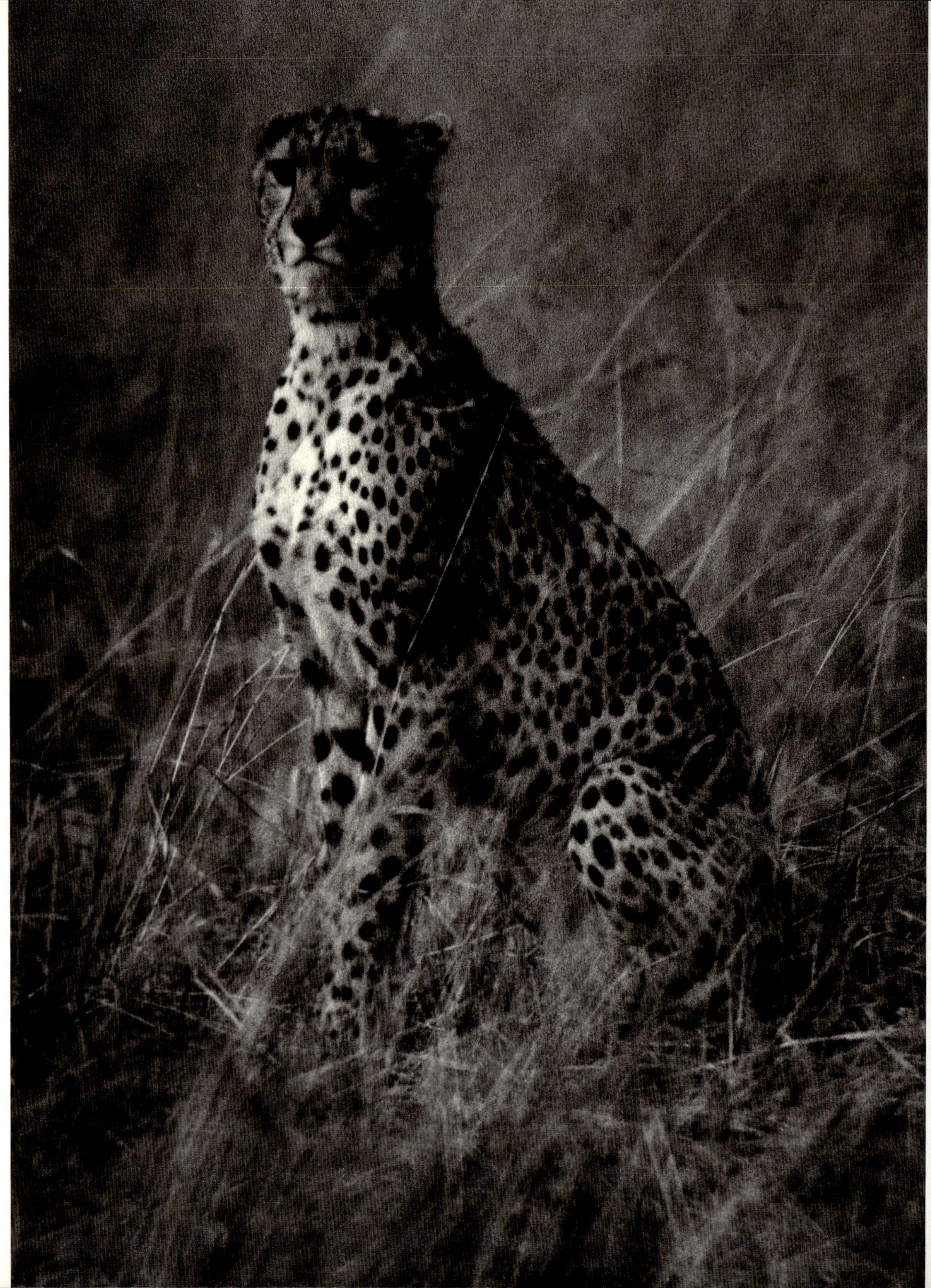

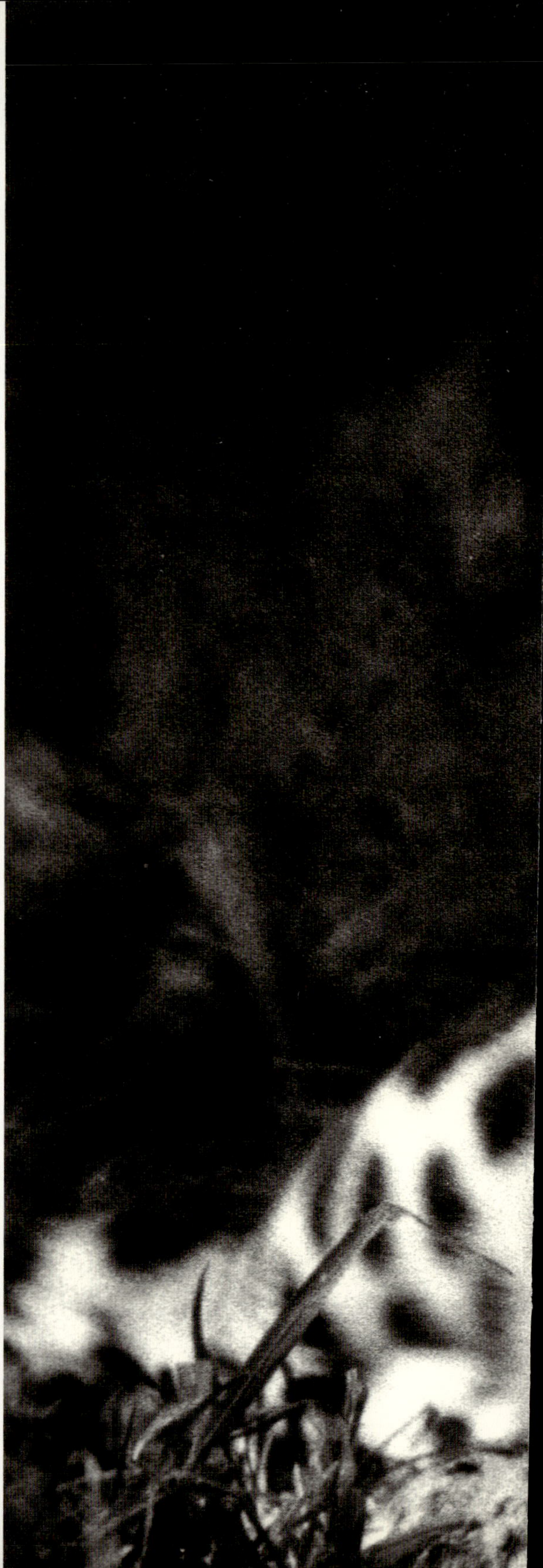

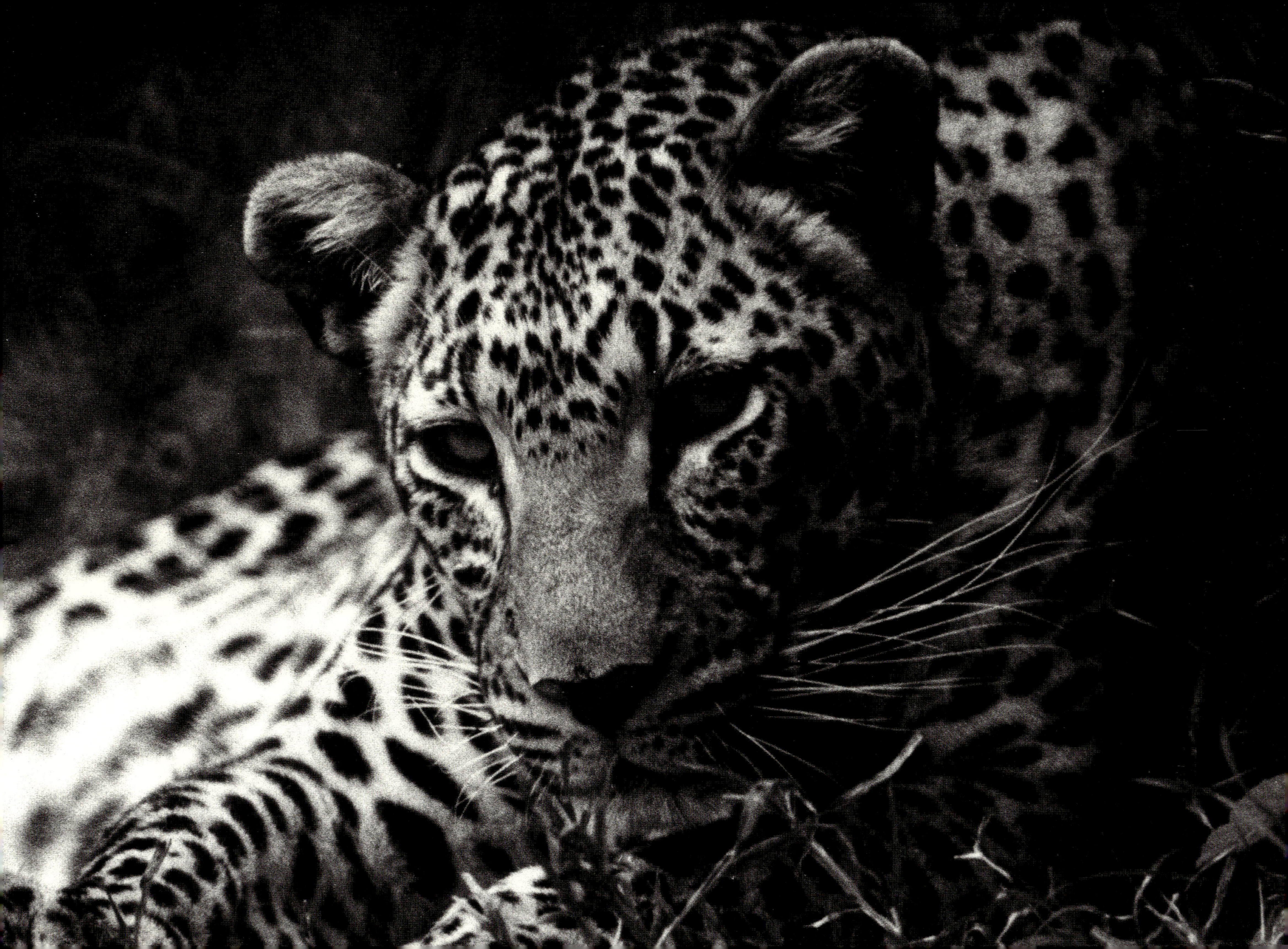

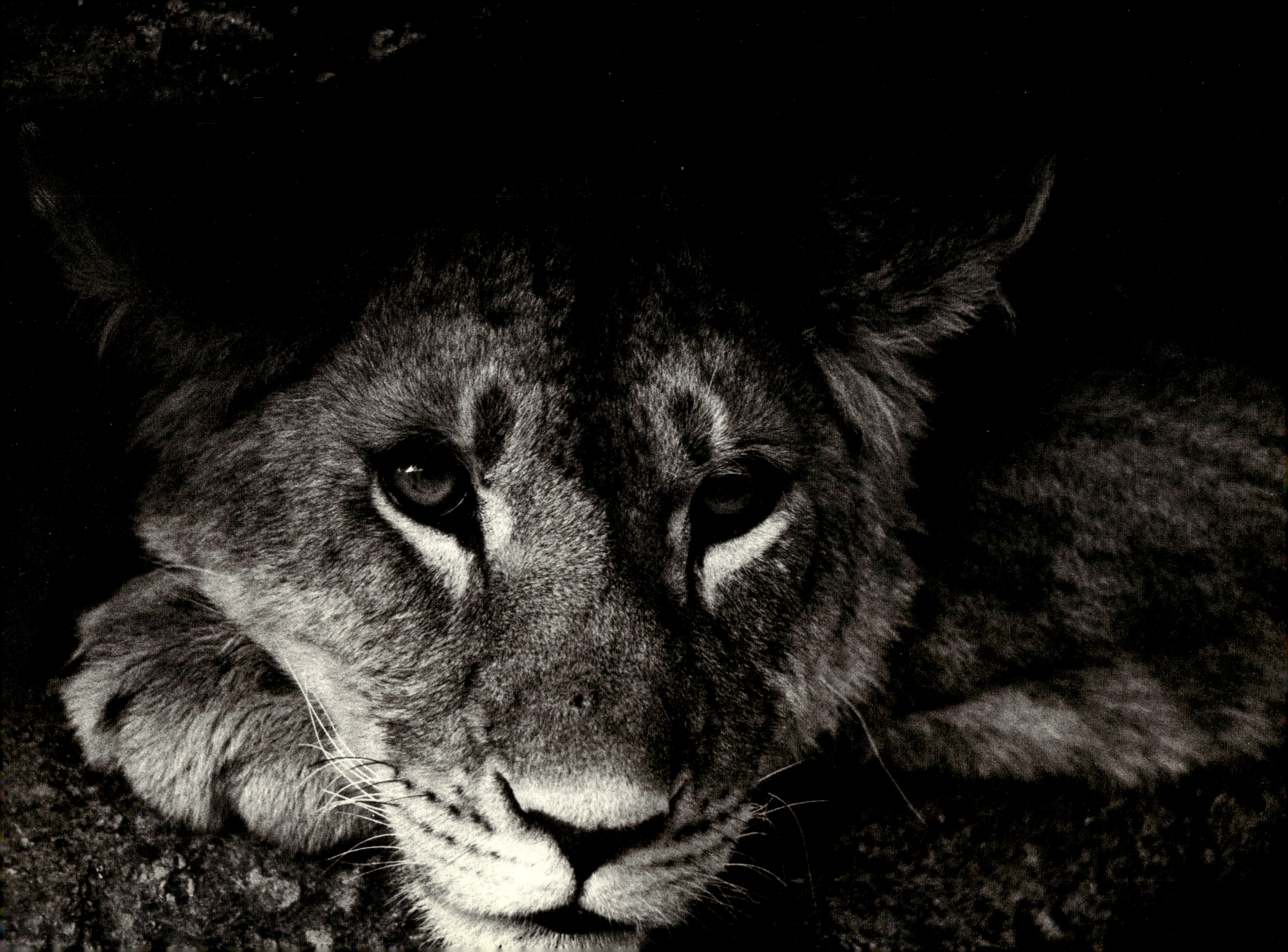

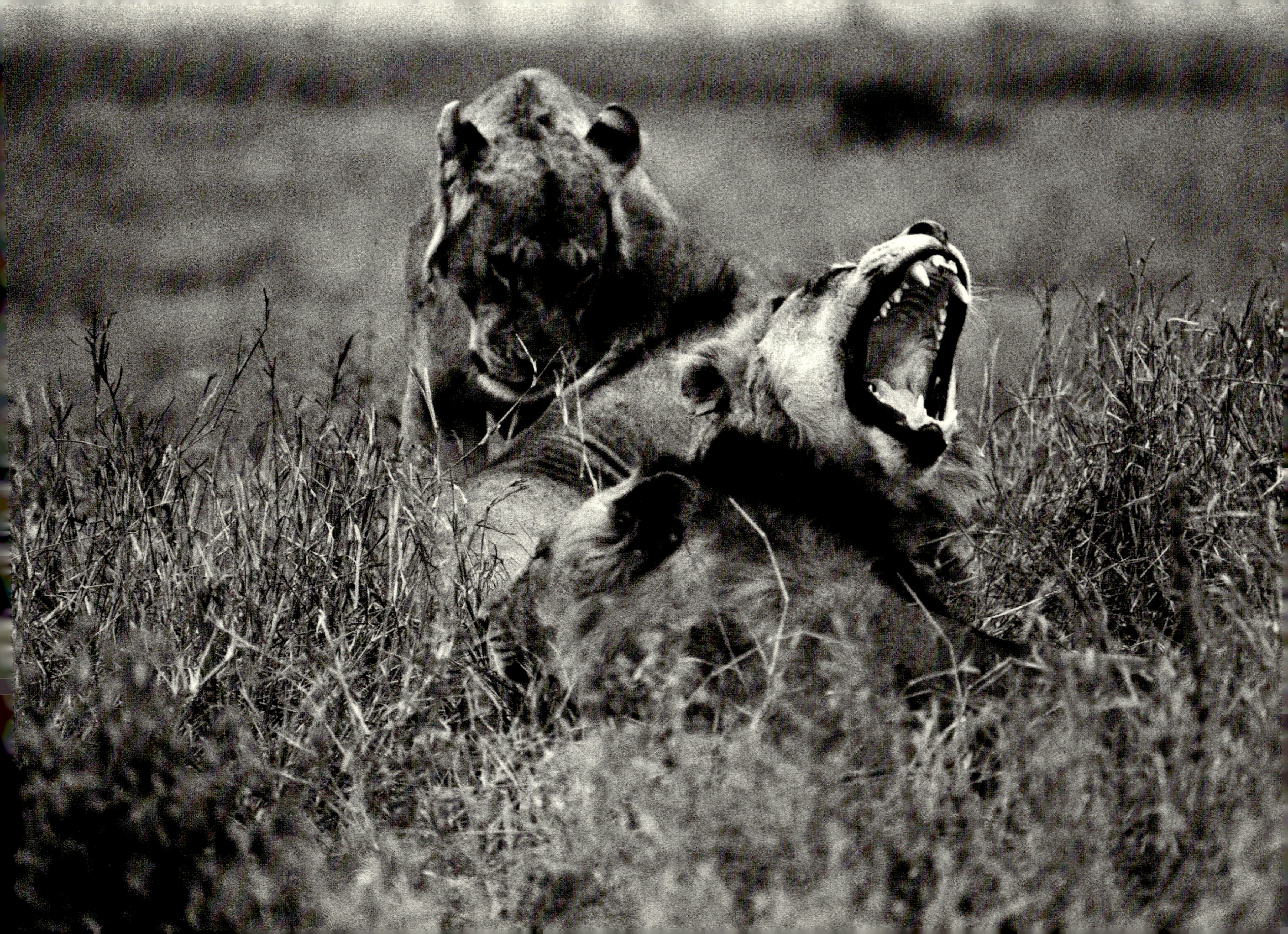

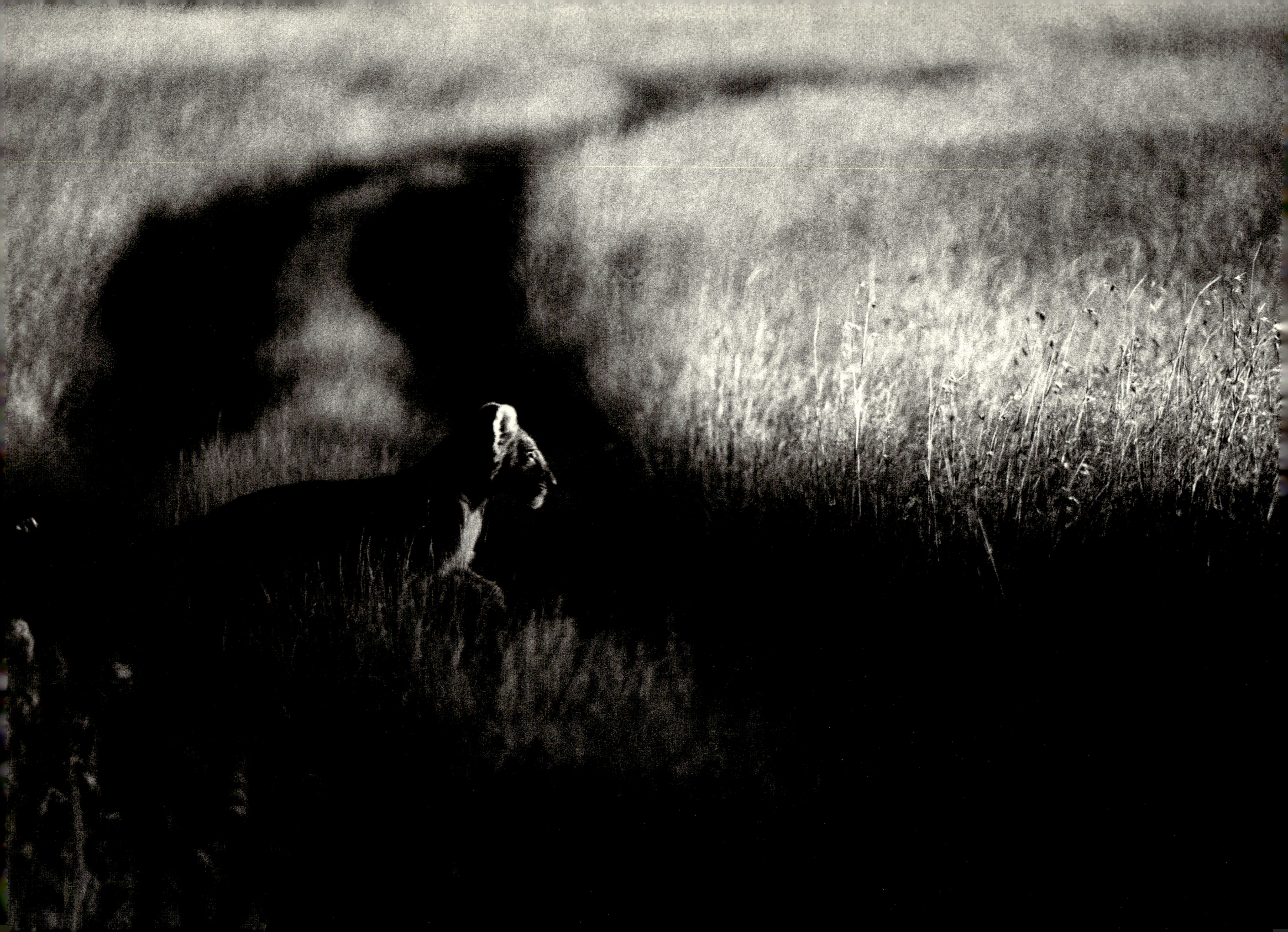

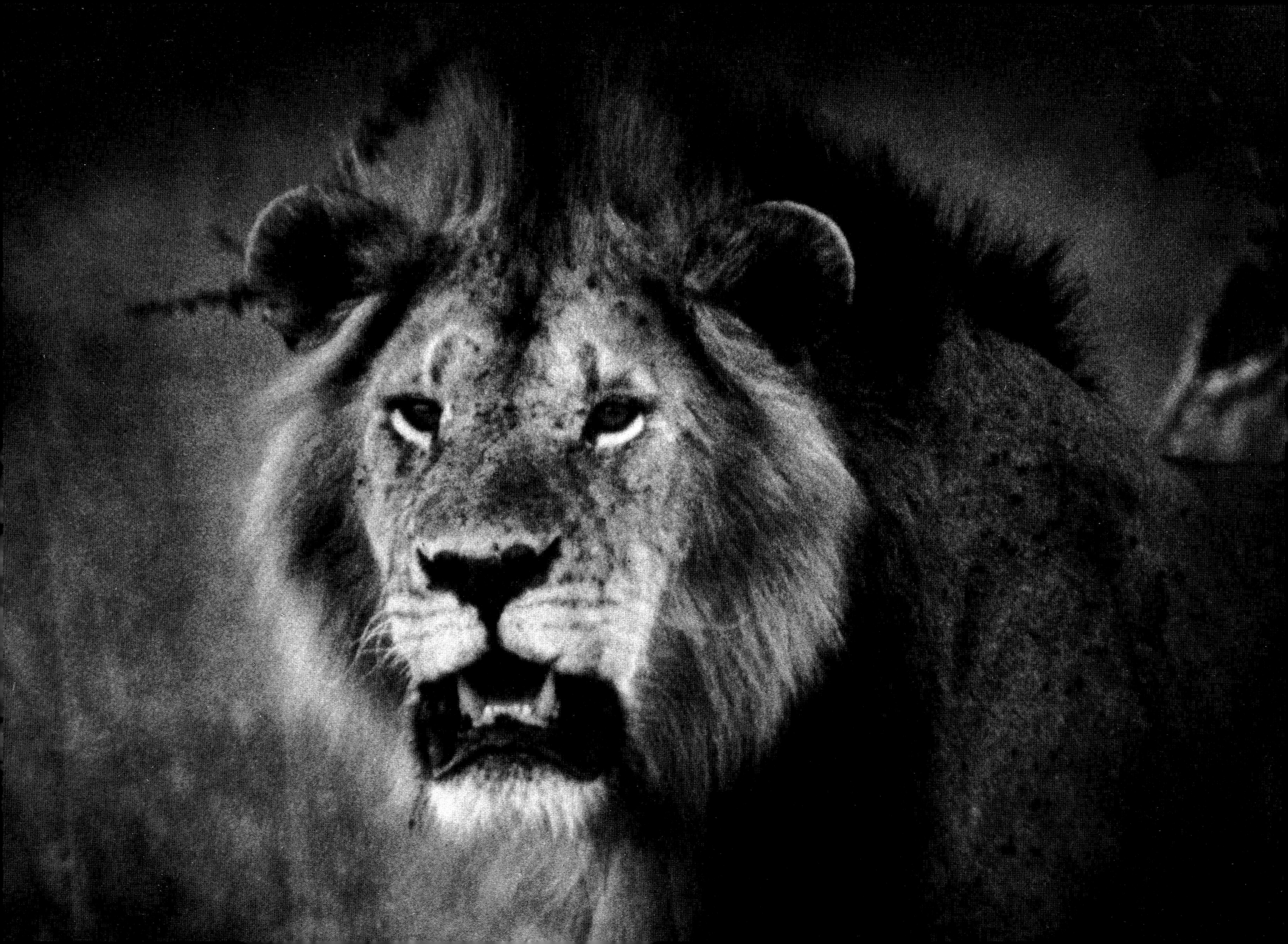

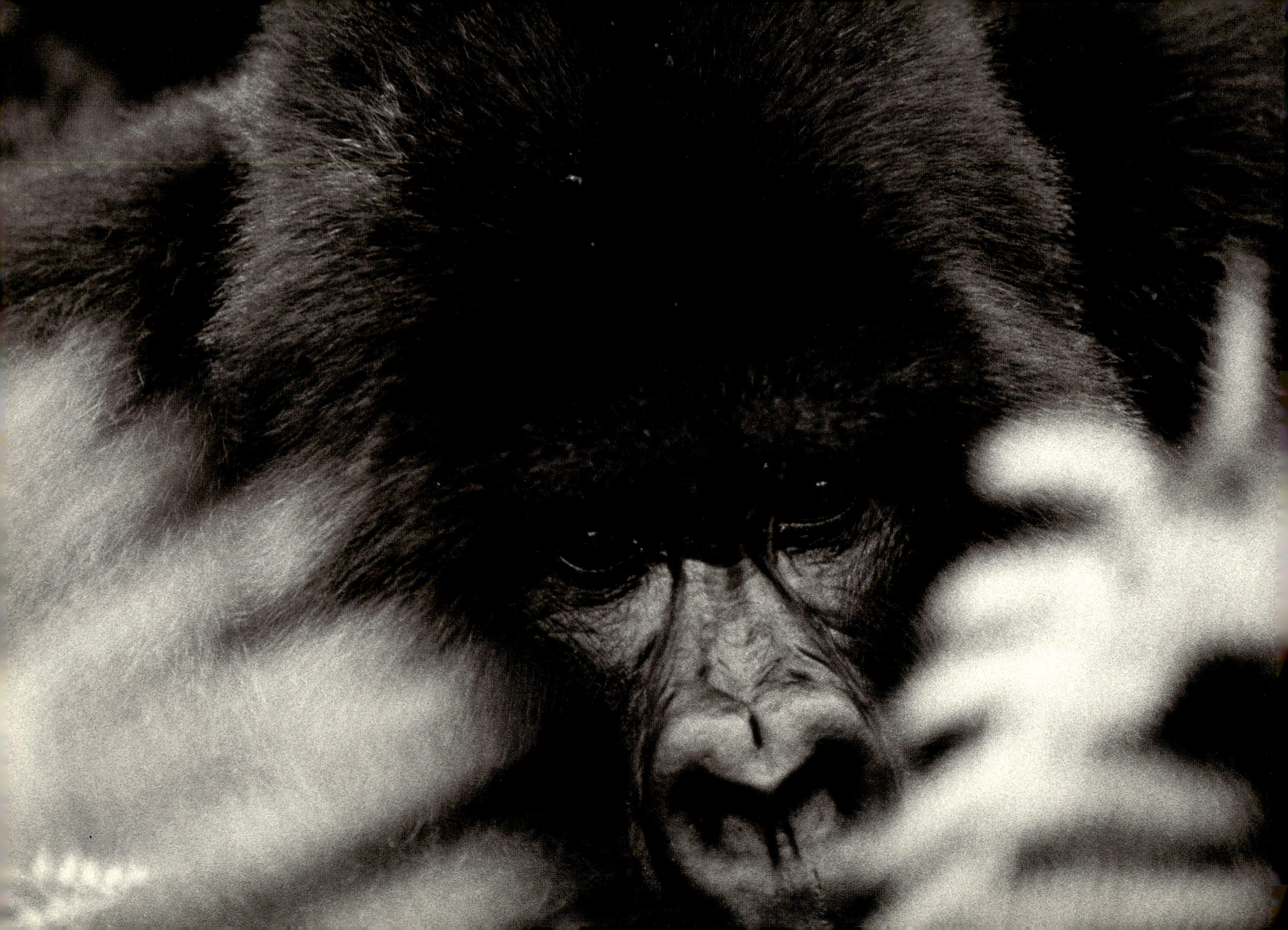

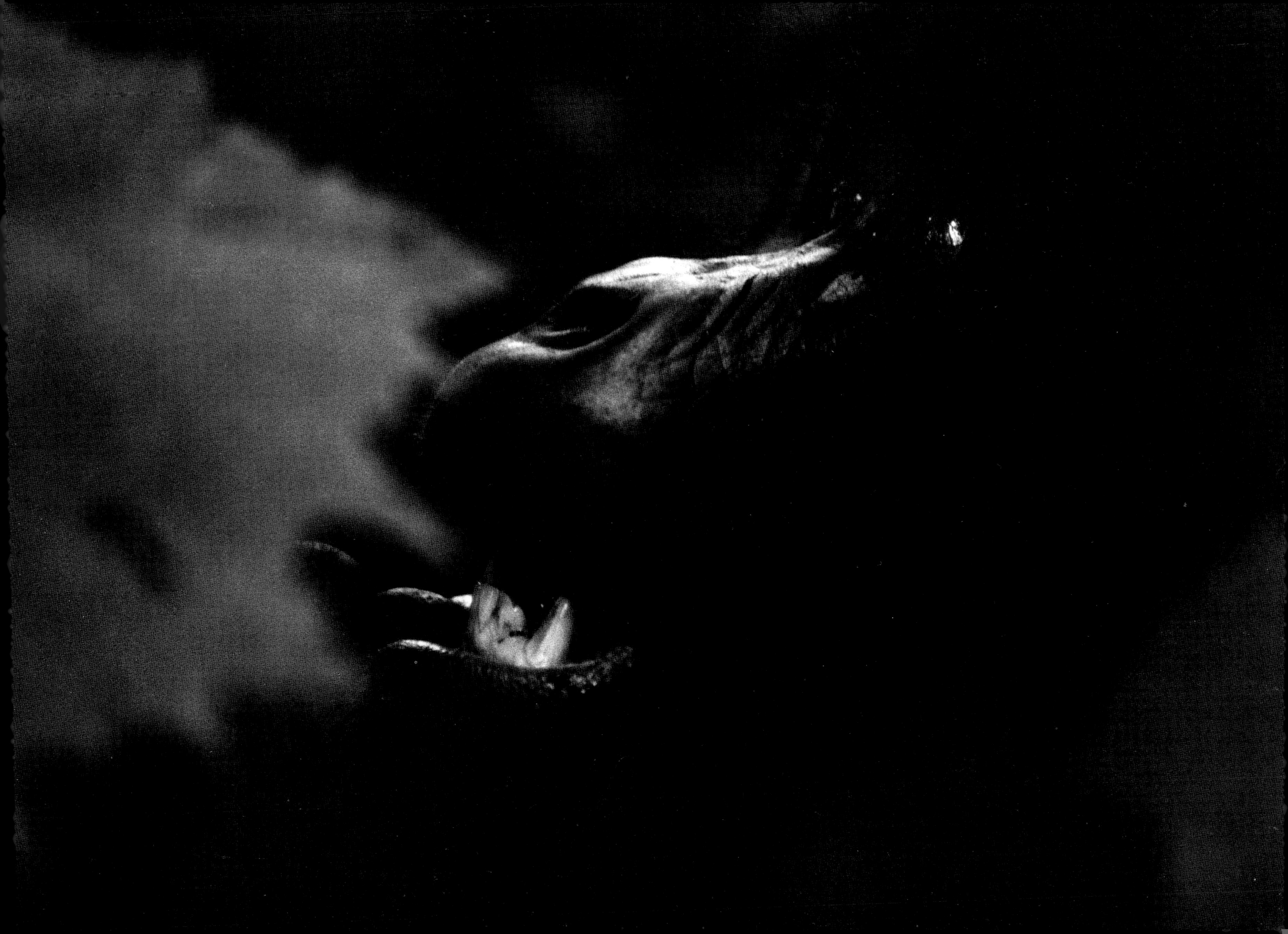

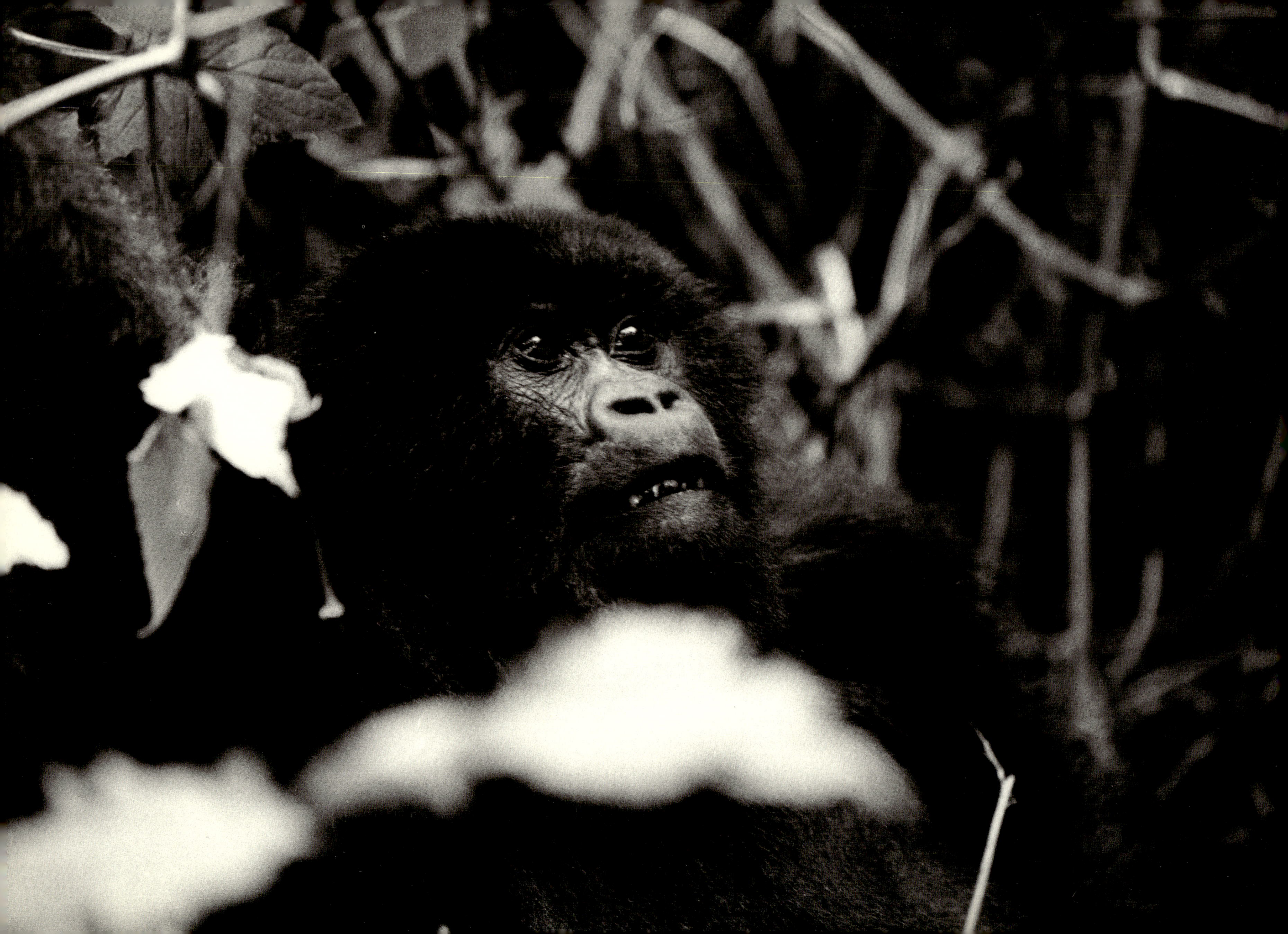

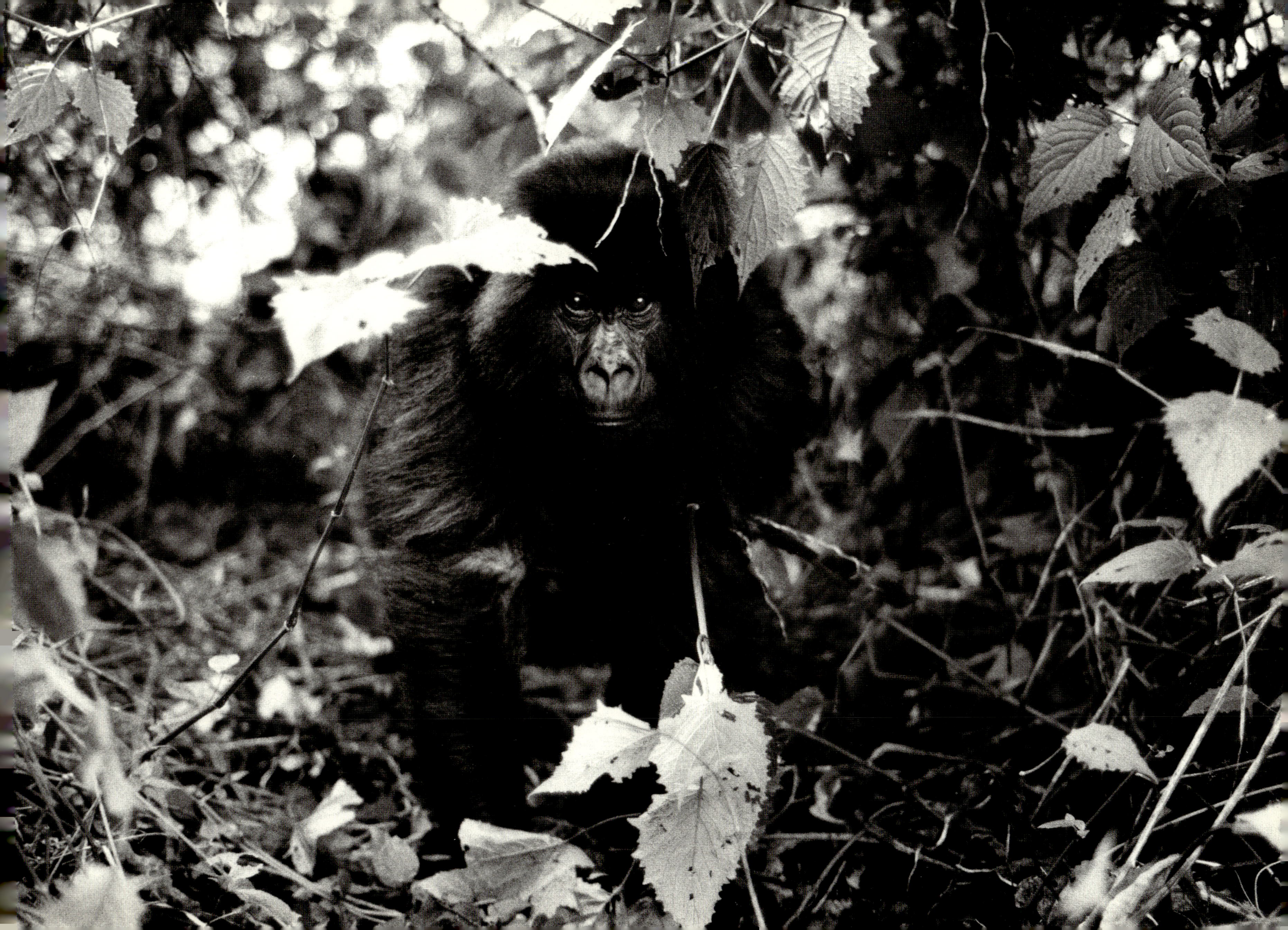

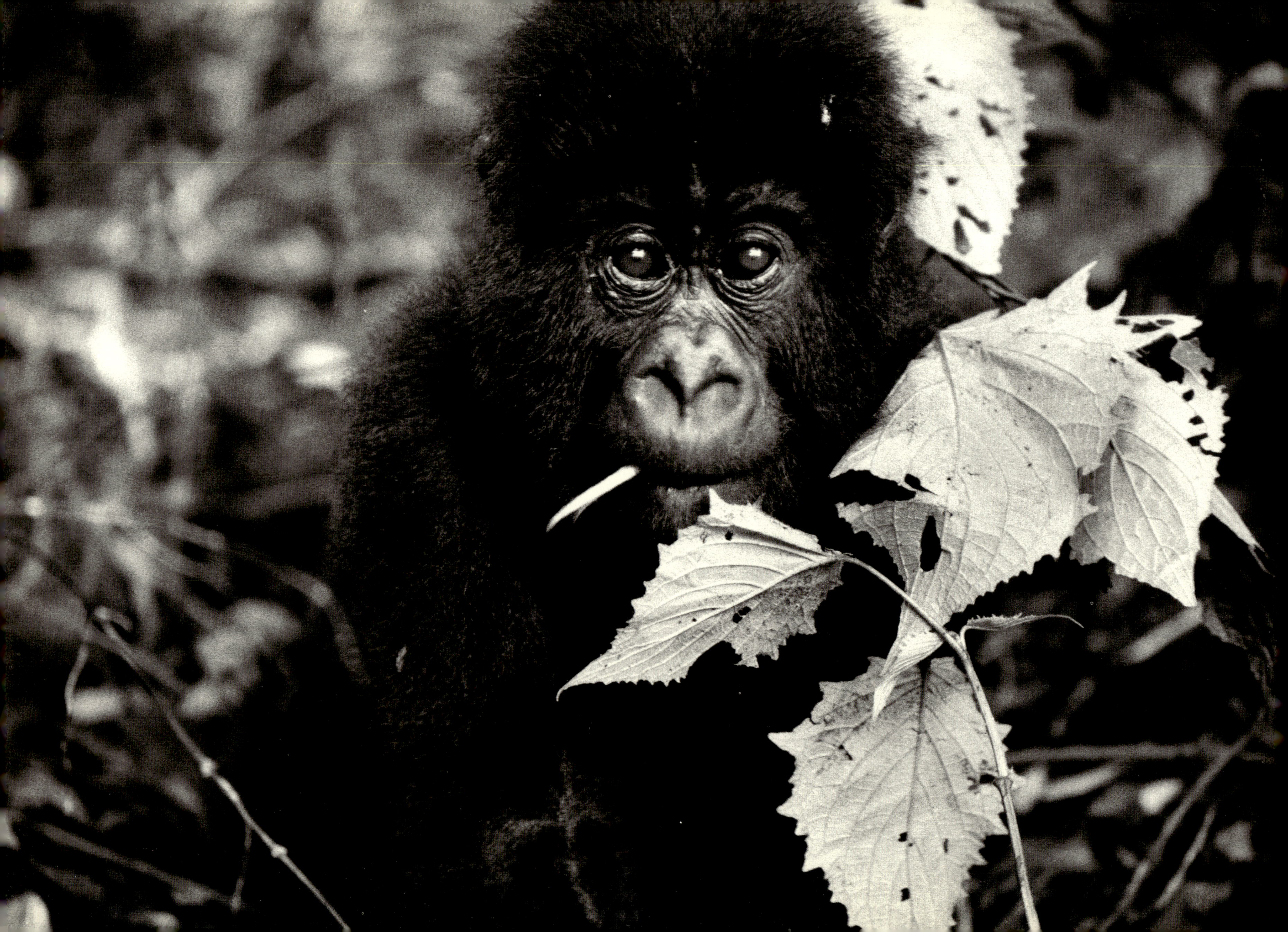

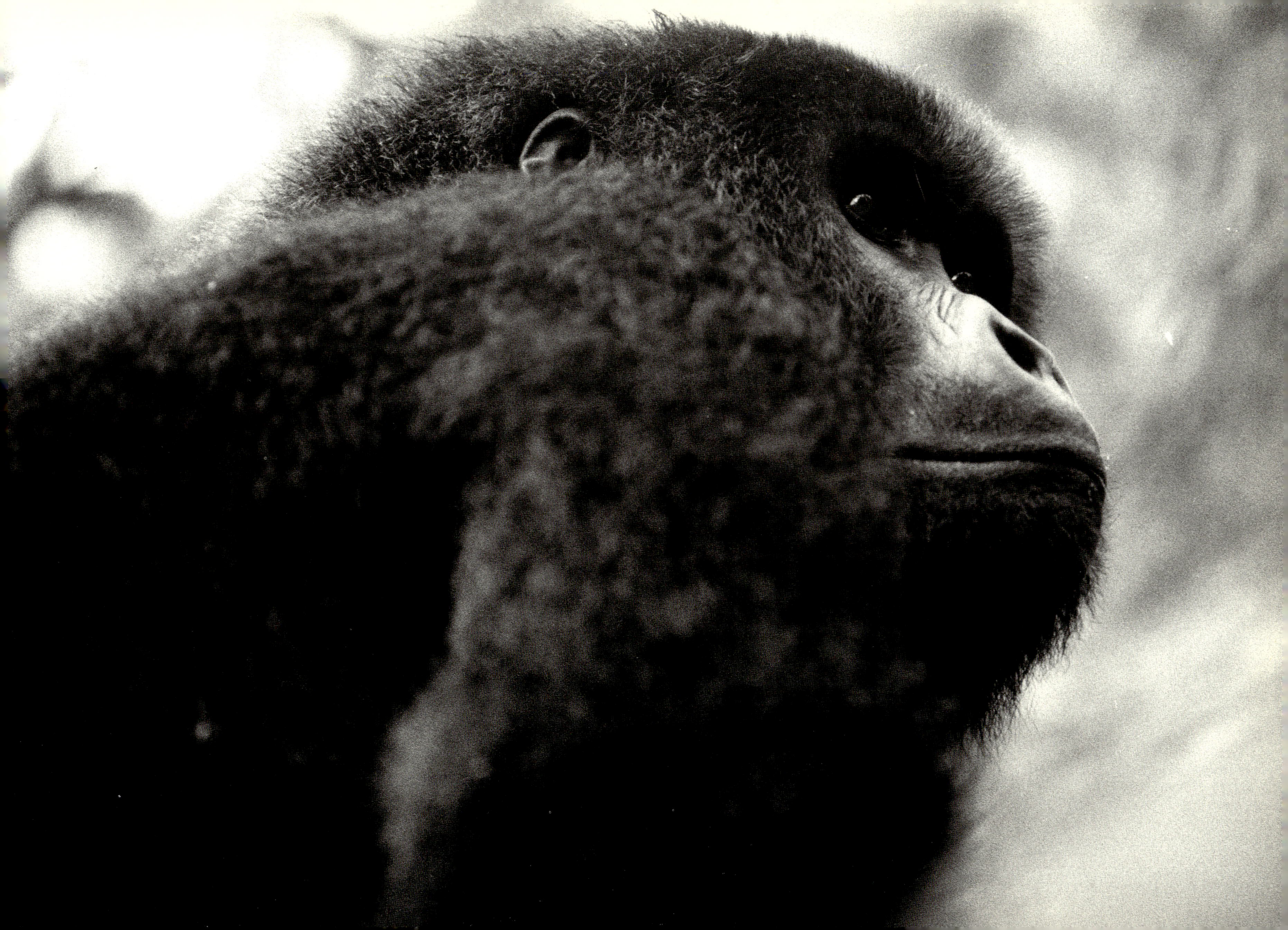

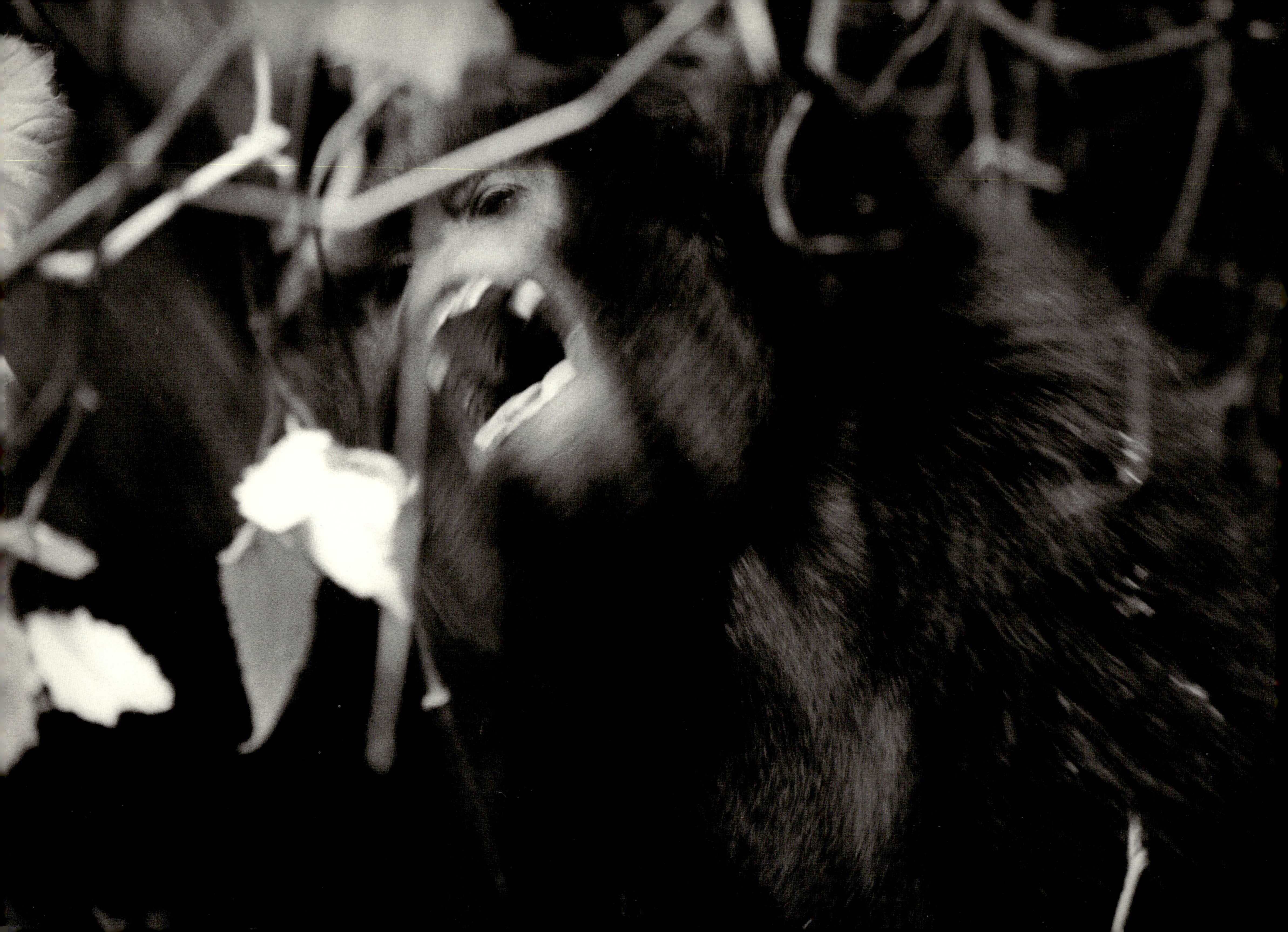

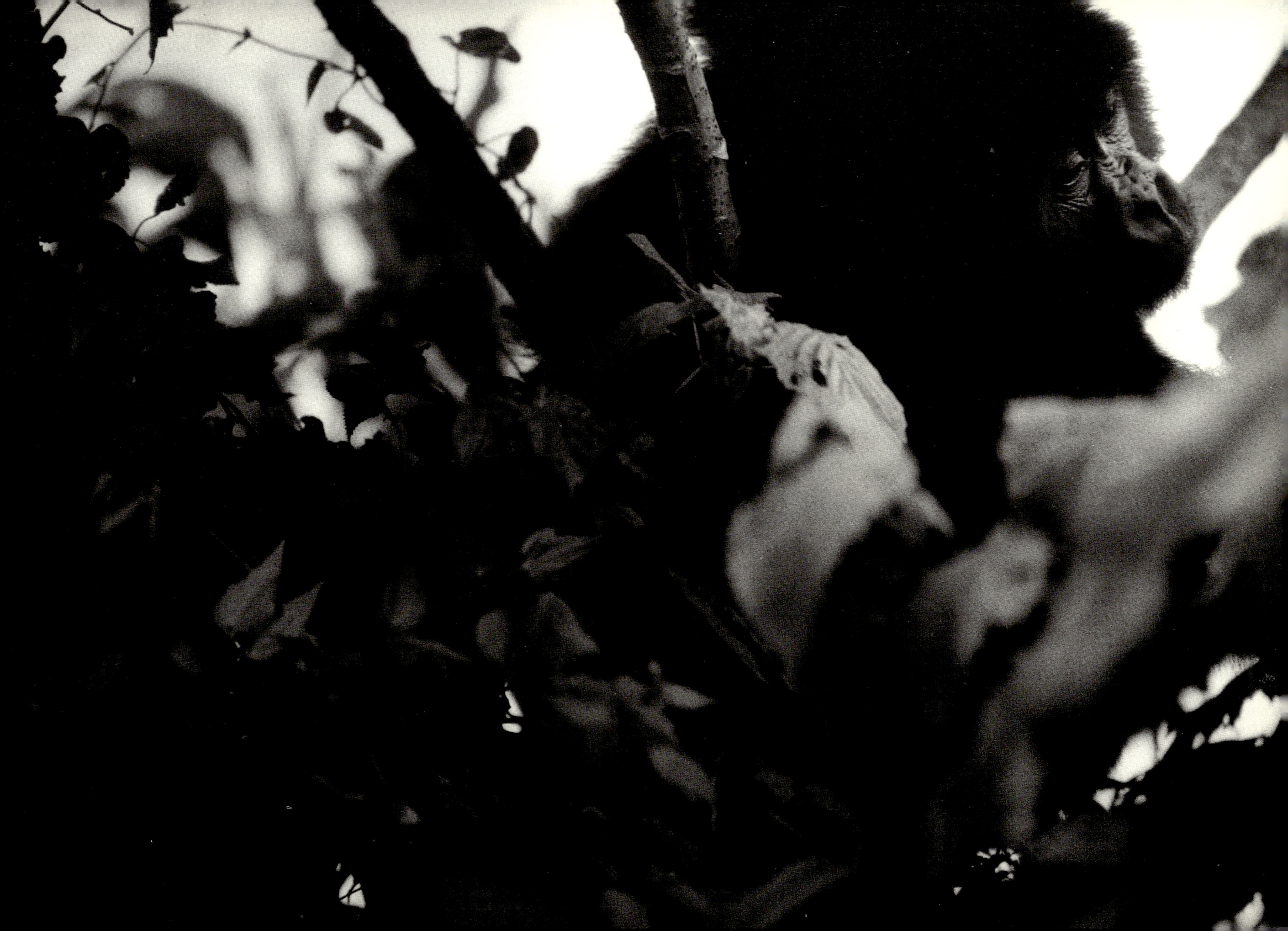

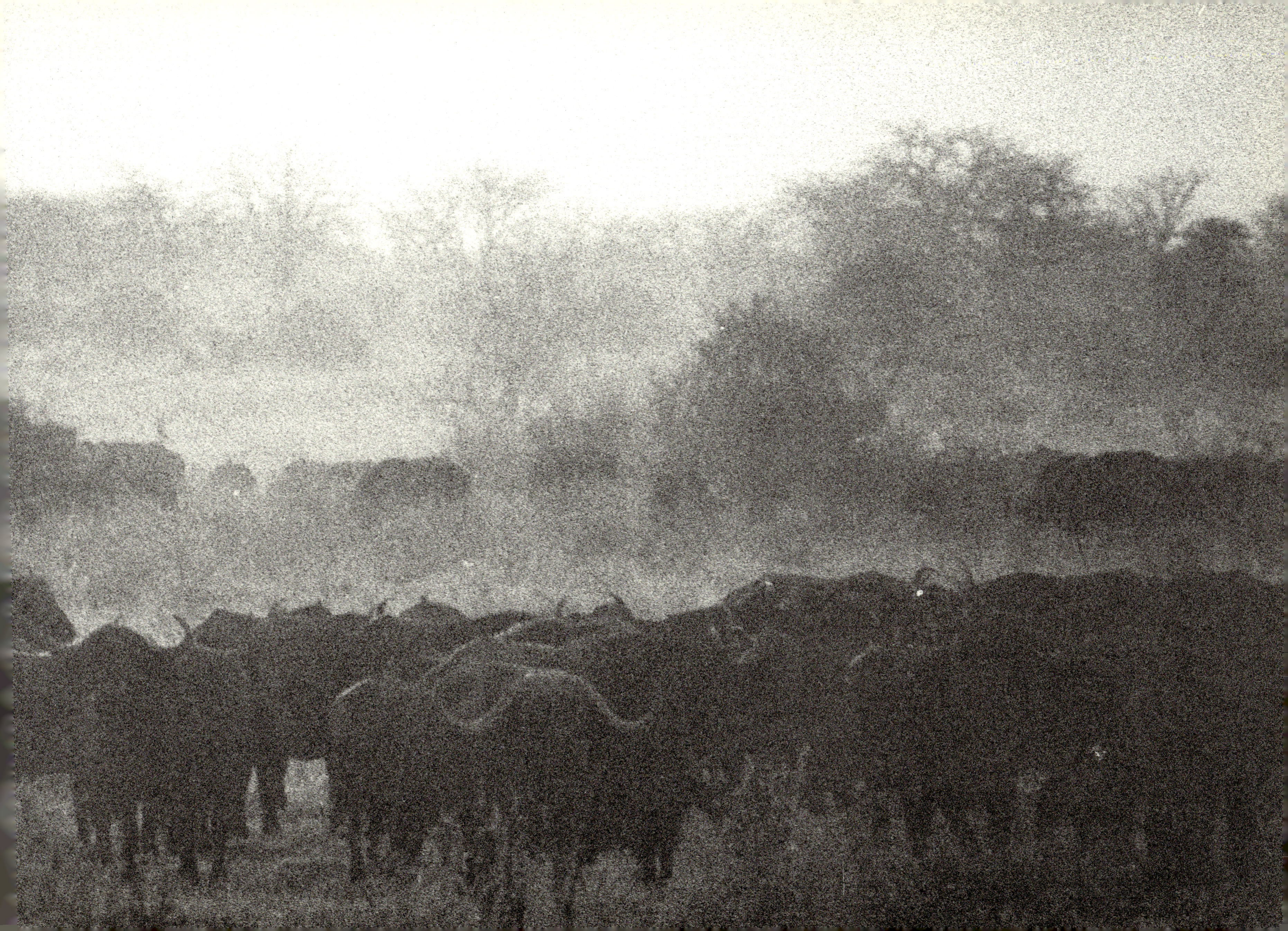

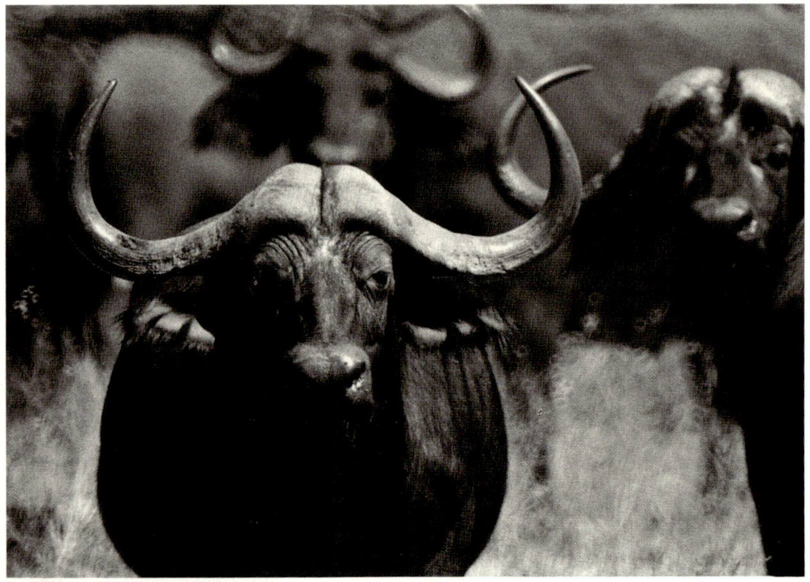

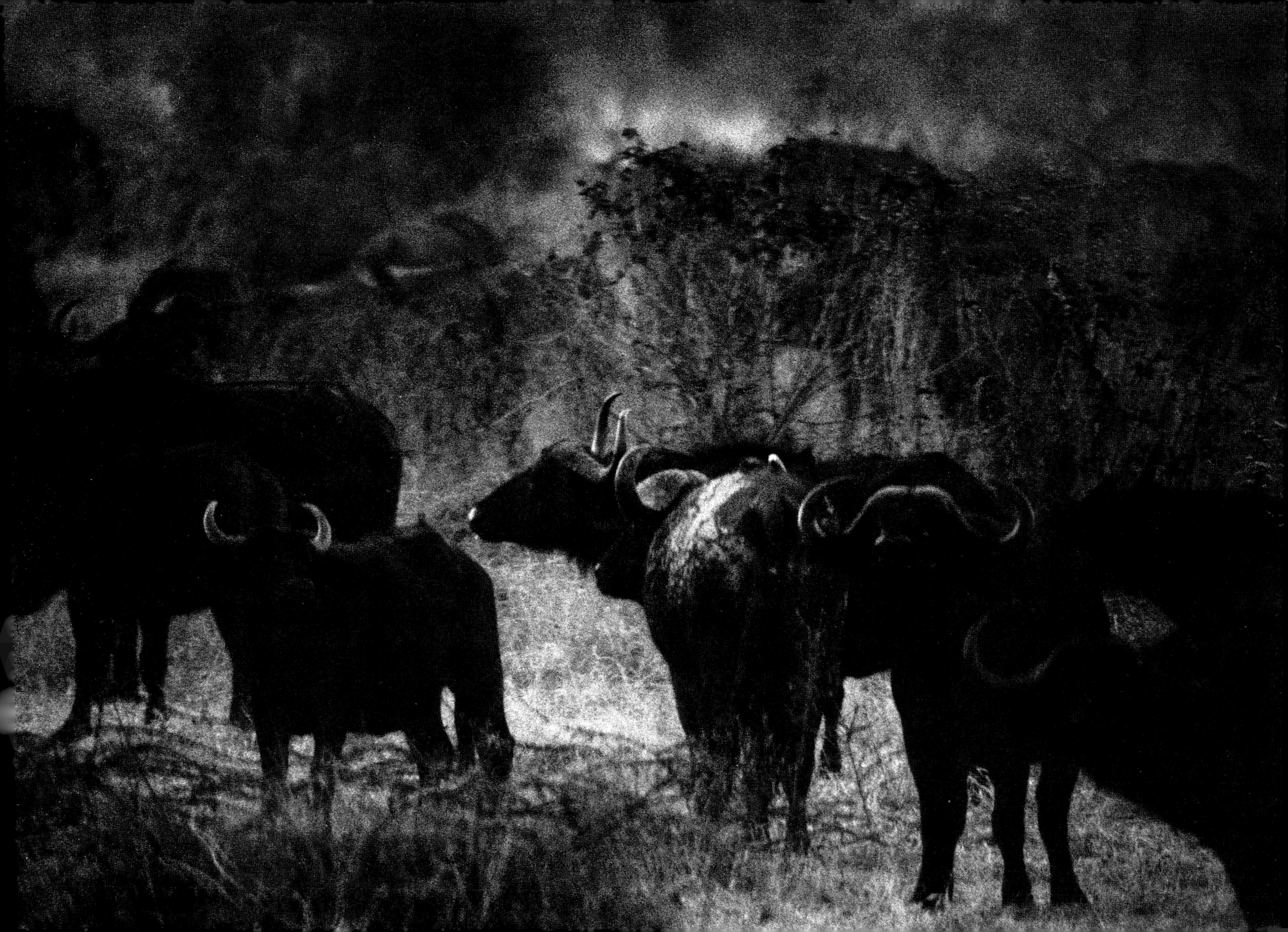

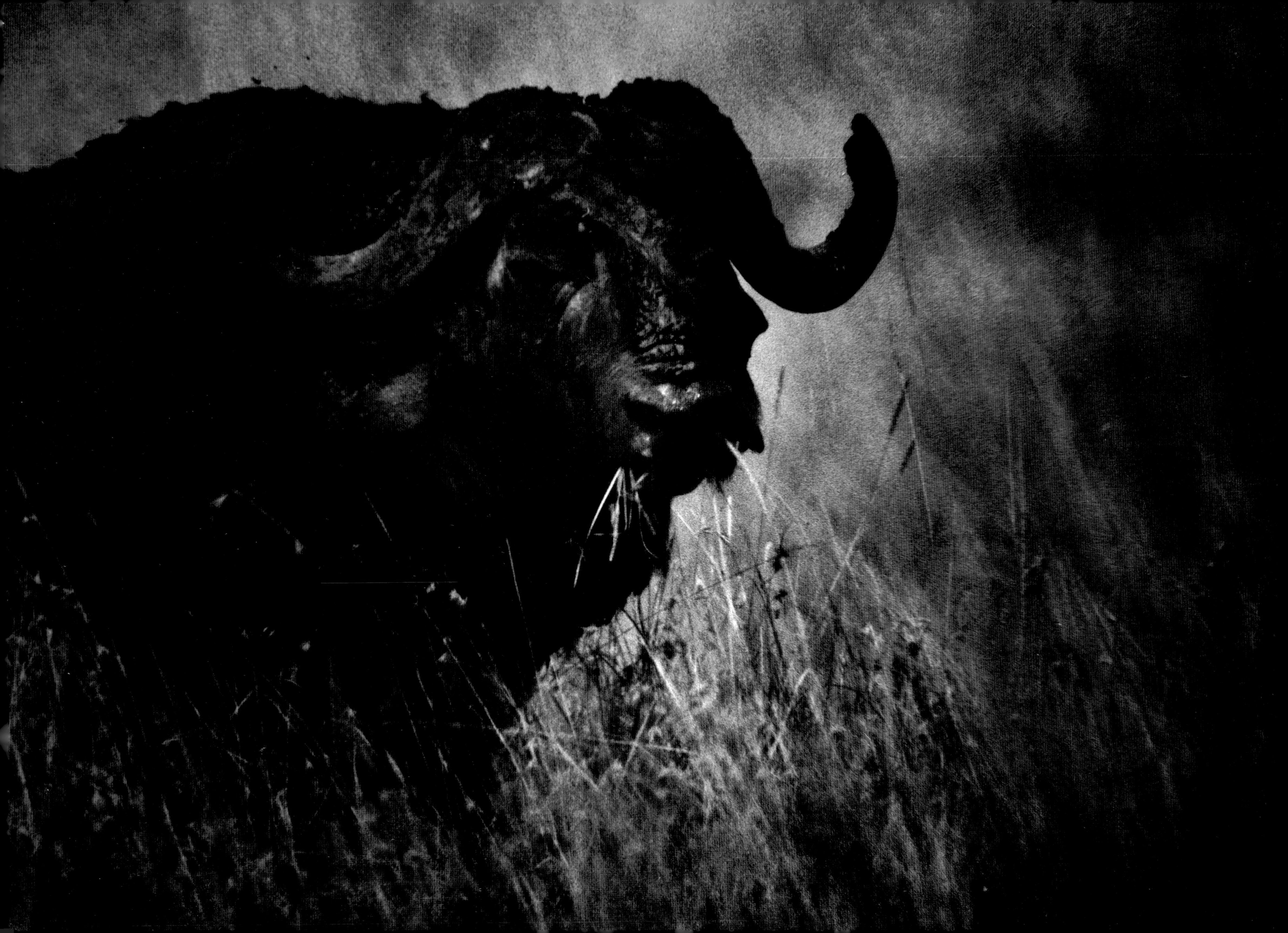

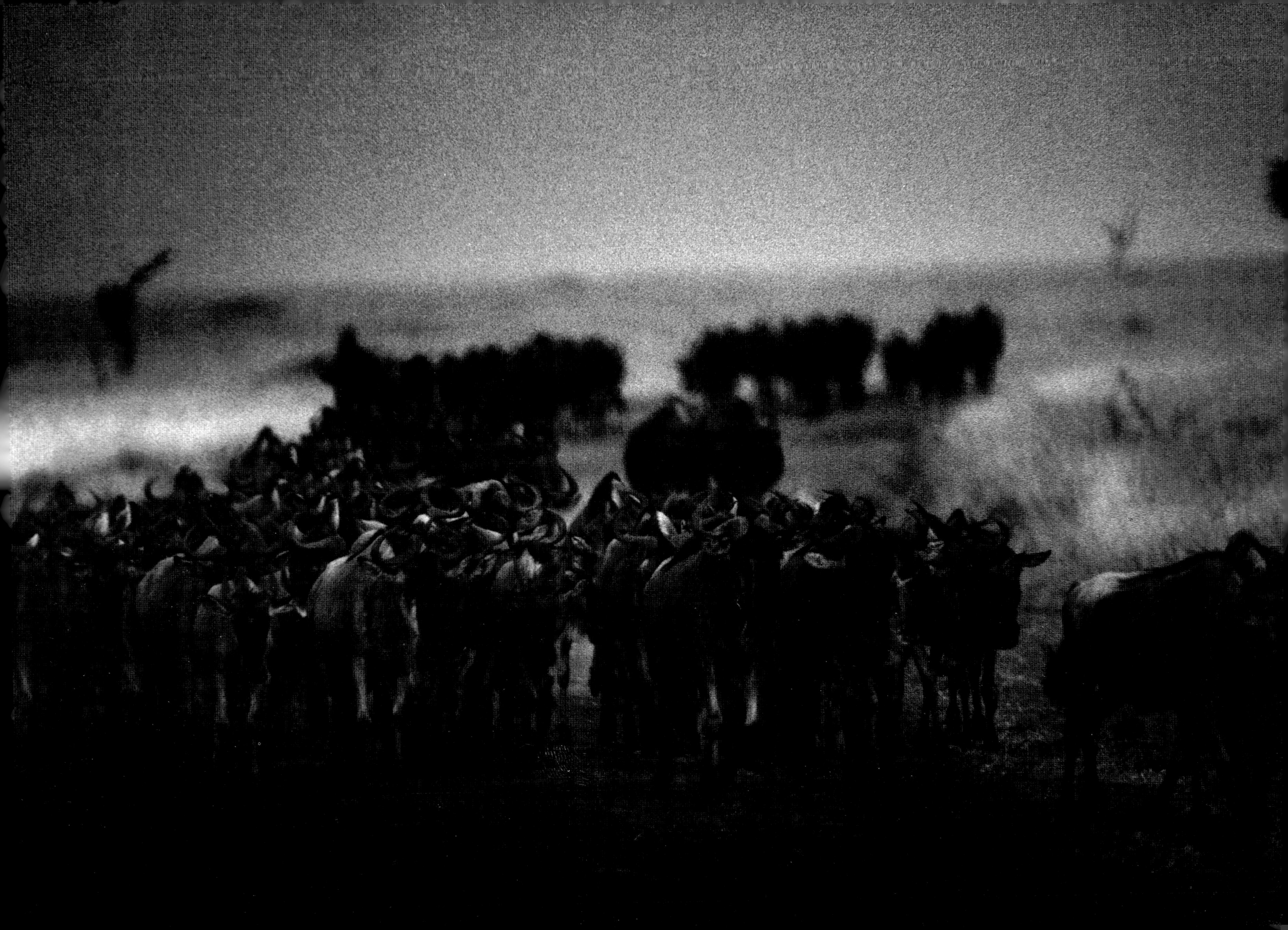

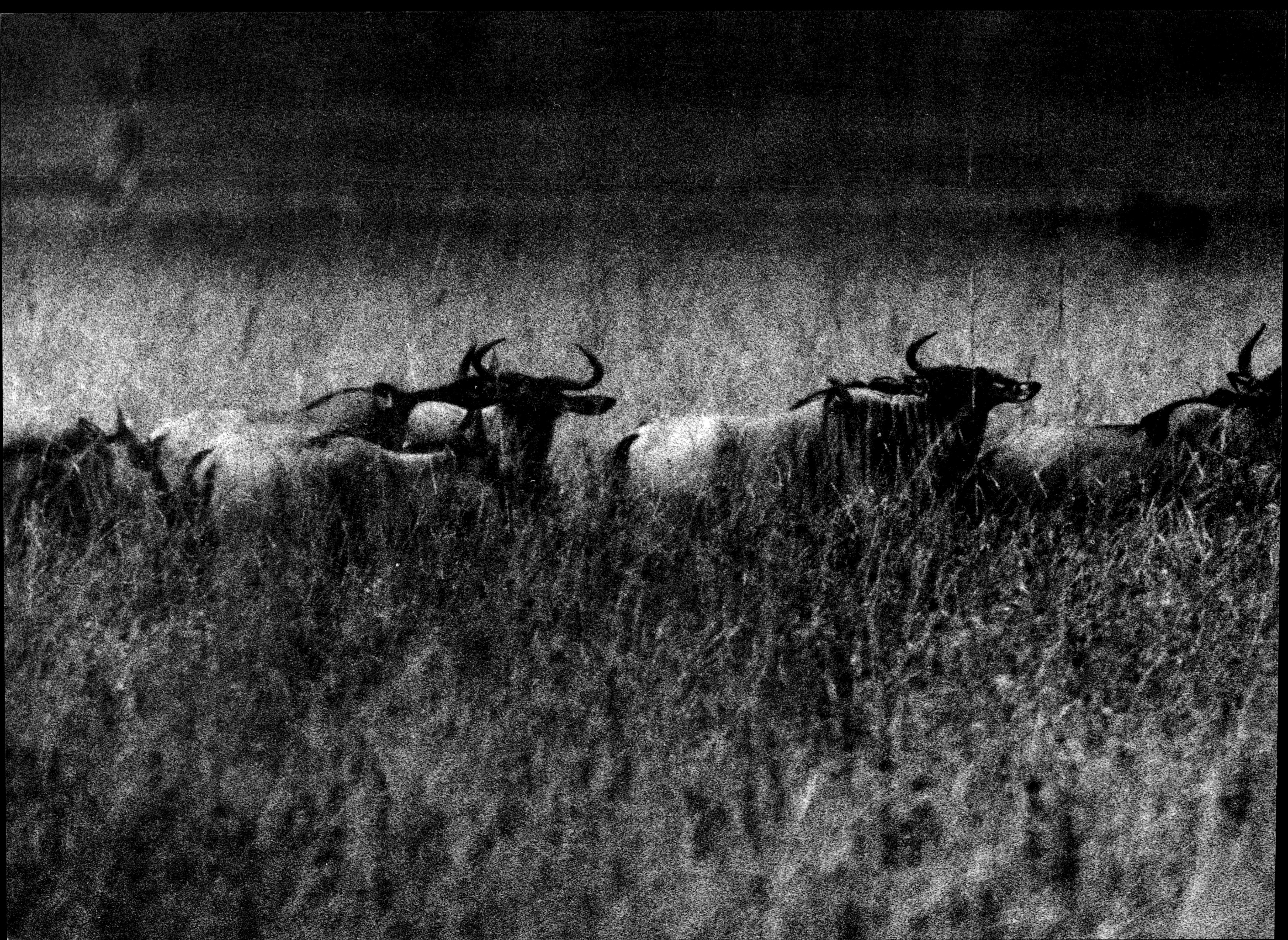

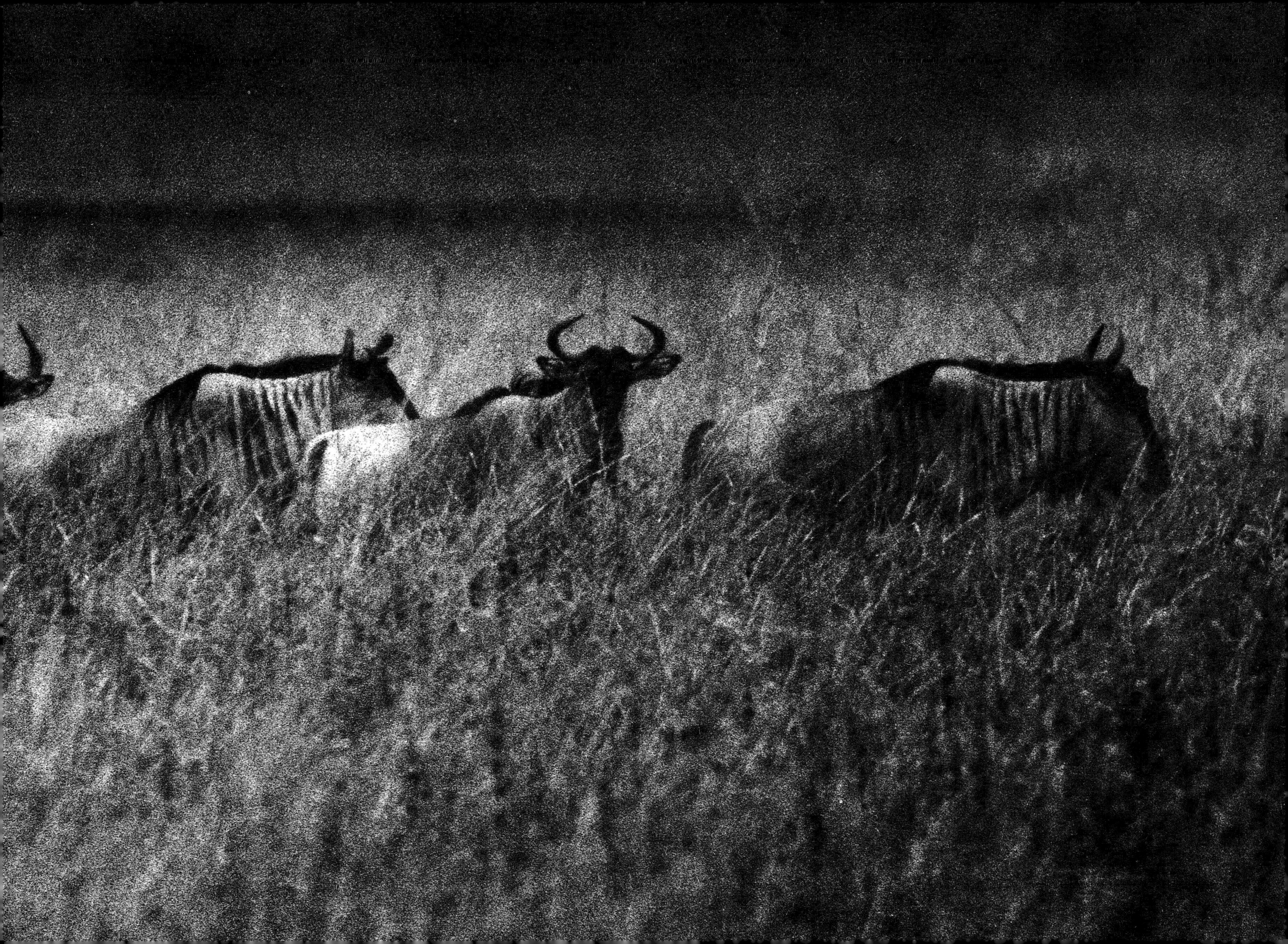

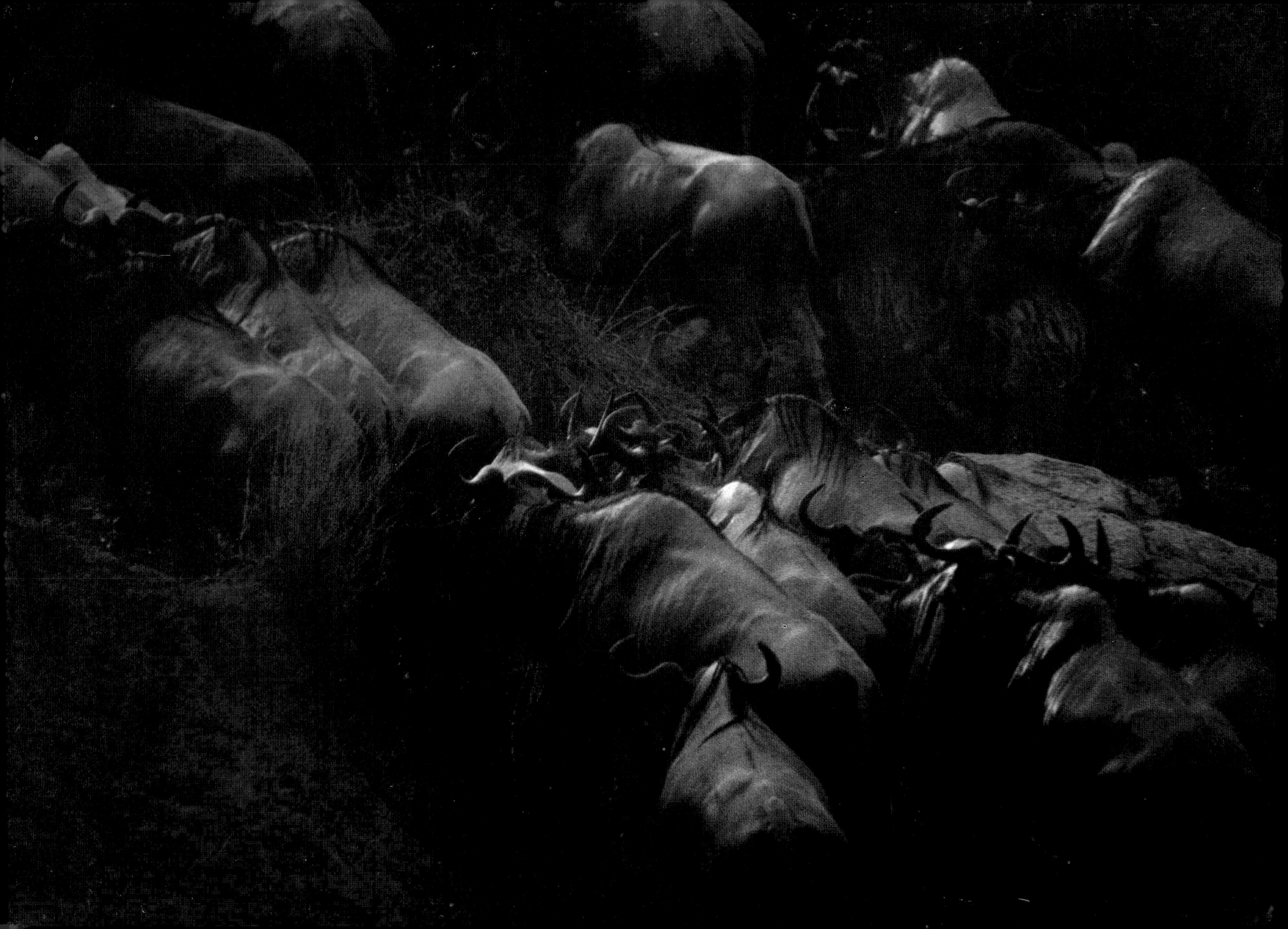

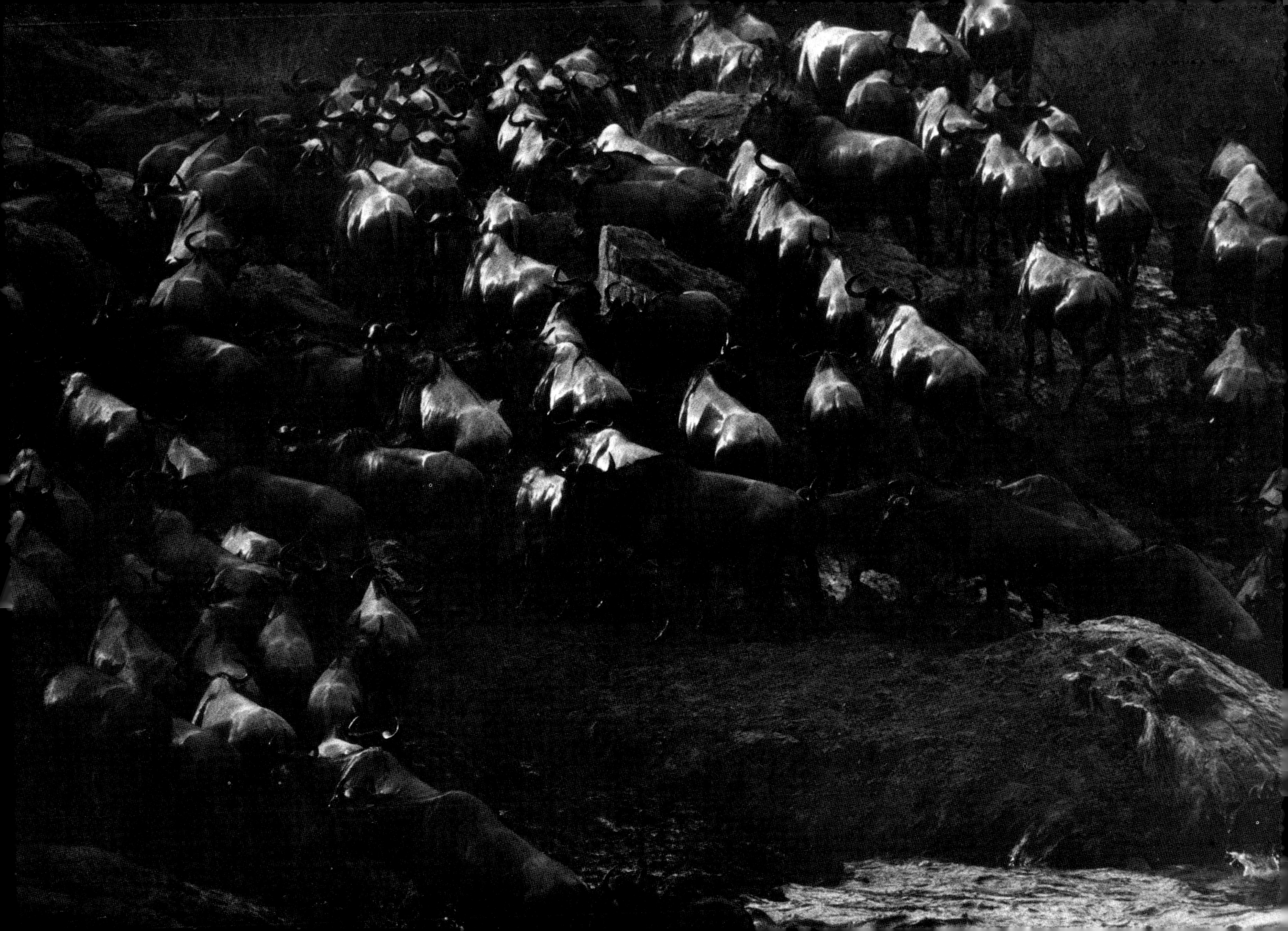

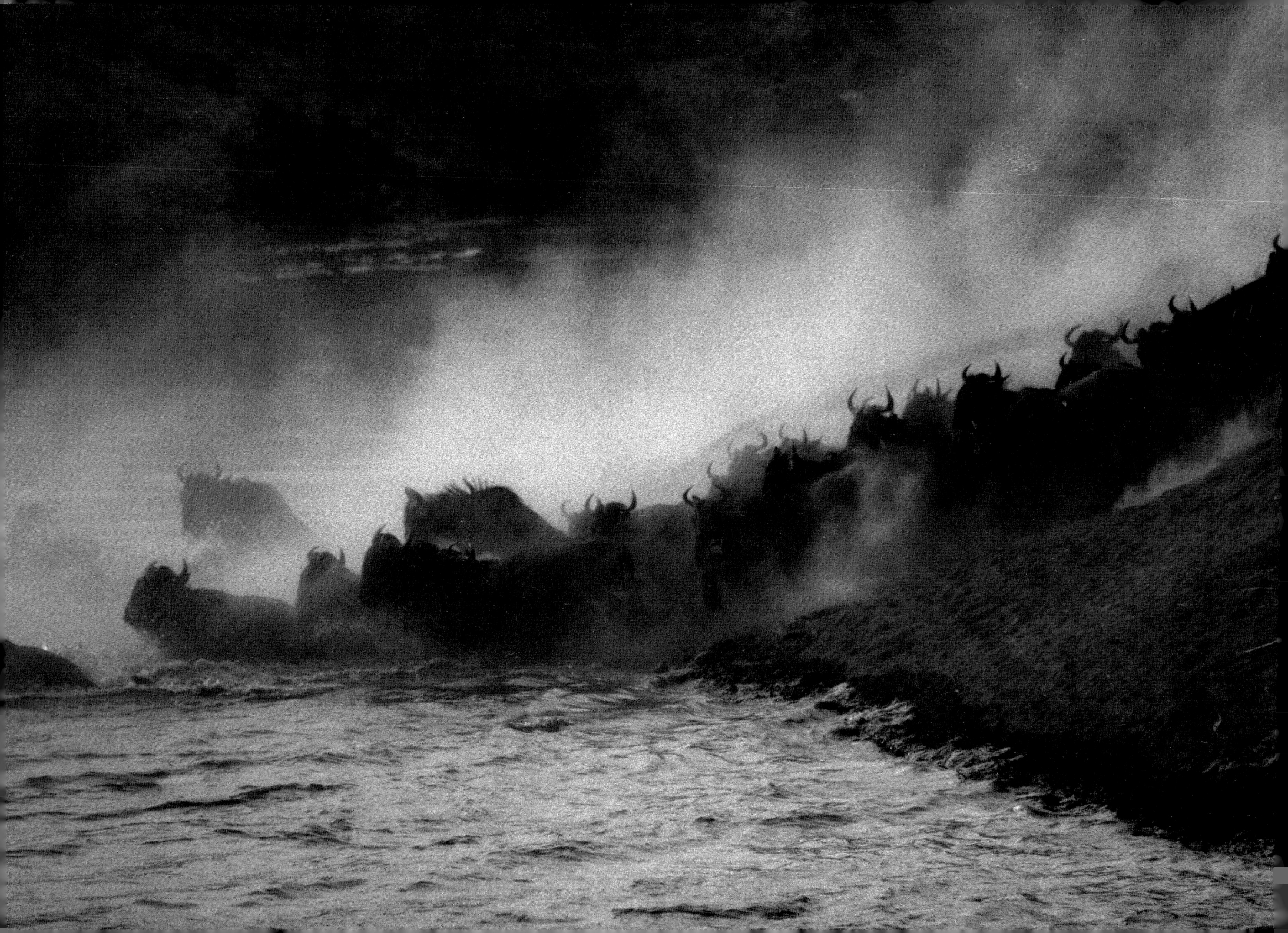

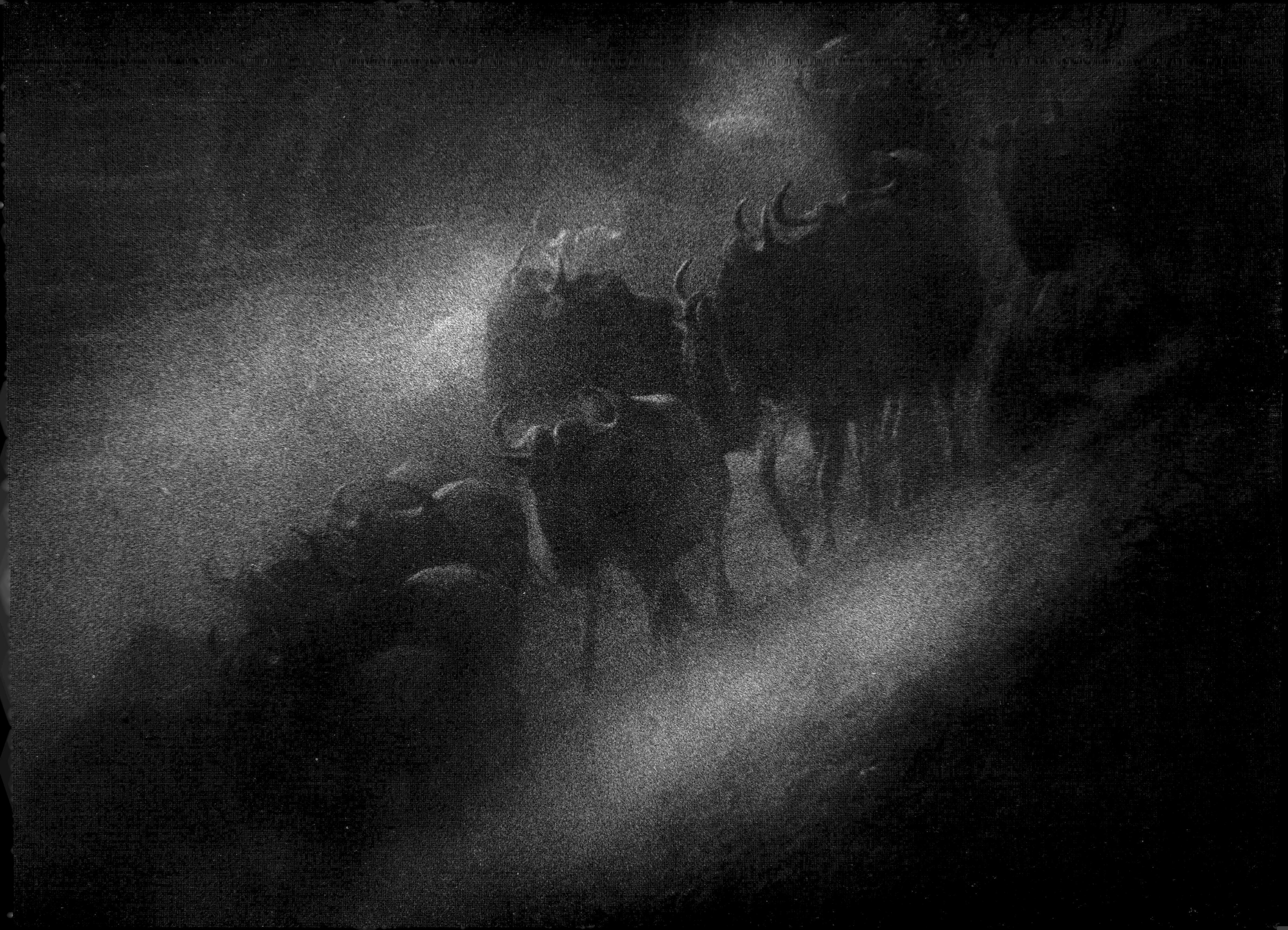

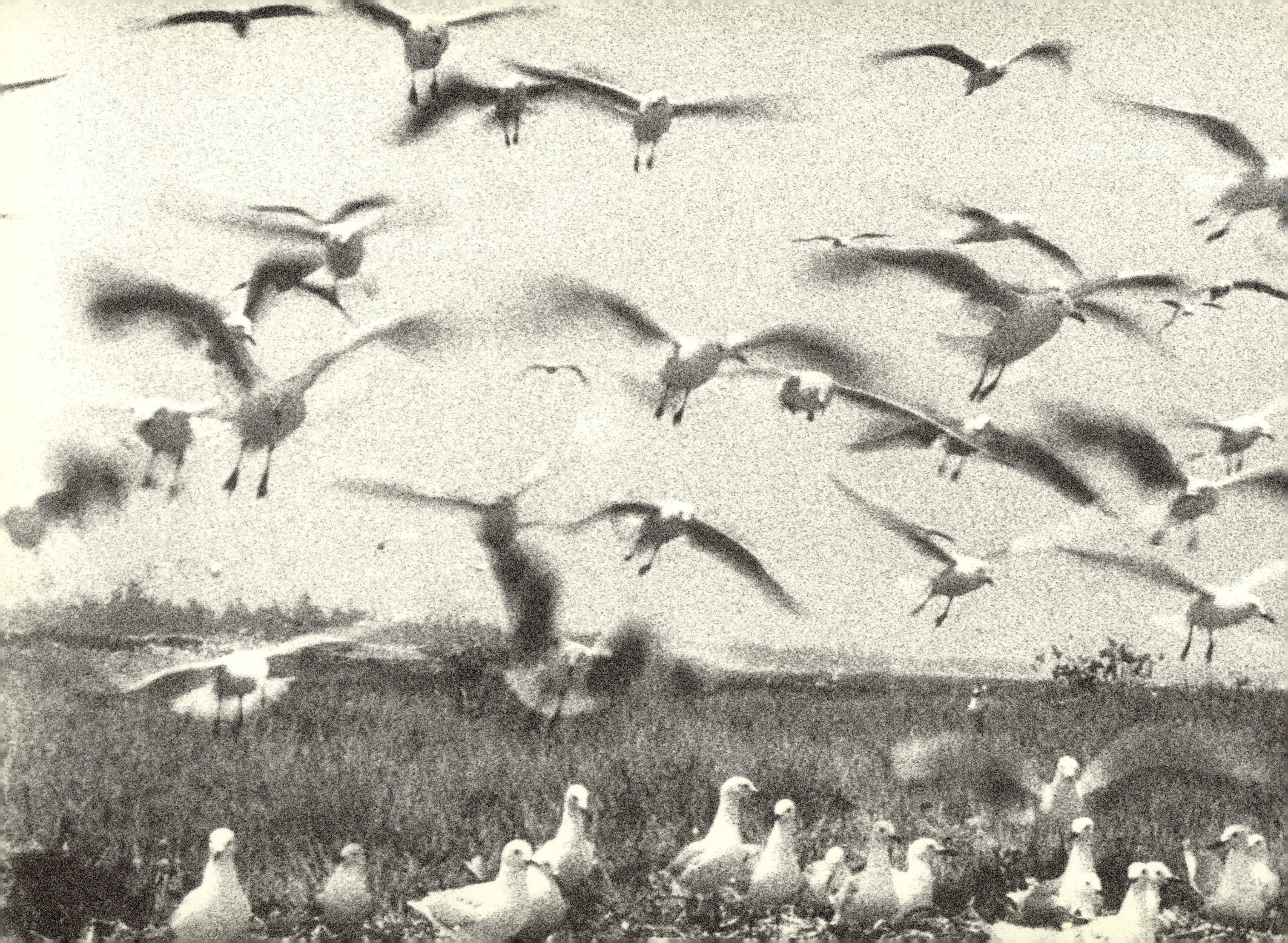

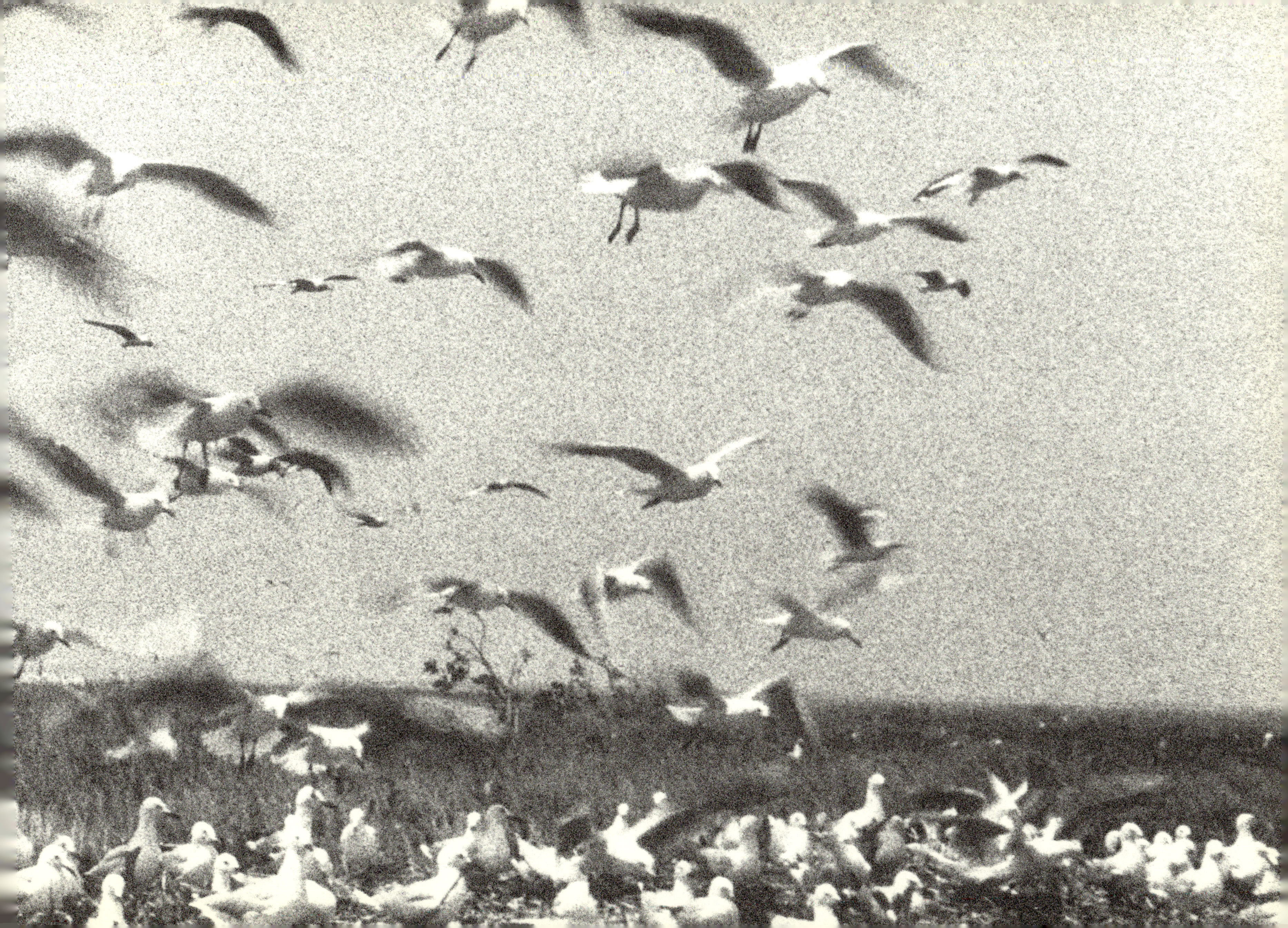

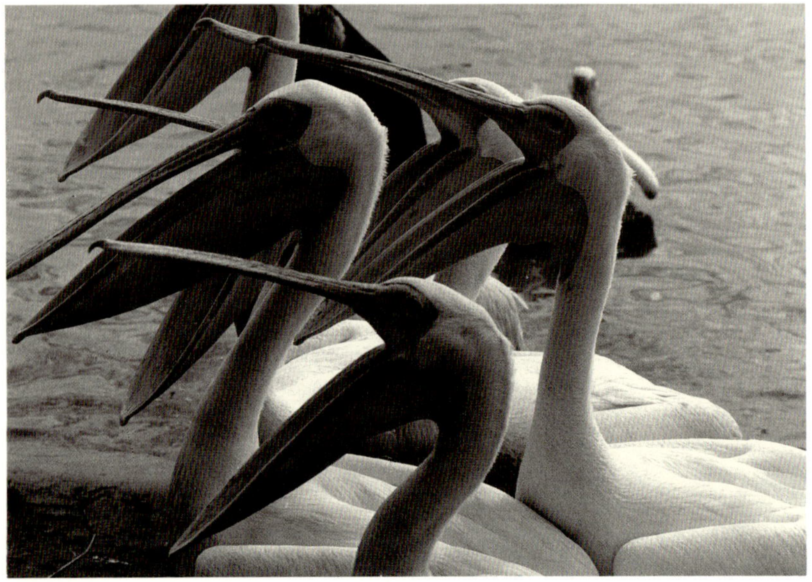

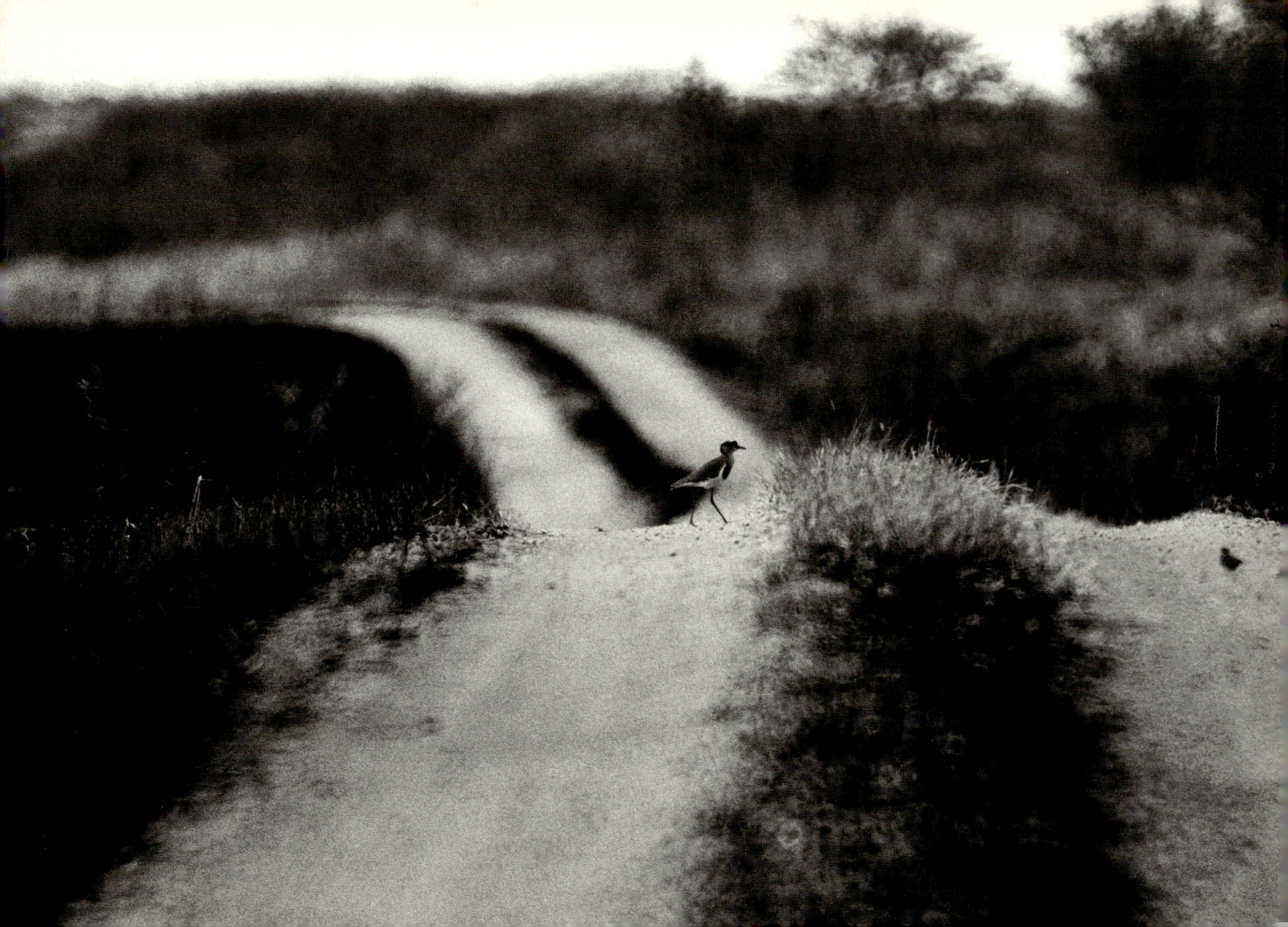

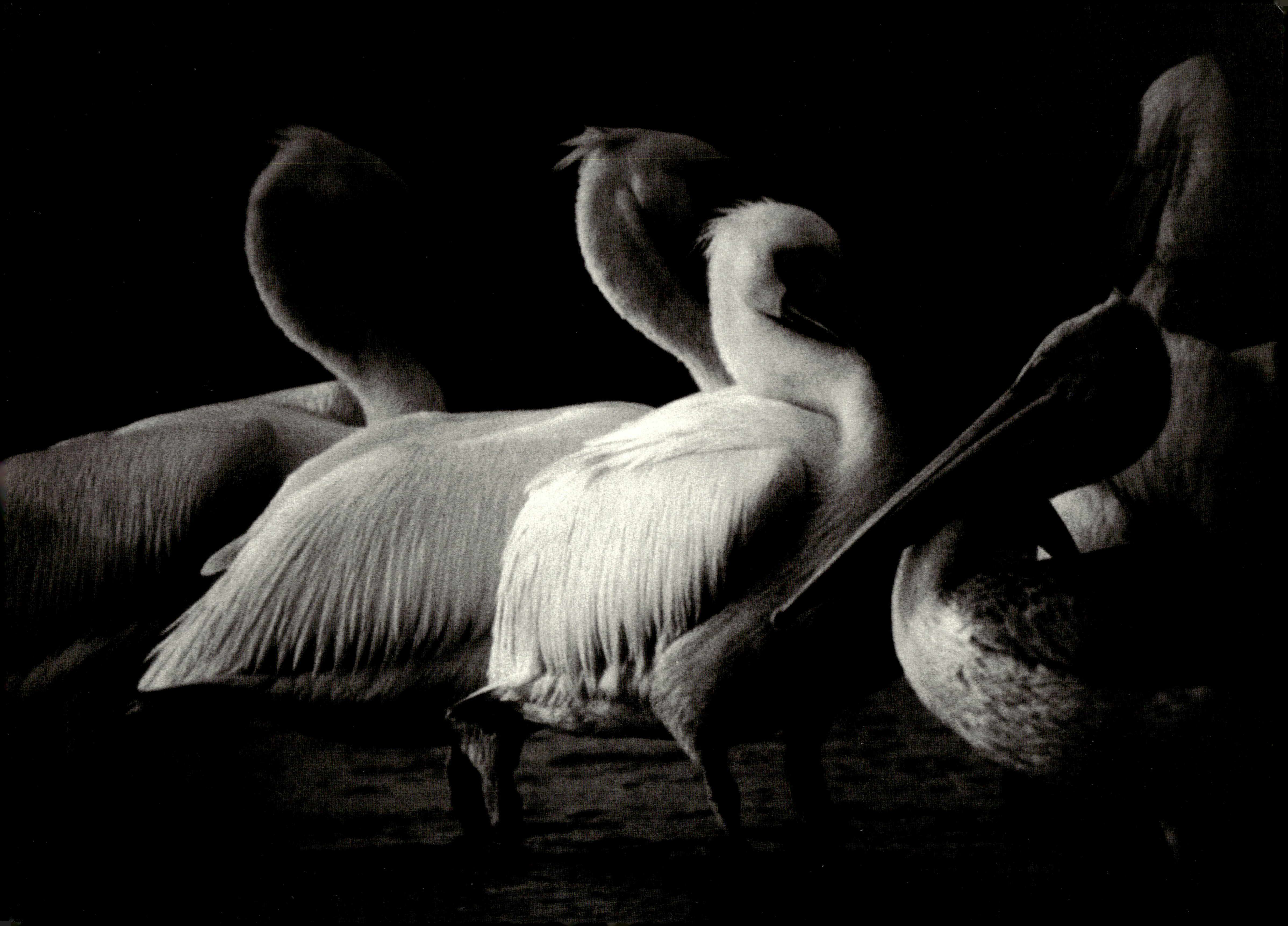

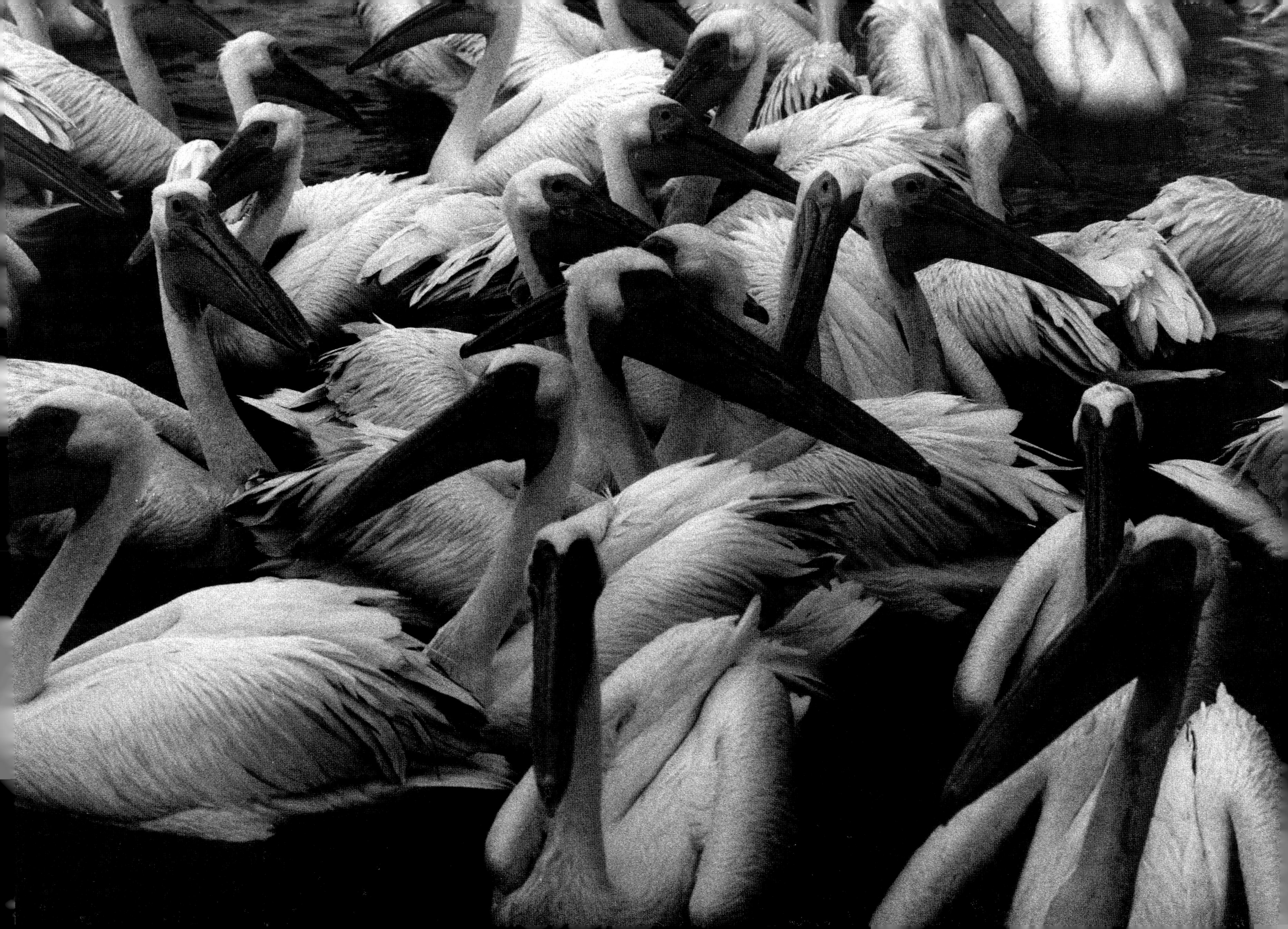

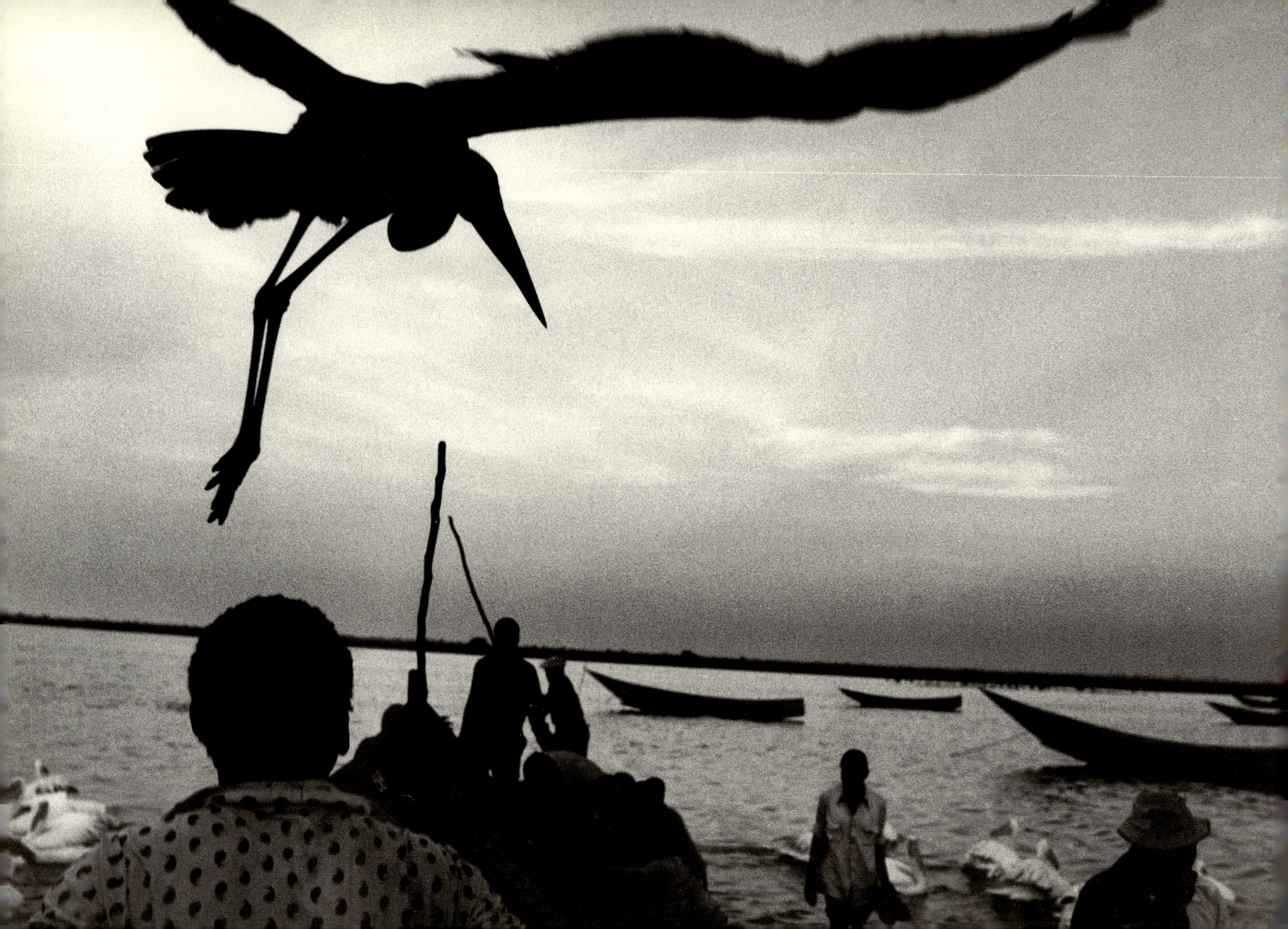

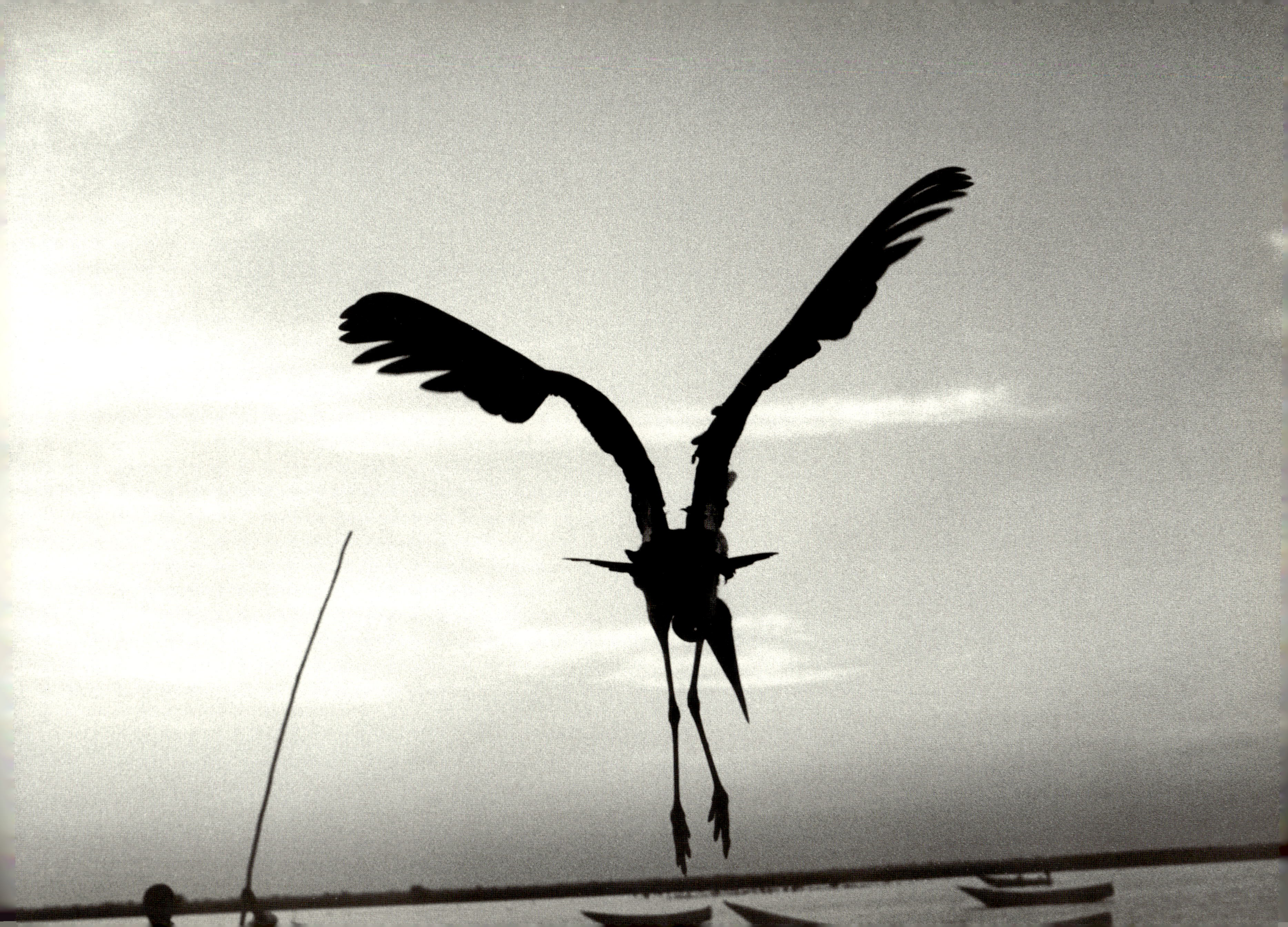

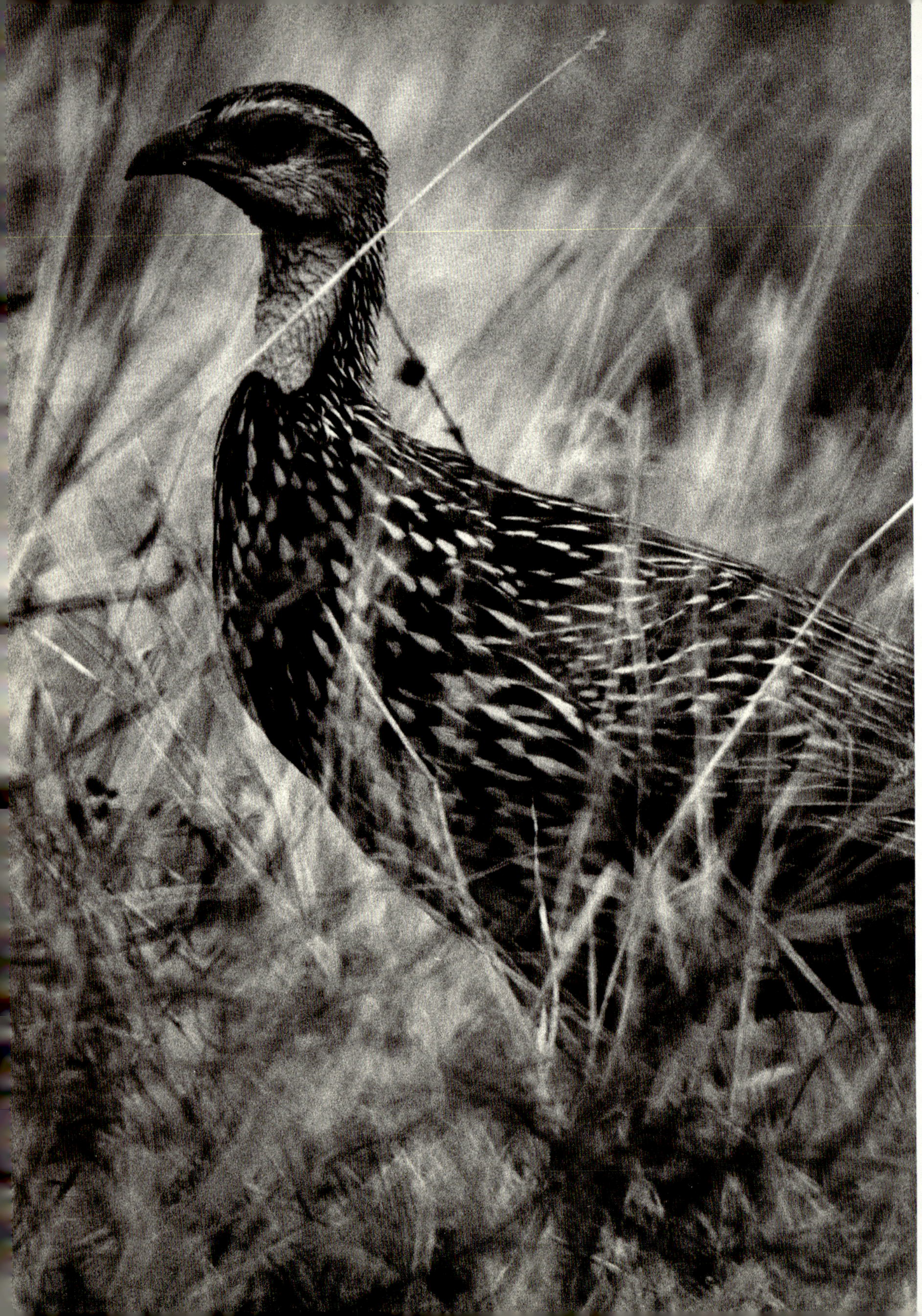
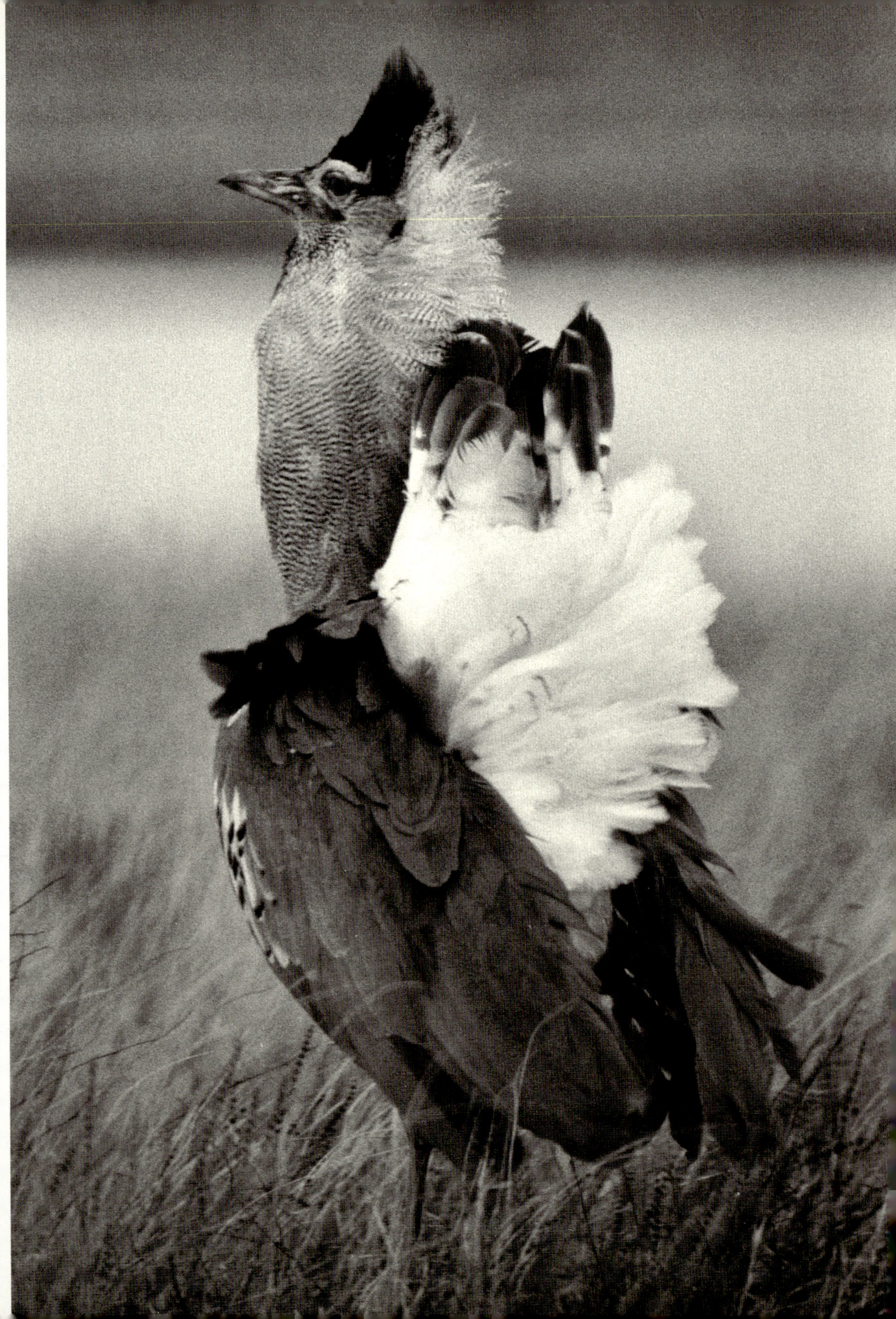

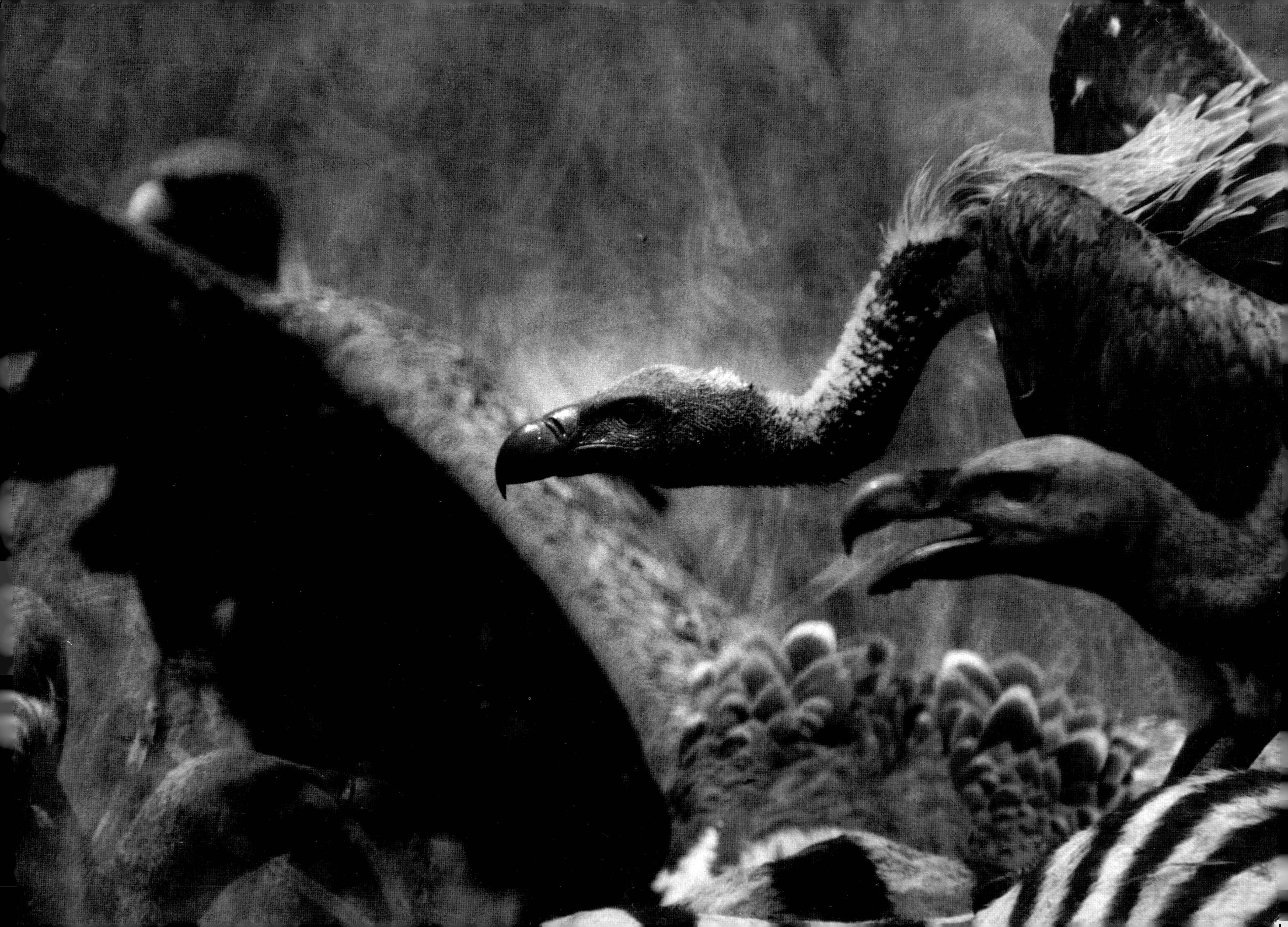

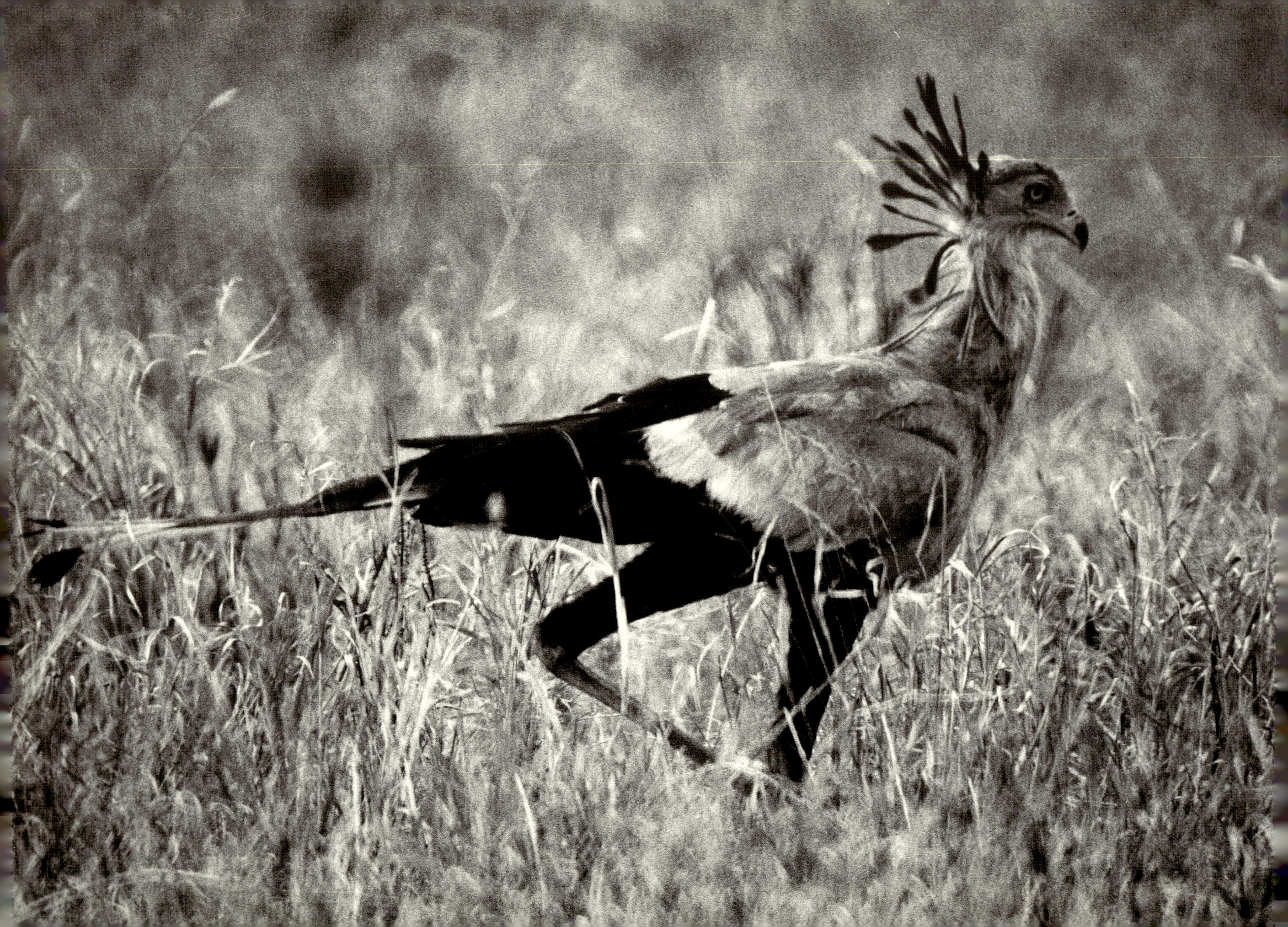

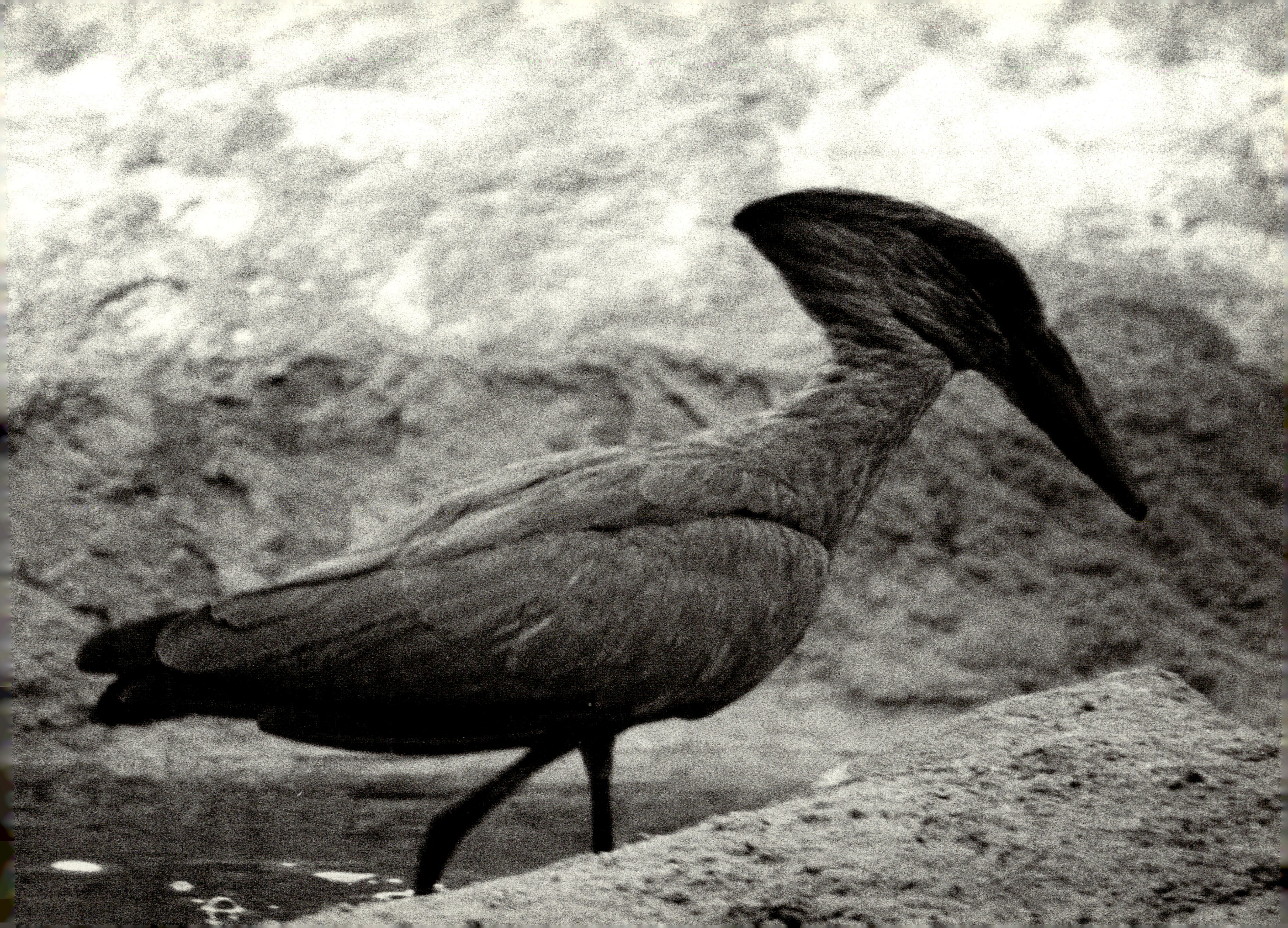

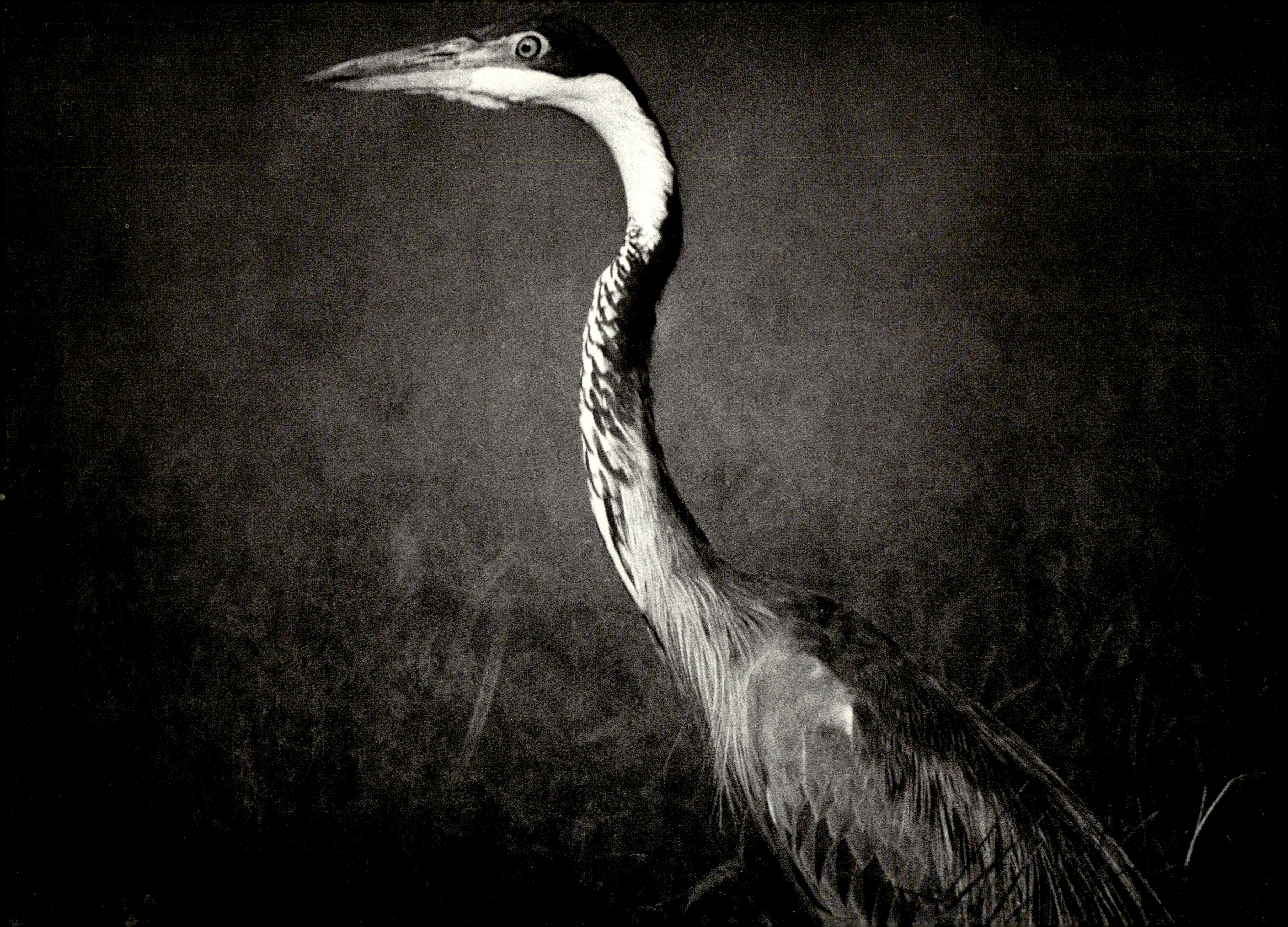

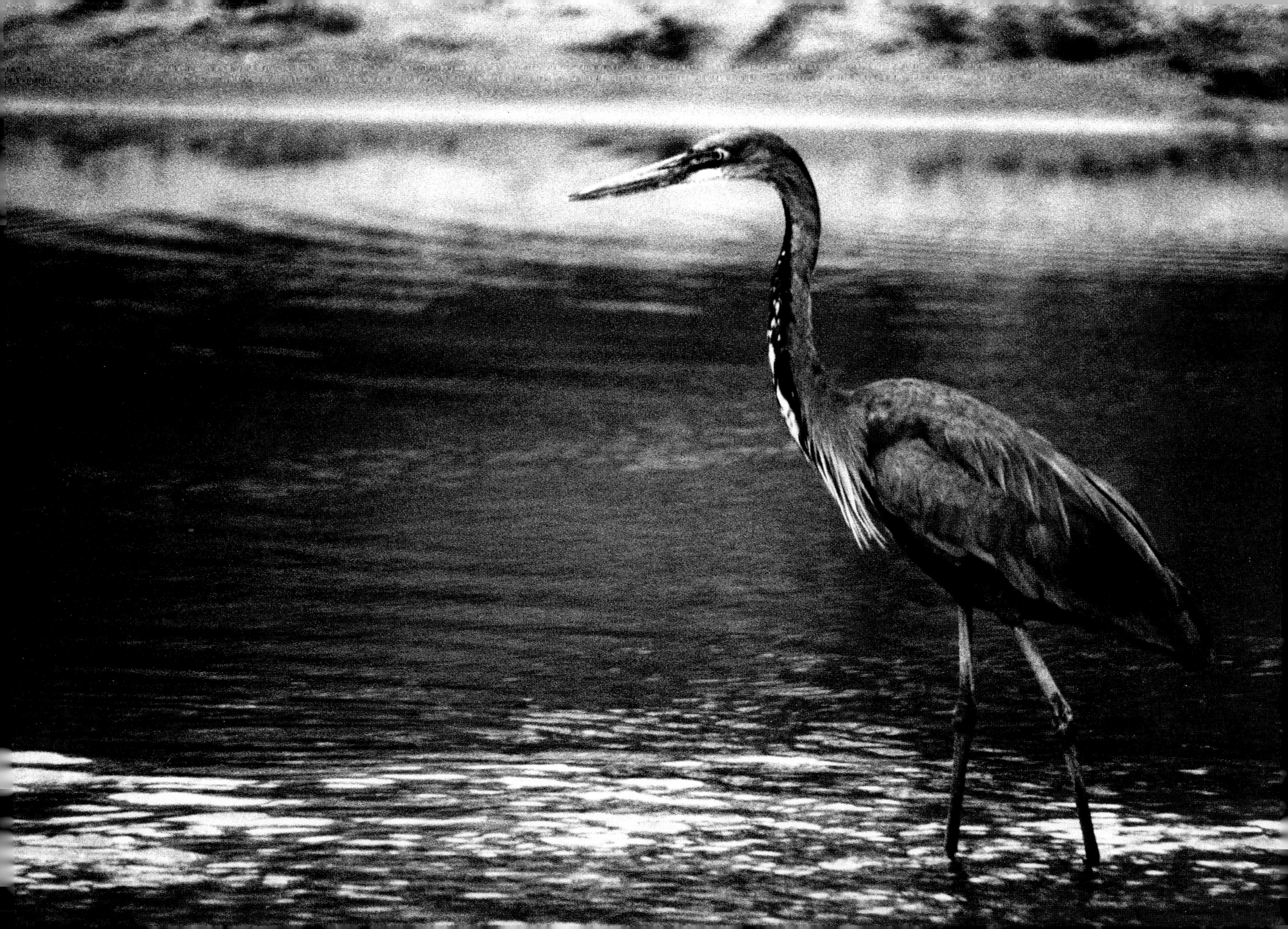

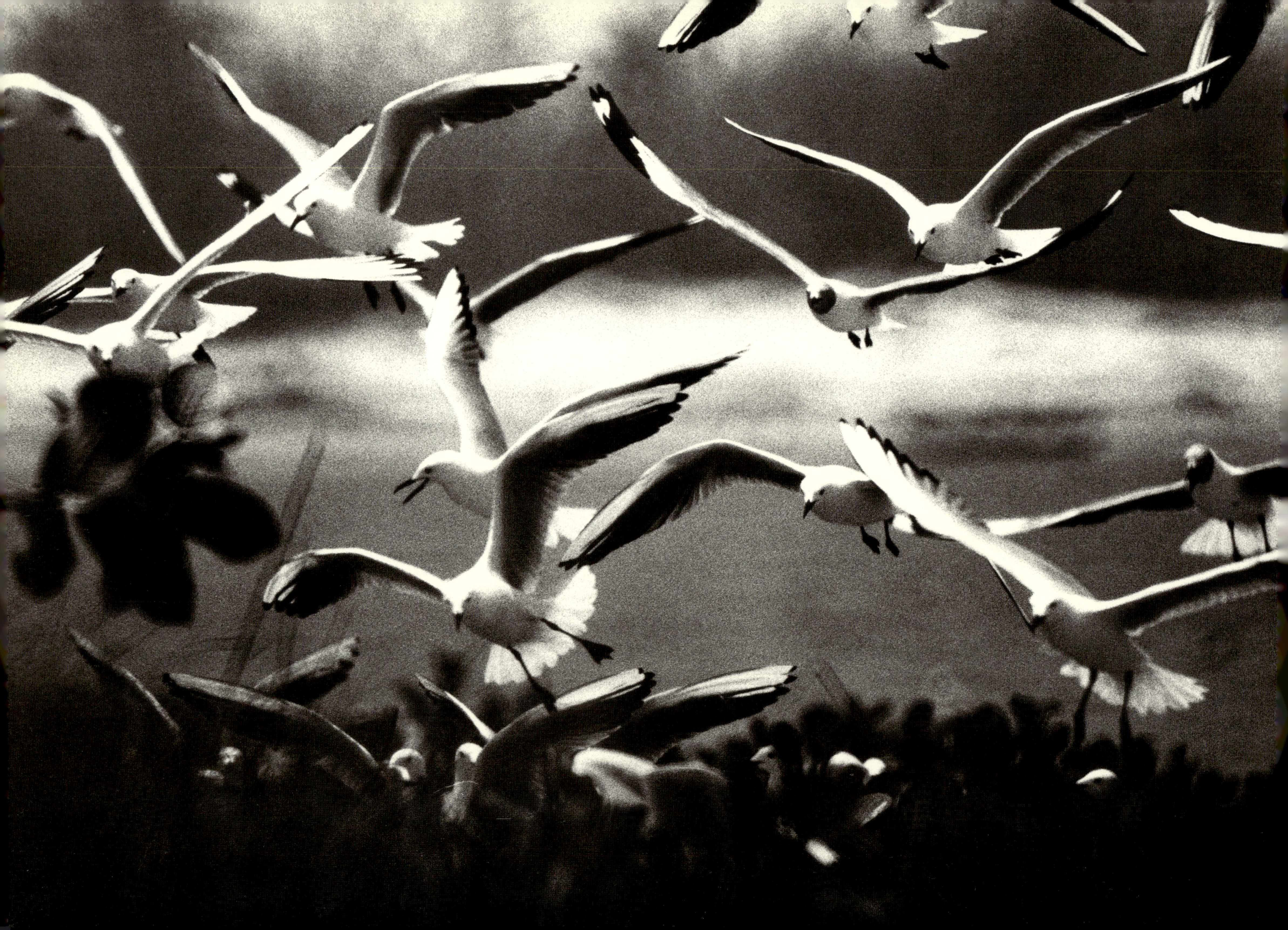

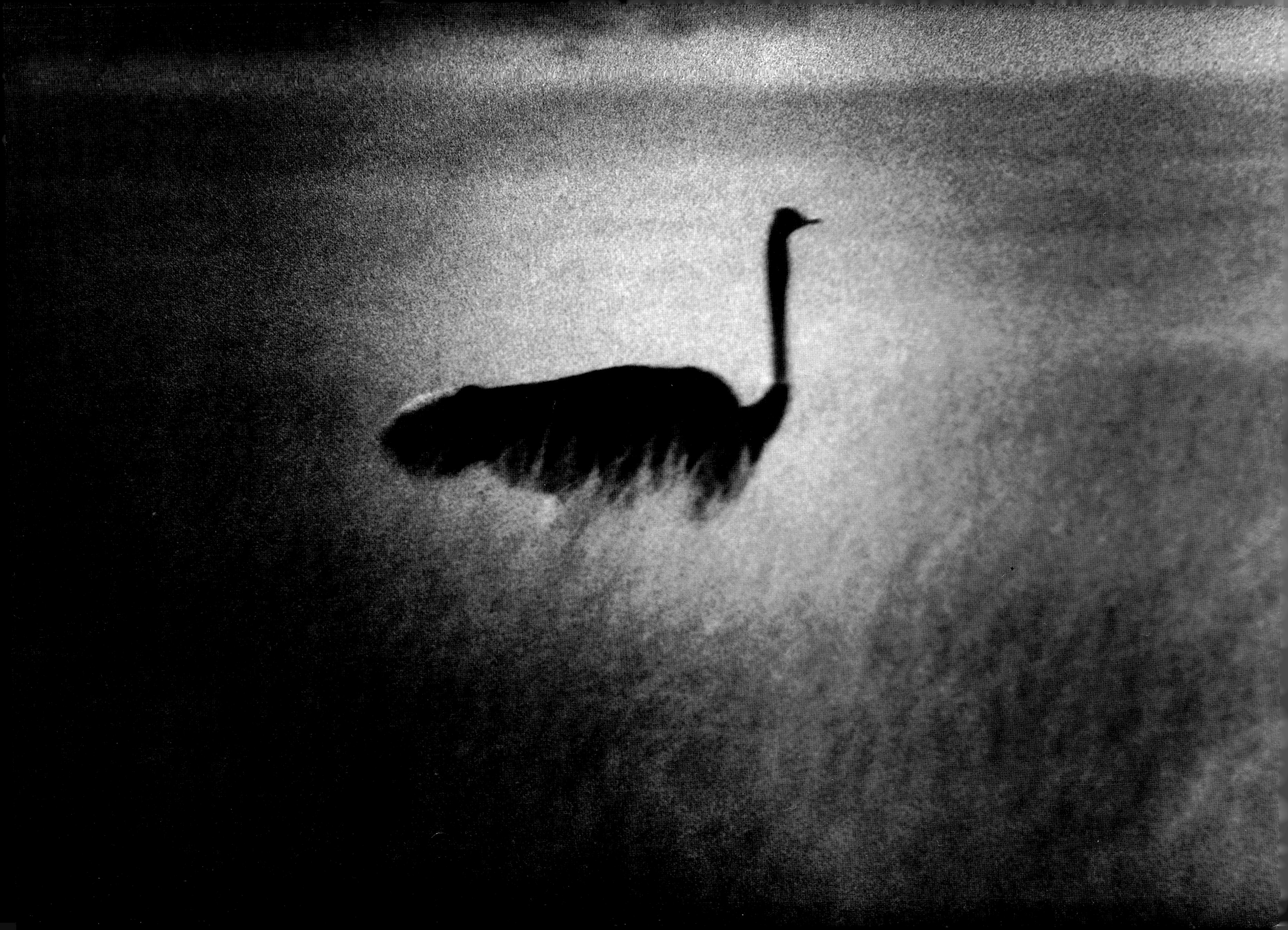

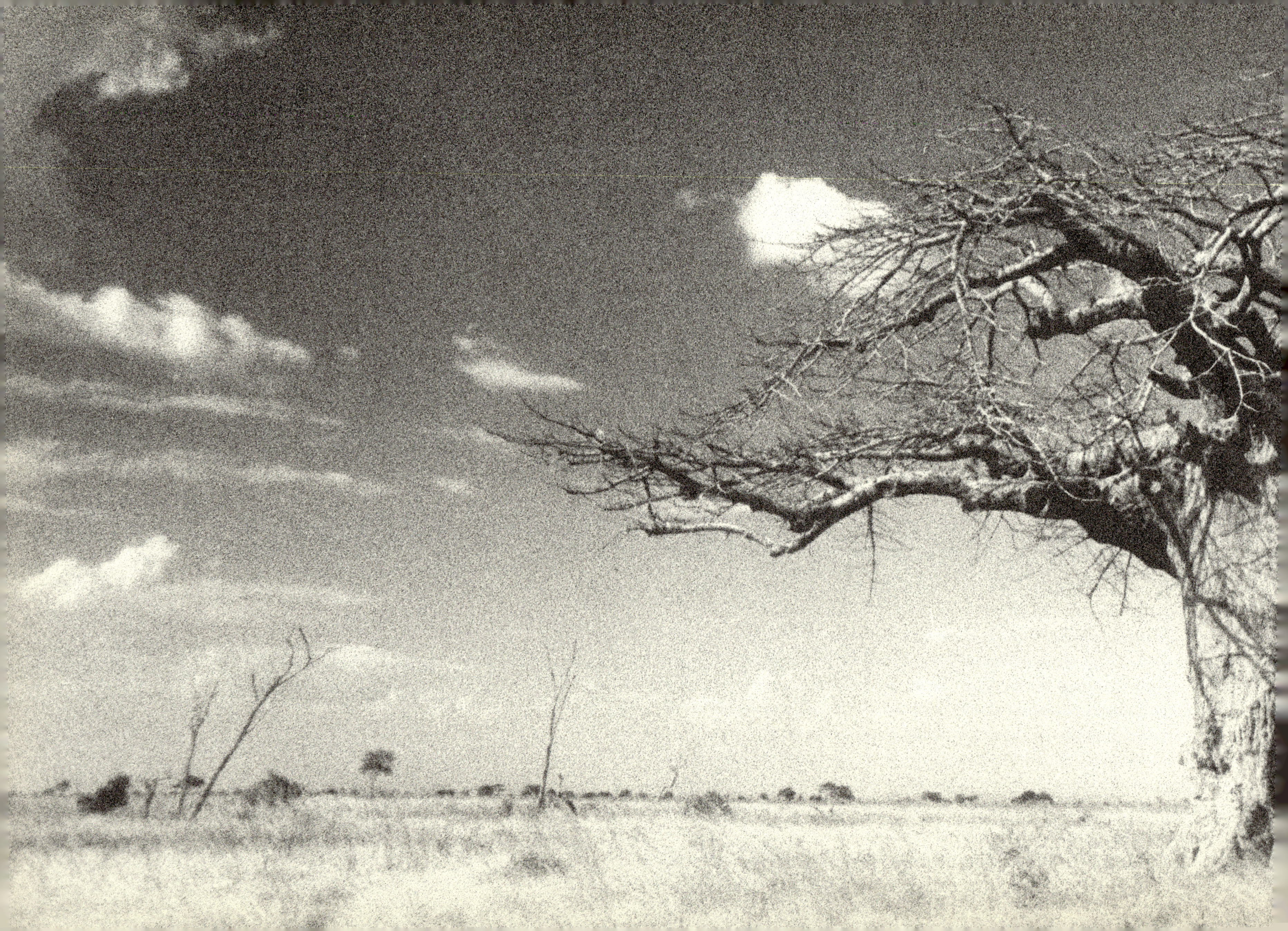

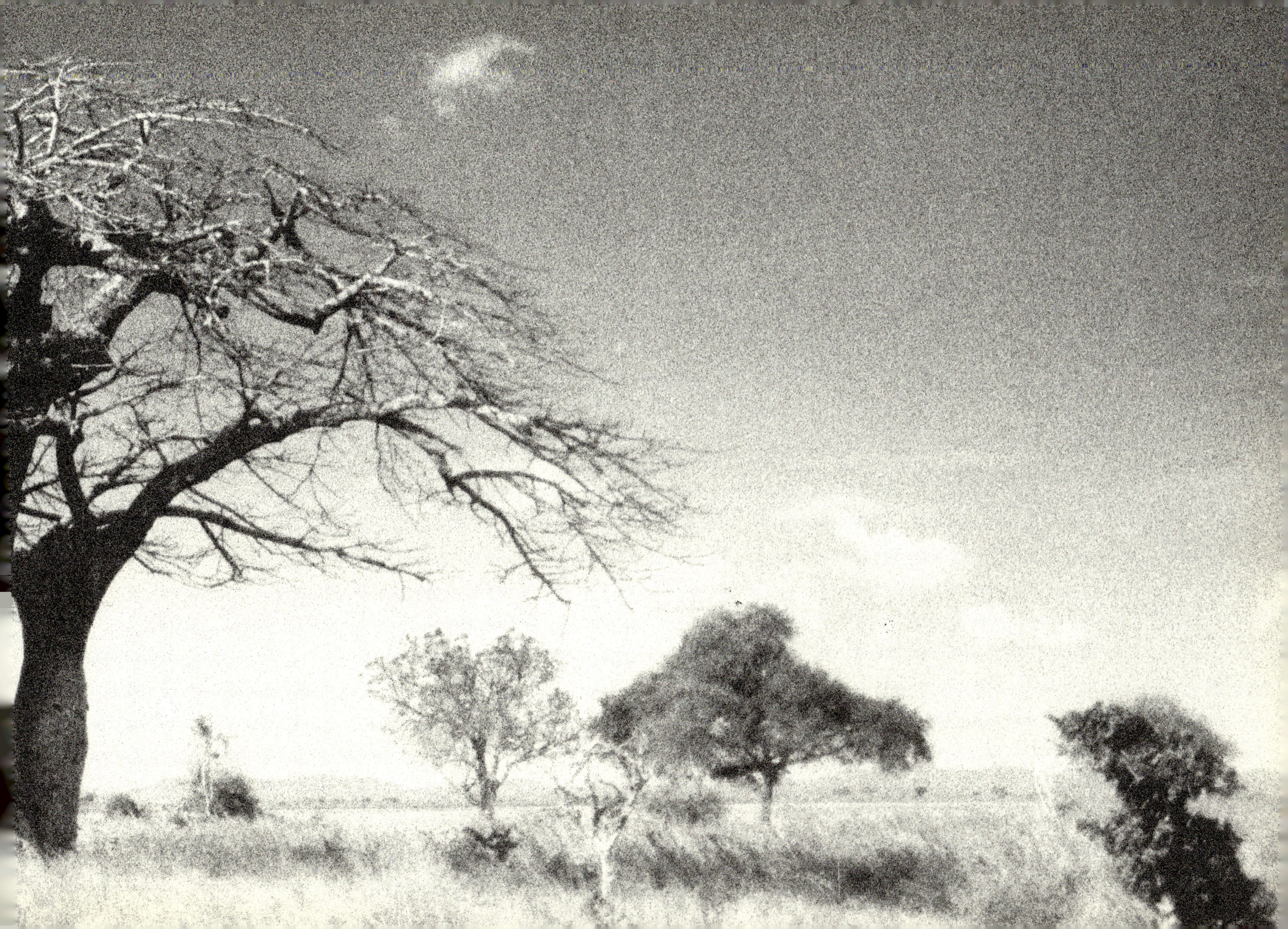

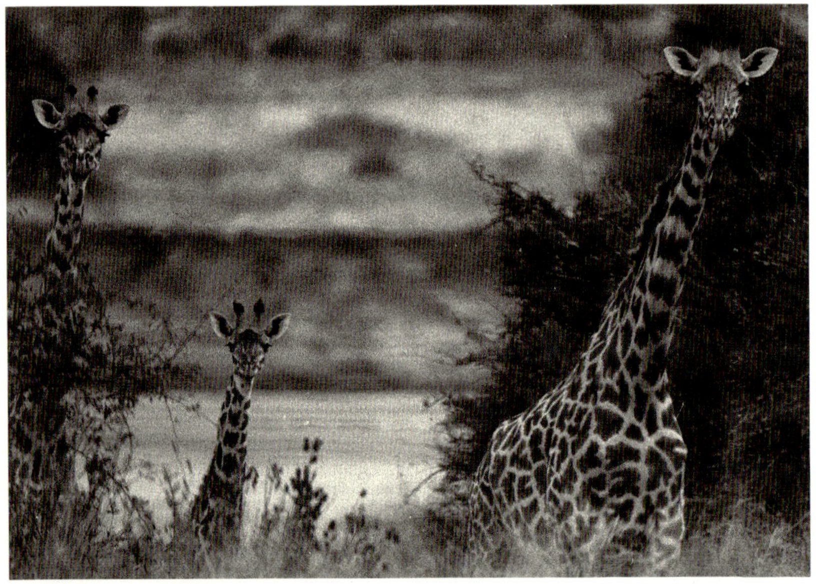

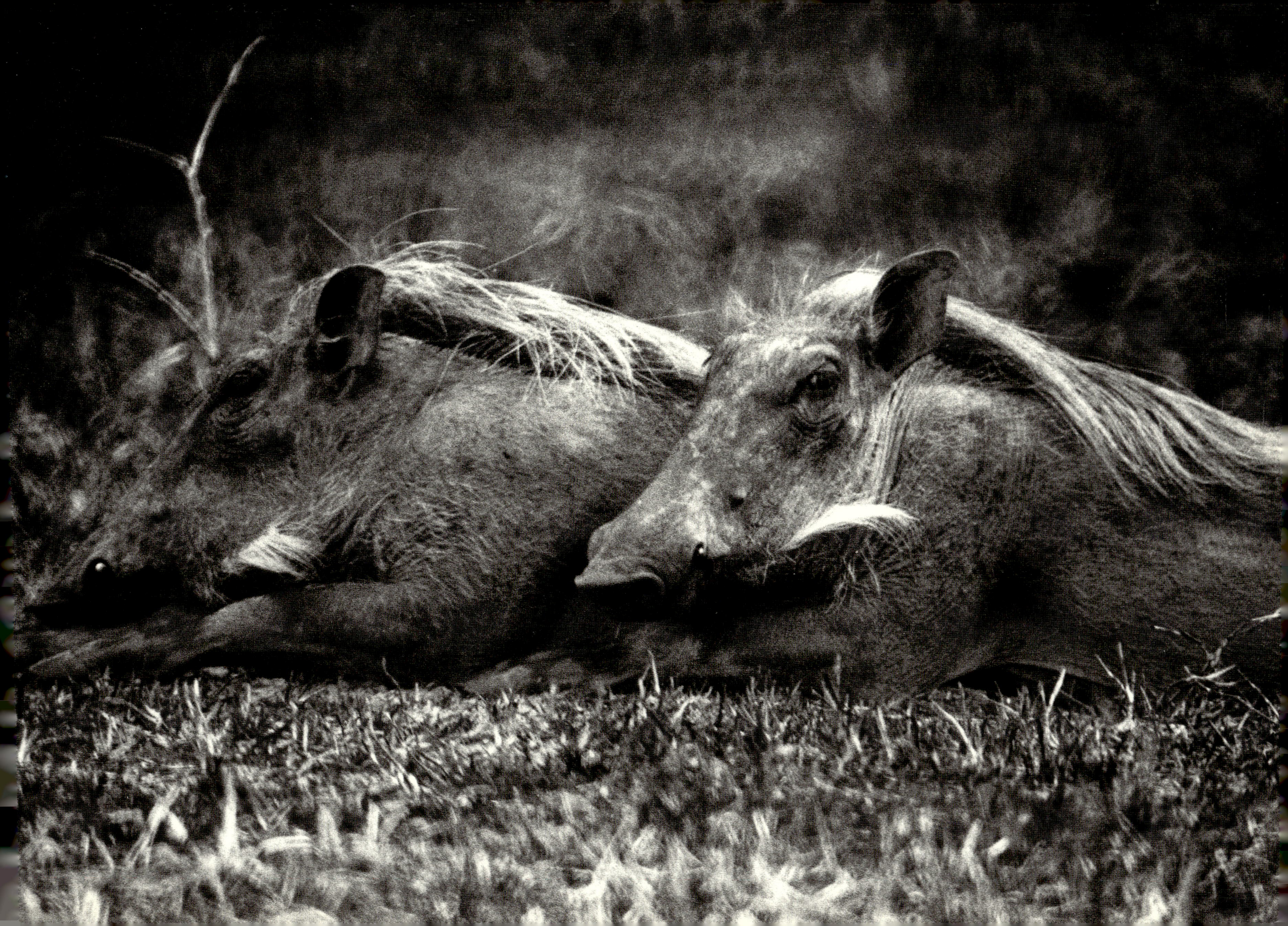

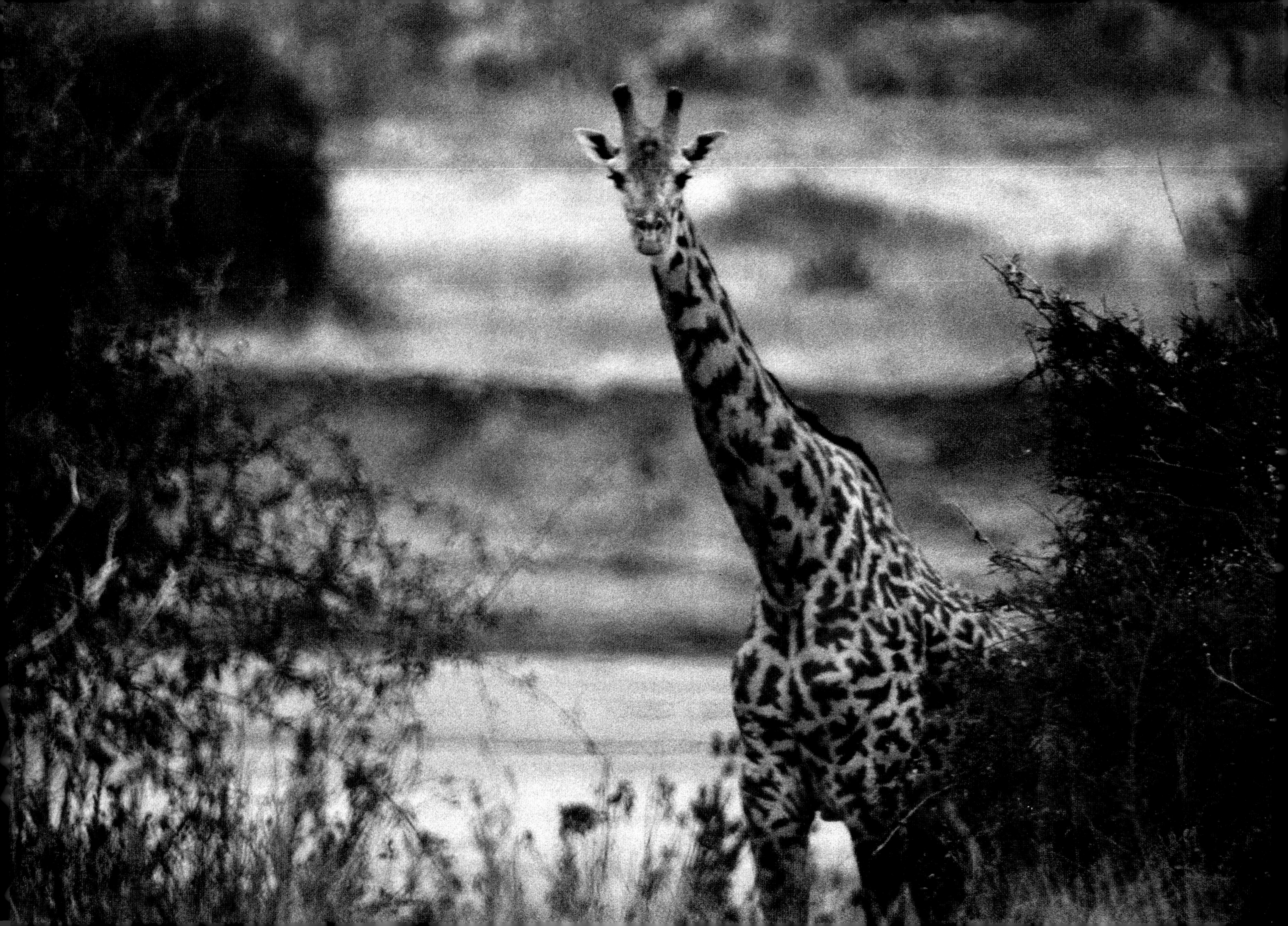

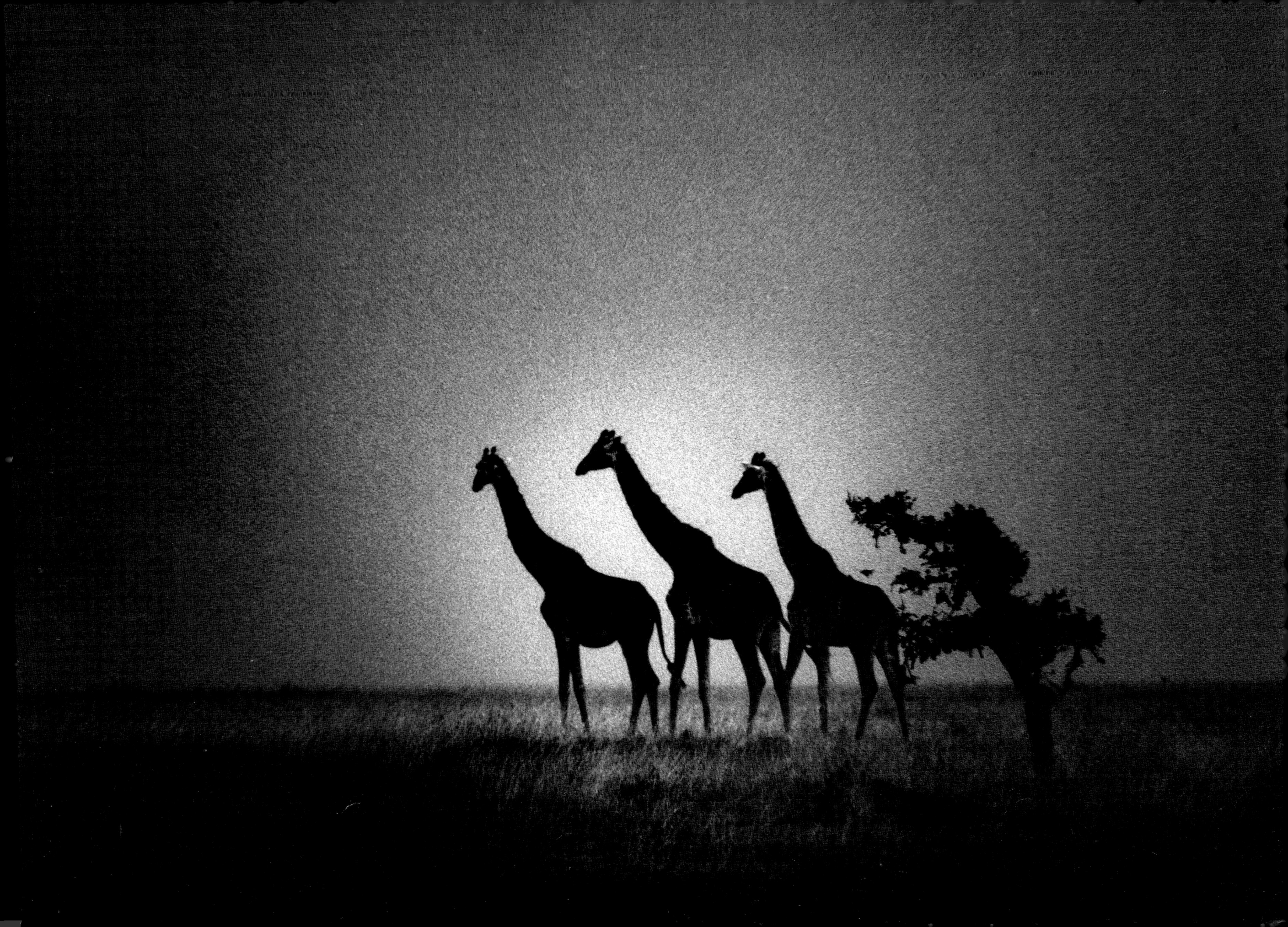

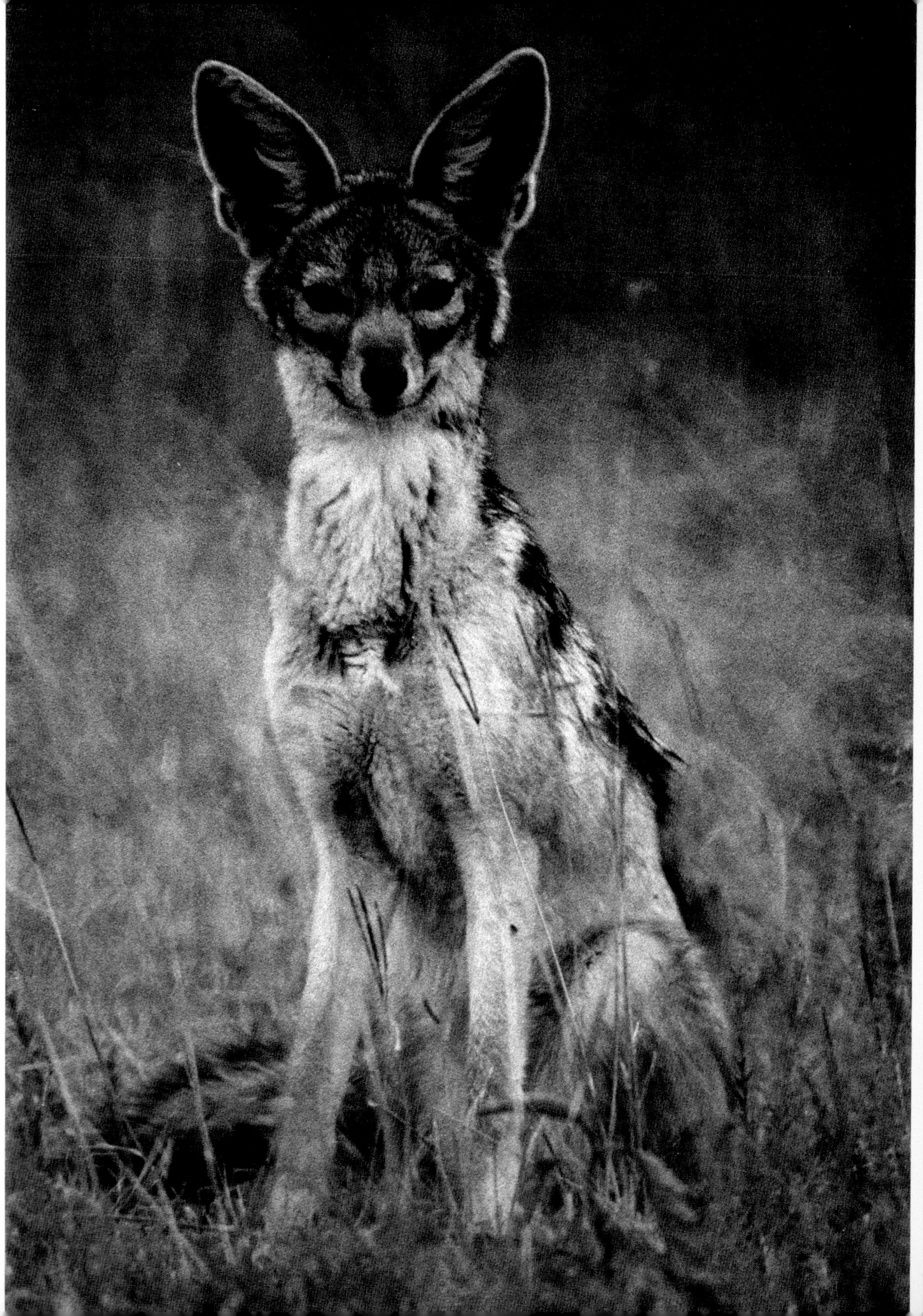

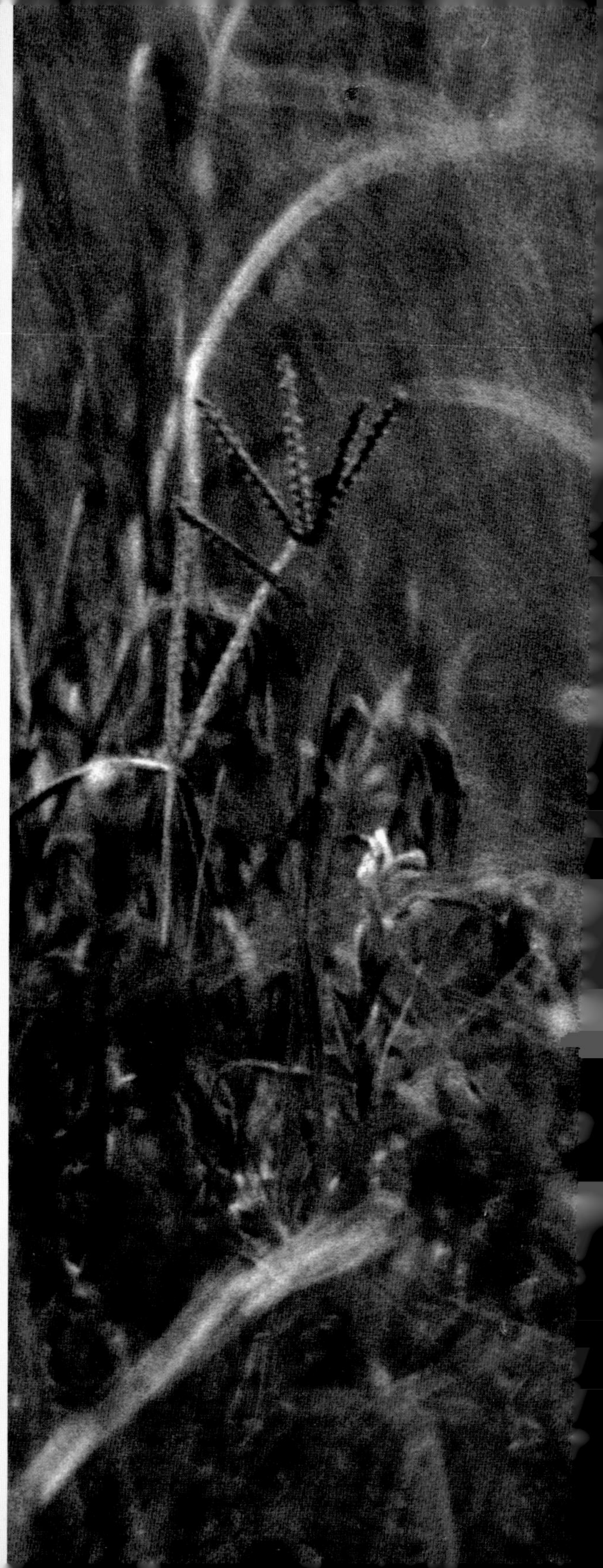

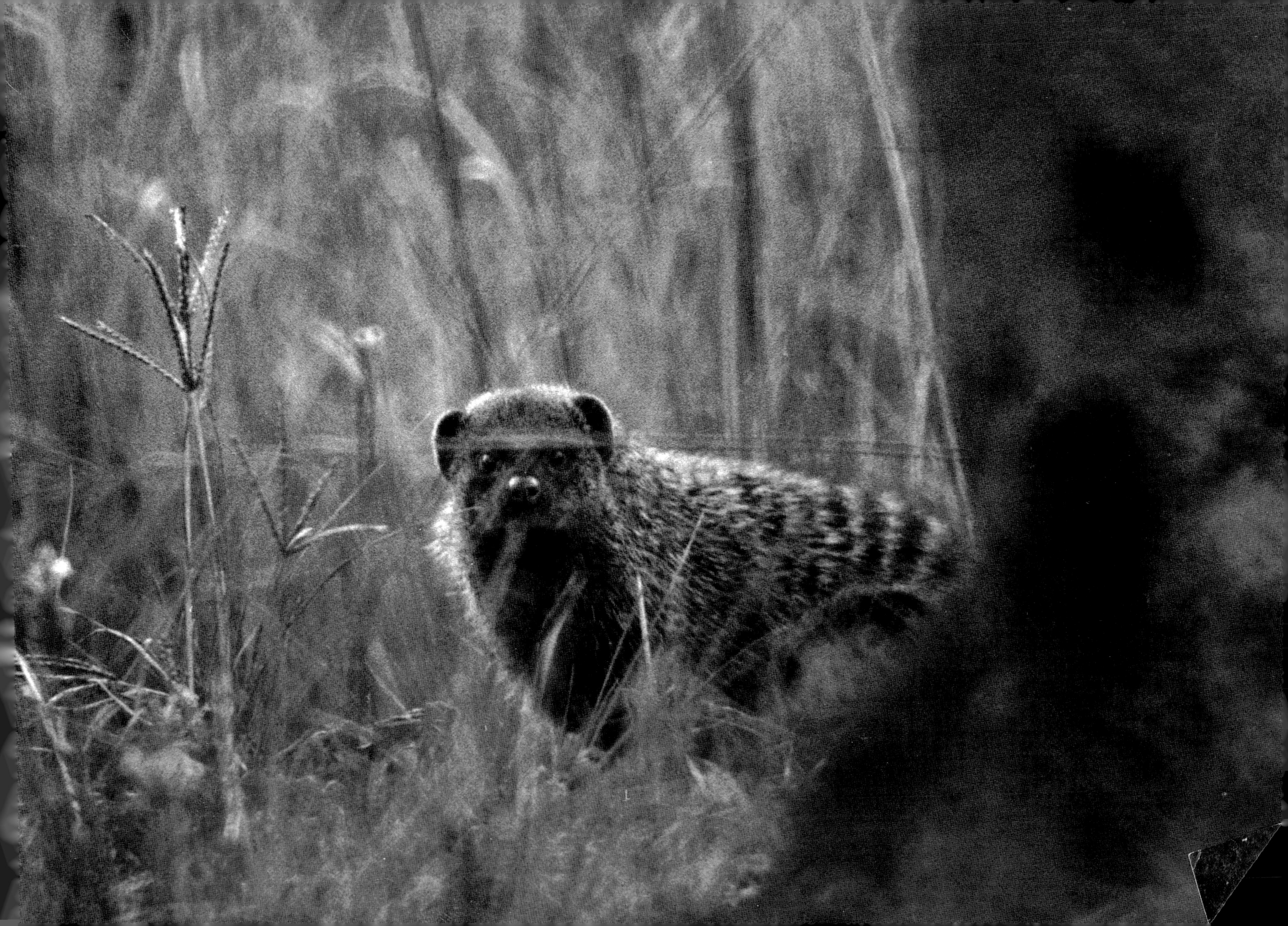

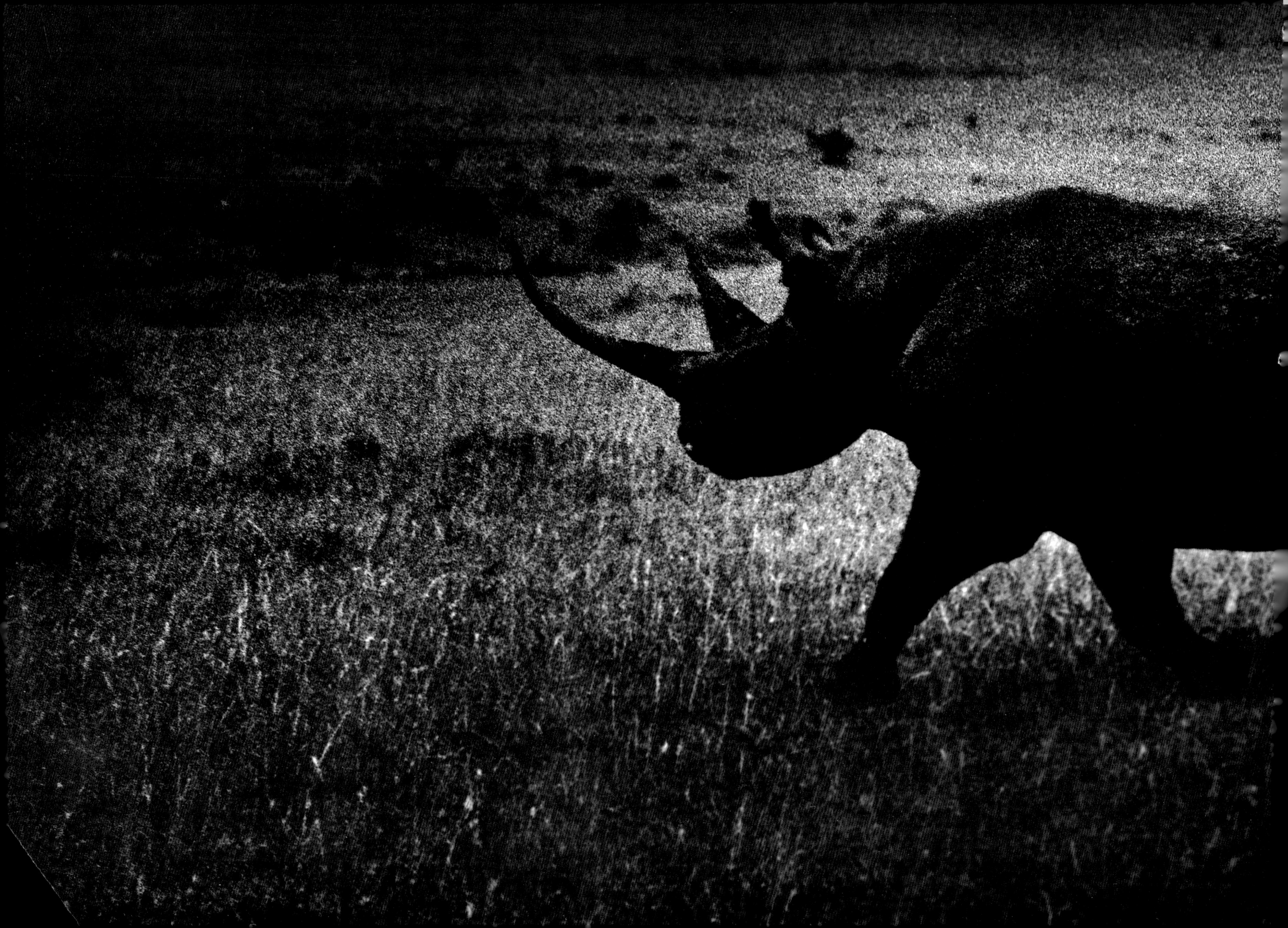

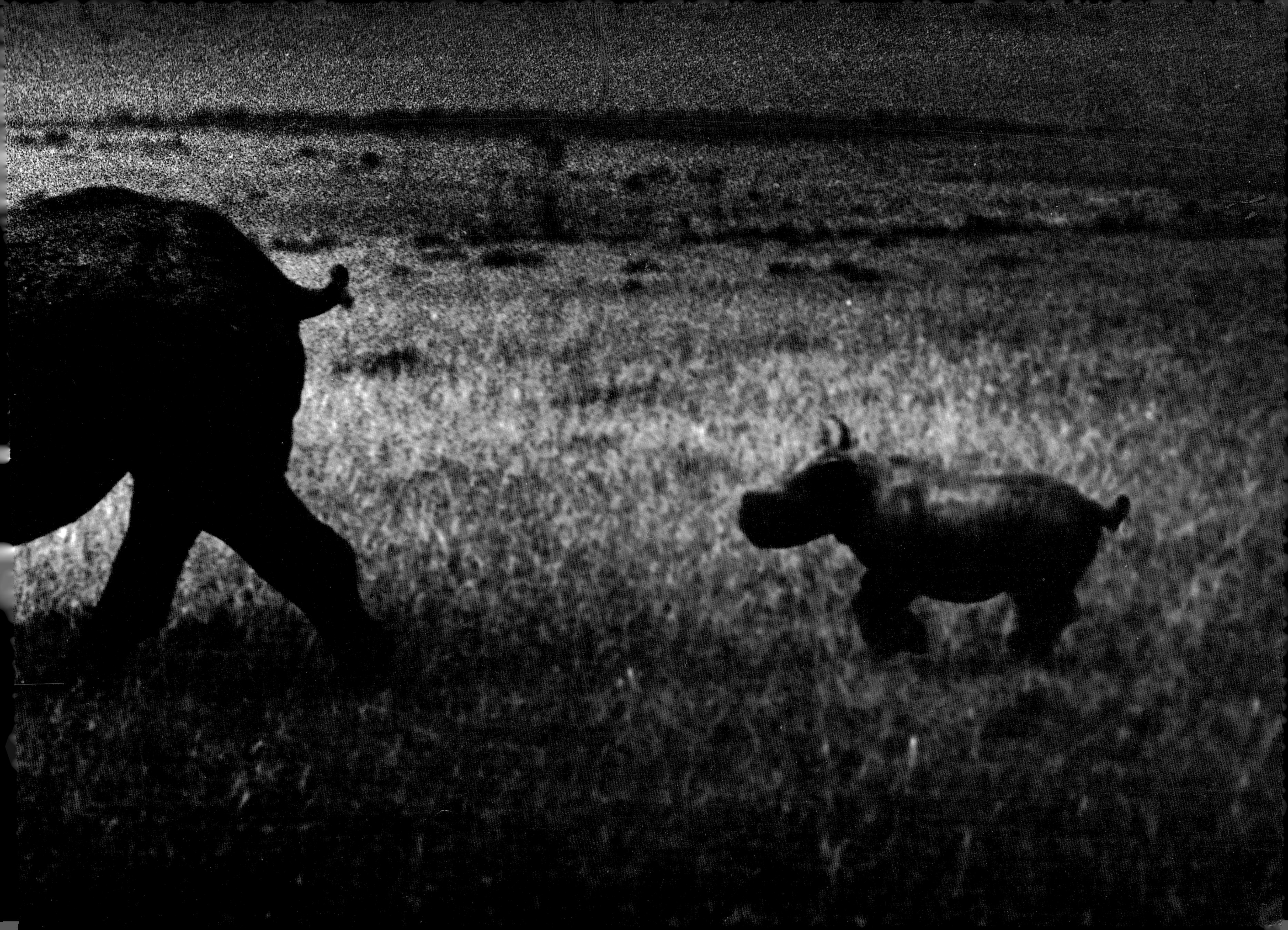

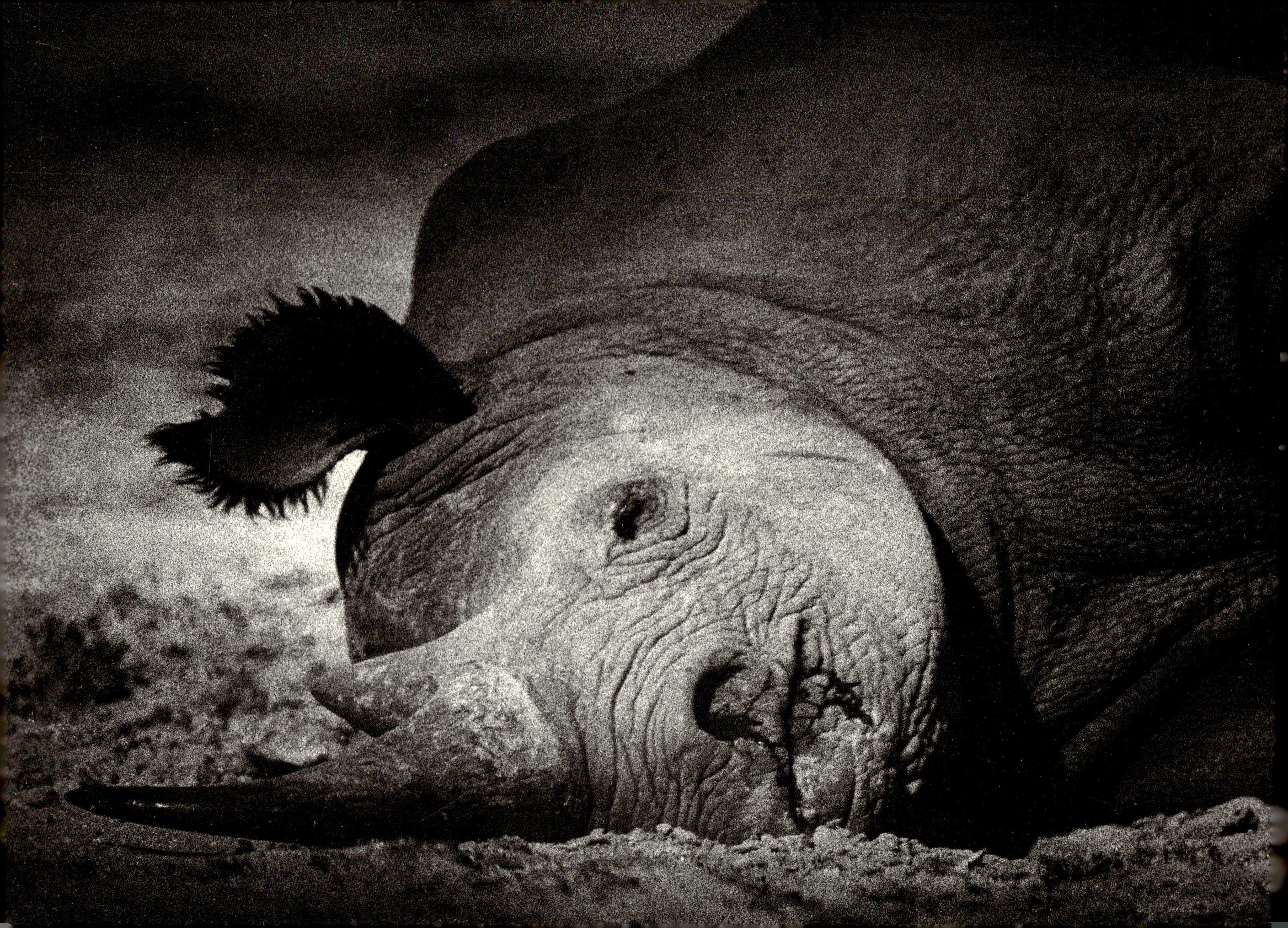

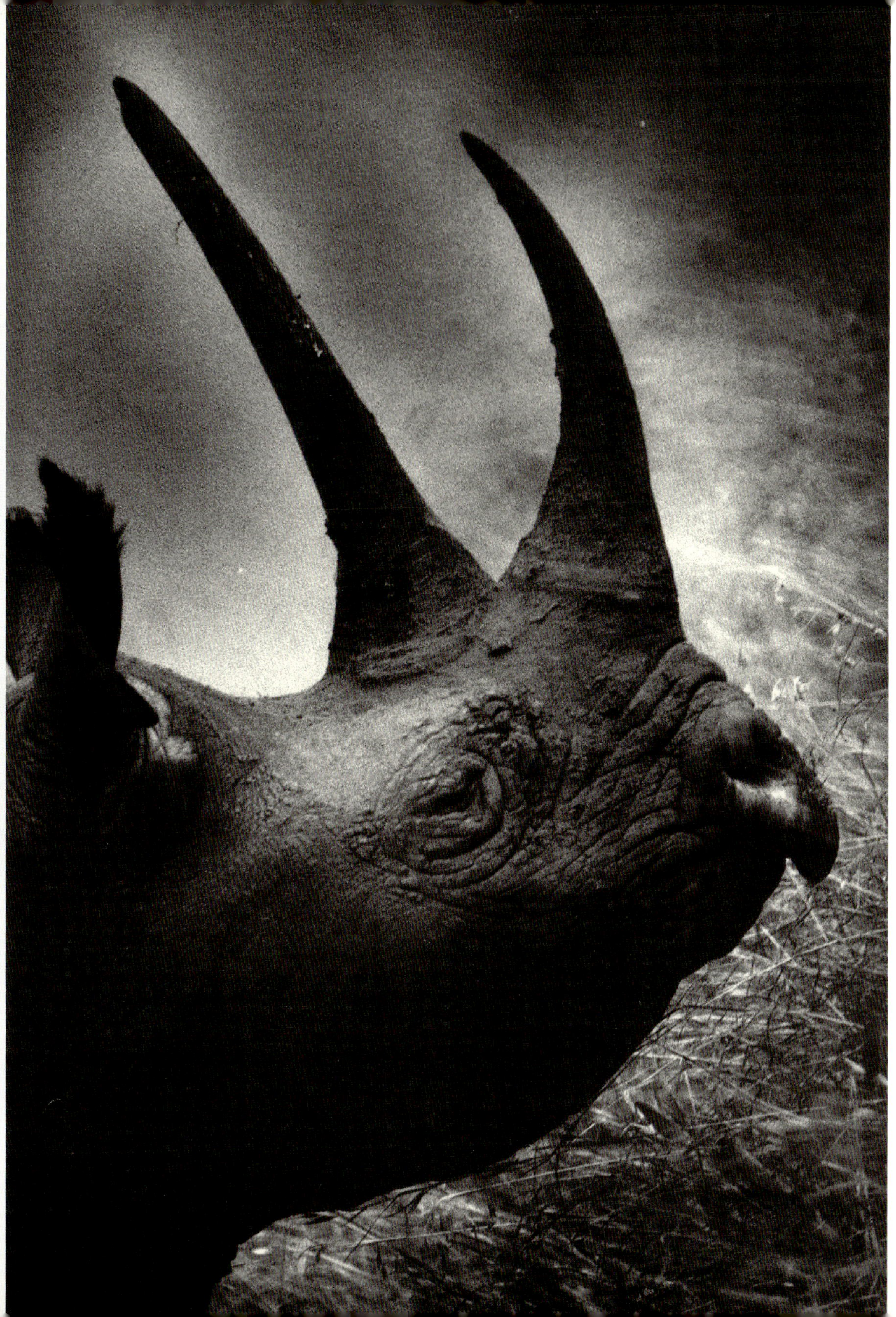

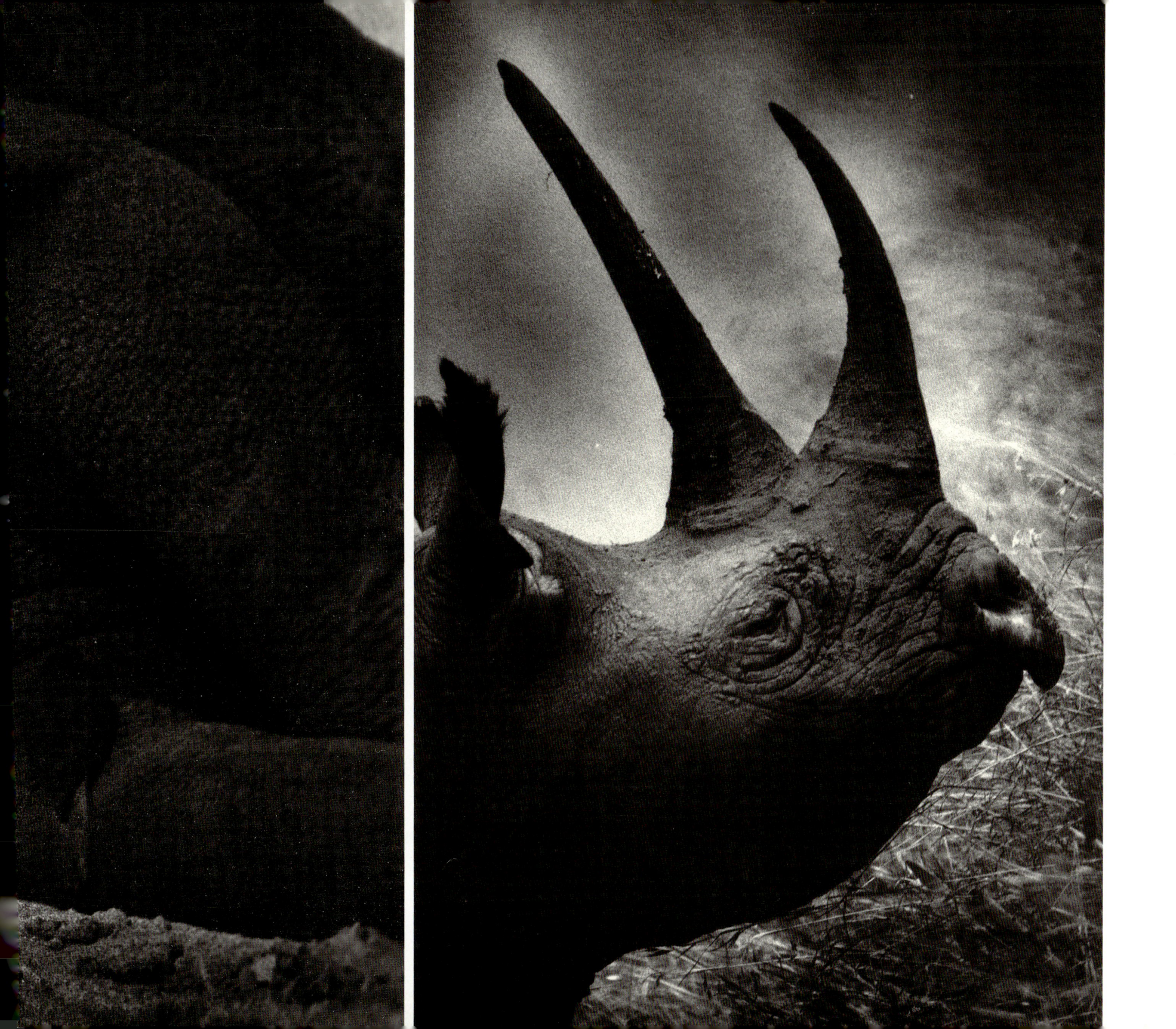

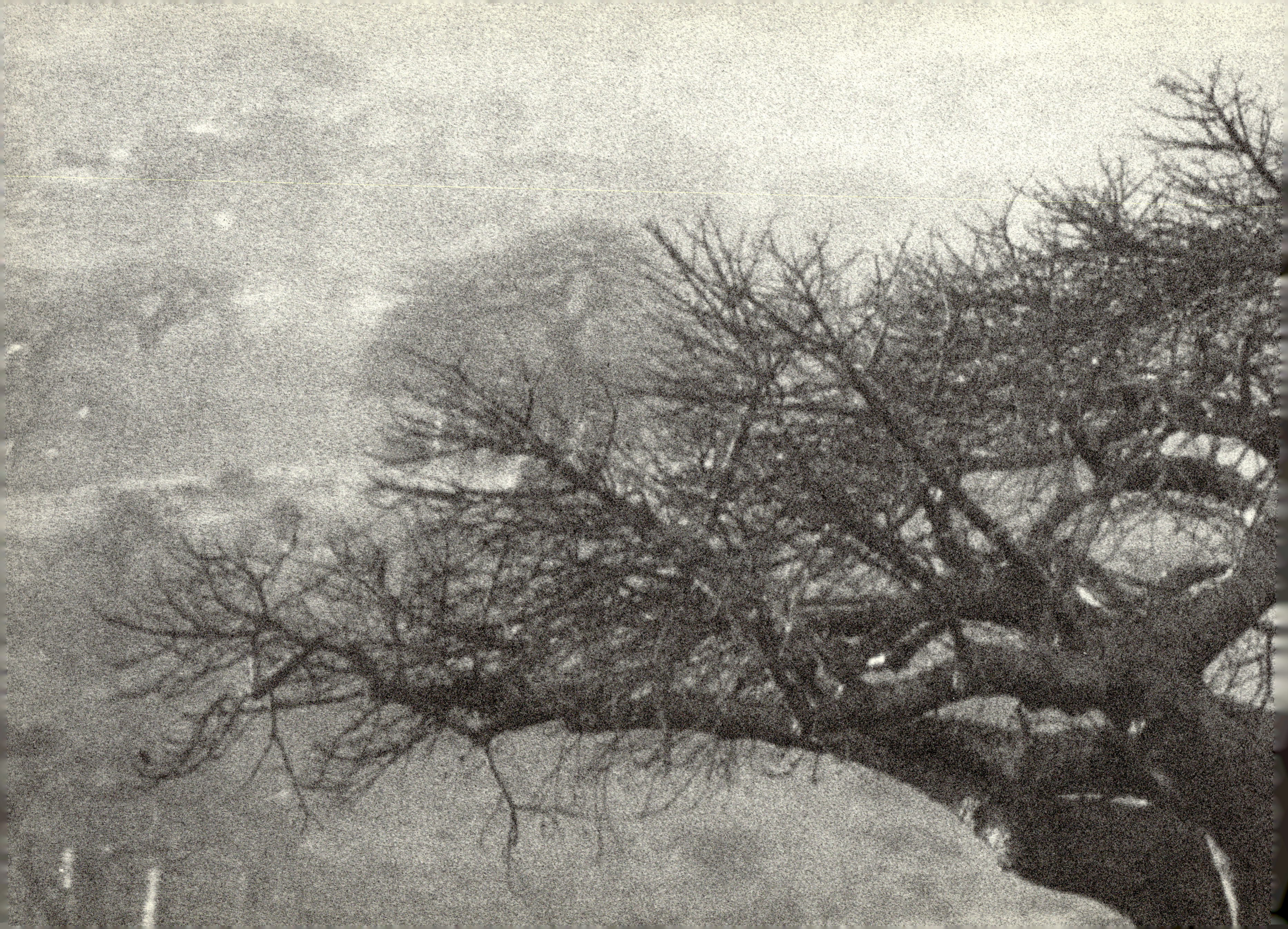

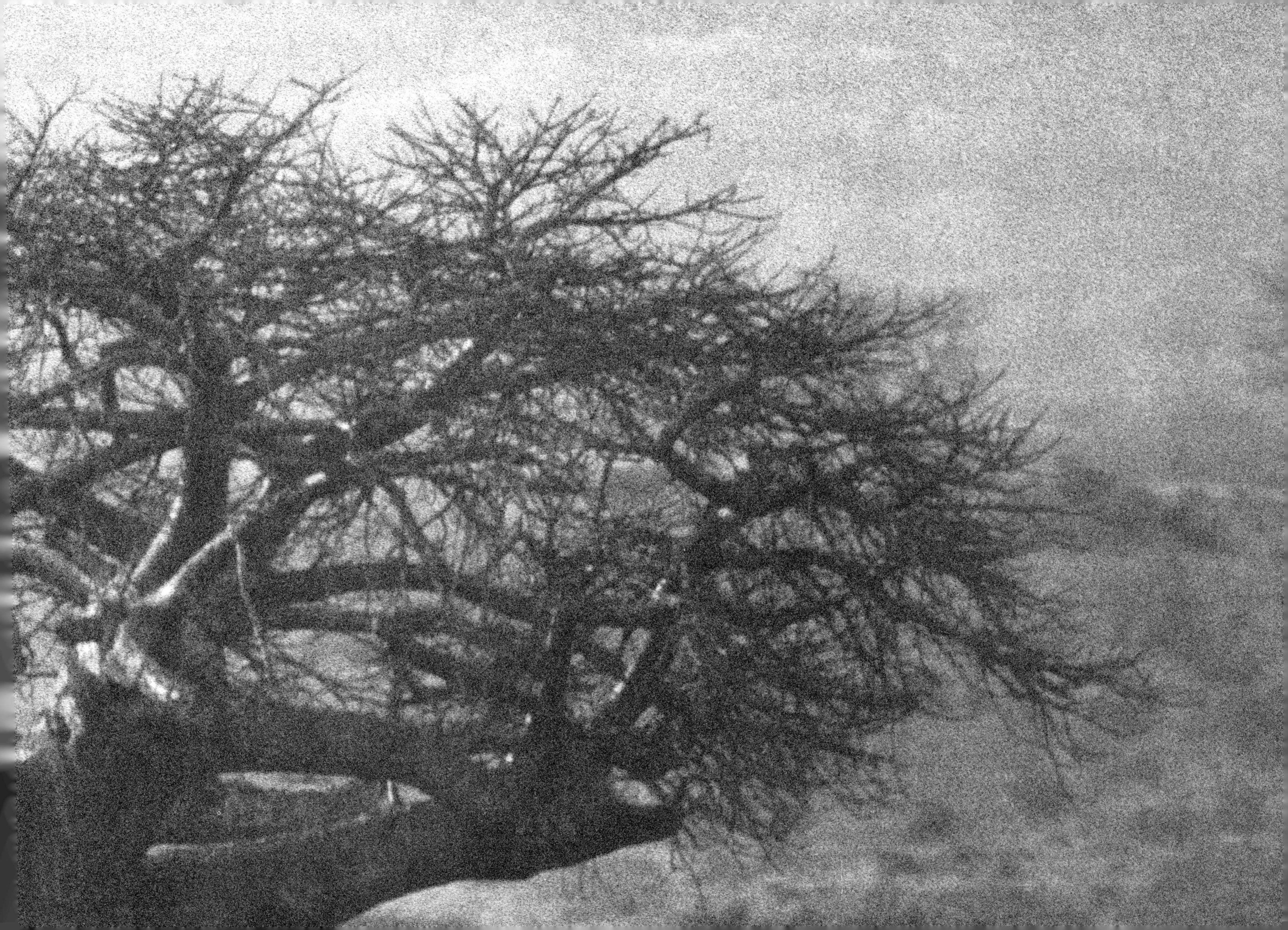

1.

2.

ELEPHANTS

LAKE JIPE, KENYA, 1989

1. and 2.: I found myself nose to nose with these elephants when I came driving around a bend. I must have been downwind from them. Braking hard, I skidded across the road. Despite my terror, I took the time to set up my tripod. Then, as I began to photograph the elephants, they picked up my scent and started to leave. The noise grew louder and louder. Soon, only the female remained behind, closing the ranks and keeping a watchful eye on me.

African elephants live mostly in large herds comprised of many families. The herd is a community for the gray giants, and an extraordinary degree of cooperation and caring characterizes relations between the animals. The central member of the family grouping is the mother, or cow, which leads the calves; as young male elephants grow up, they leave the mother troop to form separate groups. Grown male elephants create their own grouping, which usually stays close to the mother troop. Old males tend to break from the group to live solitary existences.

3.

MASAI MARA GAME RESERVE, KENYA, 1990

3.: These elephant silhouettes reminded me of animal statuary of the 1930s. As a traveler, I often recognize images in nature that I've seen in museums and childhood books.

Female elephants have calves only about once every four years. After a gestation period of twenty-two months, a baby elephant is born, weighing between 90 and 135 pounds. The calf feeds on its mother's milk until it is two years old. Adult elephants use an effective technique to protect their little ones from harm: When a predator (such as a lion or crocodile) approaches, the adults form a double-ringed circle around the calves, tusks pointing out, until the intruder retreats.

4.

5.

6.

LAKE JIPE, KENYA, 1989

4., 5., and 6.: This very curious elephant came to see us three or four times at the campground. Undoubtedly, the smell of our food attracted it. It was a joy for me to work on such striking subject matter: light, dust, the texture of the elephant's skin all came into play.

In addition to having practical functions, the elephant's ears, trunk, tail, and body express a variety of feelings. Here the African elephant spreads its large, fanlike ears in a sign of fear or anger, which makes it look particularly huge and intimidating. Ear flapping keeps insects away and cools the body. On male African elephants, the ears can be as wide as 4 feet across.

The trunk is a nose, but it is also a multipurpose tool that the animal uses in myriad ways. The elephant lifts it high in the air to pick up intriguing scents; grasps leaves, buds, and fruit from trees and stuffs them into its mouth; and uses it to suck up water. Two "lips" at the trunk tip allow the elephant to pick up small objects. The elephant produces a shrill trumpeting noise with its trunk to frighten enemies and uses the muscular, strong appendage to beat them away. On hot days, an elephant will use its trunk to give itself a shower.

7.

8.

TSAVO EAST NATIONAL PARK, ARUBA DAM, KENYA, 1987

7. and 8.: During the 1960s, the authorities intervened to stop the elephants from destroying Tsavo National Park with their enormous appetites. Ten thousand elephants were killed; it was a veritable massacre. Understandably, this herd reacted nervously to our presence as they approached the water.

Elephants migrate widely in herds, constantly searching for food and water. They need to drink water every day and are always hungry; an adult elephant can eat as many as 600 pounds of leaves and grass in a day. In the rainy season, when vegetation is in abundance, a herd will travel from 8 to 20 miles a day. But in dry times, elephants may have to range for 30 miles to find enough to eat. The animal's favorite food is overripe and fermenting fruit, which can sometimes lead to apparent drunkenness.

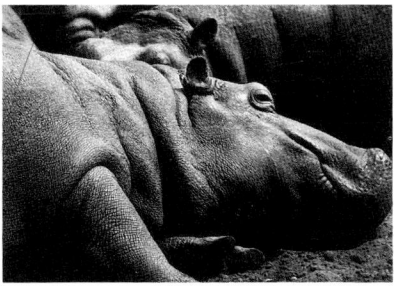

9.

HIPPOPOTAMUSES

LAKE MANYARA NATIONAL PARK, TANZANIA, 1990

9.: I like the mood of this photograph, taken at two or three o'clock in the afternoon. It's very rare to find hippopotamuses lying about like lizards in the hot sun. The sun burns their skin.

This hippo is enjoying a nap in the sun. Hippopotamuses are amphibious, living mostly in lakes and rivers bordered by flat, sandy banks. During the day, they are often submerged under water and can go for as long as fifteen minutes without breathing. With eyes, ears, and nostrils situated atop their heads, hippos can see, hear, and breathe, while keeping cool in the water. At night, they head for land to graze on short, soft grasses and other plants in nearby meadows.

10.

VIRUNGA NATIONAL PARK, ZAIRE, 1972

10.: We bought a Land Rover in Chad and drove across the Central African Republic to get to Zaire. In Virunga National Park, I saw my first animals. I was 21 years old and knew nothing about the behavior of hippos. Immediately, I wanted to get to work photographing this subject matter: the wrinkles, the reflected light, and the mud.

Hippopotamuses are formidable creatures. On land, only elephants rival them in size. Fully grown hippos can weigh as many as 4 tons and newborns weigh between 40 and 60 pounds. The hippo's appetite is also enormous. An adult can eat up to 100 pounds of food a day. Hippopotamuses are entirely vegetarian. The animal's skin, smooth and hairless, is actually rather tender. It can dry out and crack easily in the sun. This explains why the animal spends so much time in the water, and why it so often wallows in the mud when on shore. Mucous glands in the skin secrete a reddish fluid that helps keep the hippo moist.

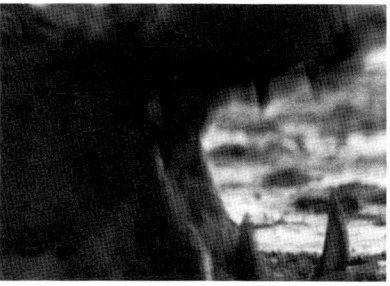

11.

12.

13.

14.

15.

VIRUNGA NATIONAL PARK, ZAIRE, 1987

11., 12., 13., 14., and 15: Fifteen years after my first trip to Virunga National Park, I went back again. I knew I needed more hippopotamuses for my book. Uganda was off-limits for political reasons, and I had to go around Lake Victoria and through Tanzania and Rwanda. With a pang of emotion, I rediscovered the marsh where I had started out, that muddy sea under a low sky (the park is at 6,560 feet above sea level). There had been many more animals the first time.

In fifteen years, my work-style had evolved. I had increased my speed and learned to zero in on one isolated animal or on others in groups. During this second trip to Virunga National Park, I gave preference to behavior rather than poses. I distanced myself considerably from the car to get near the animals. In the viewfinder, I could see dramatic intensity: the striking combination of black and white, the violence of the hippos' movements, the threat of their very sharp incisors.

When a hippopotamus opens its mouth, it's either yawning or conveying a threat. Its mouth is gargantuan, second in size only to that of a large whale. Razor sharp incisors inside grow to an average length of 20 inches while tusks grow to 30 inches. The top and bottom incisors meet at angles, cutting through grass or the flesh of an aggressor in a scissor-like way. Hippopotamuses are generally peaceable animals, but the males will sometimes vie with each other for the right to mate with a particular female or for dominance over territory. Female hippos will fight to defend their young against such predators as crocodiles and lions. To convey inferiority and submission within the hierarchical order, a hippo will wag its tail back and forth in a sharp, jerking motion.

16.

REPTILES

LAKE TURKANA, KENYA, 1972

16.: We had to wait patiently to photograph these crocodiles. I could have spent an hour photographing just the texture of their skin and the steely gaze of their eyes. It's hard not to be impressed by these prehistoric animals—they've hardly changed over the course of 130 million years. When a flock of plovers heralded our presence, the crocodiles rushed into the water with a great noise: The charm of the moment had been broken.

I can't rid myself of a certain mistrust of crocodiles. I've heard so many sinister stories about them, all of which remind me of the reptile's cruelty and unpredictability.

The crocodile's teeth are effective for seizing and holding on to prey, but not for tearing flesh apart or chewing it. To rip flesh from a corpse, the reptile plants its teeth firmly in its victim and rolls over in the water with it. The crocodile may stash a corpse underwater beneath the riverbank so that its flesh will become soft and chewable. Crocodiles feed only in the water.

17.

SERENGETI NATIONAL PARK, TANZANIA, 1972

17.: The first time I tried to photograph crocodiles, I scared them off. I didn't know that the animals could be more alarmed by my presence than I was by theirs—at least on this river in the Serengeti. I've heard that in other areas, such as on the Omo River, a man can run extreme risks.

While crocodiles can walk on dry land, they move with ease in water. Typically, they live along the shores of freshwater rivers and lakes in the world's warmer regions. The Nile crocodile of Africa swims in the ocean as well.

18.

18.: When I returned the following day, I stopped the car well away from the river. While walking silently, I heard a violent cracking noise in the water. I stopped in my tracks. A little further along, two crocodiles were fighting. One minute later, one of them glided across the river with a newly killed rabbit in its mouth.

The diet of young Nile crocodiles consists of dragonfly larvae, worms, crickets, beetles, and other insects. As the croc grows larger, it advances to toads, crustaceans, small birds, turtles, and the like, while mature individuals prefer to eat other reptiles and mammals.

19.

20.

MALINDI, KENYA, 1972

19. and 20.: It's possible in Malindi to find snakes on your bedroom window. These photos were taken directly from the hotel where I spent a night near Malindi. The entire coastal region—tropical, humid, and full of dense bush—is a veritable snake zone.

The speckled sand snake is called the "karimojong" throughout part of its range in the low-lying arid regions of eastern Africa. Handsome and sleek, the serpent has a gaudily colored skin that can be both speckled and striped.

21.

22.

SERENGETI NATIONAL PARK, TANZANIA, 1976

21. and 22.: One finds snakes in the most unexpected places. I came upon this one between the tent and the canteen where we kept our food.

The boomslang is a member of the Colubridae family of snakes. It can be vivid green tinged with yellow, or it can be olive green. This fast-moving snake prefers meals of lizards, chameleons, frogs, large eggs, and small rodents. A mature boomslang can be as long as 7 feet. The snake will inflate its neck when harassed, and its extremely poisonous bite can be fatal to humans. Boomslangs are primarily arboreal.

23.

24.

25.

26.

27.

28.

29.

NANYUKI, KENYA, 1978

23.: This snake bit the chameleon over and over again. The chameleon stiffened and contracted in spasms but continued to breathe for many minutes—a painful, extended death.

This speckled sand snake dines on a chameleon. The snake's diet consists of small rodents and lizards. Sand snakes move fast and frequent sandy, dry thornbush regions. During breeding, a combat dance can ensue among males when they compete for a female.

24.: The high-casqued chameleon is a favorite food item of boomslangs and various birds of prey.

The high-casqued chameleon, like most other chameleons, has the ability to camouflage itself by changing color. Its eyes can also swivel in complete hemispheres independently of each other. This lizard's most fearsome weapon is its tongue, which shoots out in lancelike fashion to fell passing prey. A sticky substance on the tongue's tip ensnares the chameleon's victim.

SERENGETI NATIONAL PARK, TANZANIA, 1973

25.: We discovered this python sleeping on a tree. We had time to calmly count out the eight loops of its length, each about 3 feet long, and to take some photos. When we came back three hours later, the snake had killed a Thomson's gazelle. I made the mistake of getting too close, and it immediately attacked the car, striking against the fender with its head. The noise was impressive. Without hesitation, I backed away.

The African rock python inhabits the central and southern regions of Africa, mainly in the open bush, scrub, and rocky outcrops. Monkeys, small antelope, wild pigs, and other small game are its favorite diet. The African rock python can grow as long as 32 feet.

ZEBRAS

TARANGIRE NATIONAL PARK, TANZANIA, 1987

26.: I was often astonished by the way these animals seemed to melt into the tall grasses of the Tanzania savanna—without seeming to even touch the invisible ground below. It seemed as though these zebras floated in a halo of light.

A subspecies of the plains zebra, the Grant's zebra lives from southern Sudan and southern Ethiopia down through Tanzania. It can be recognized by the particular width, closeness, and extent of its stripes, and by other subtle anatomical distinctions. Unlike the quagga zebra, which became extinct in the latter half of the nineteenth century (the last individual died in 1883 in the Amsterdam zoo), Grant's zebras and other northern subspecies number into the hundreds of thousands.

RUAHA NATIONAL PARK, TANZANIA, 1987

27., 28., and 29.: It took us three days of driving to get to Ruaha National Park: three days of bush as far as the eye could see and rows of baobabs bending against the wind. With my eyes on the ochre color of laterite, my spirit wide awake in spite of physical fatigue, I was only worried about one thing: engine trouble. I had all the necessary equipment with me to deal with a breakdown, including some 50 gallons of gas and 25 gallons of water.

In Ruaha National Park, the grass is dry and there are enormous quantities of dust. We met immediately with hordes of zebras, which were extremely curious about us. They rubbed against each other continually, noses against rumps.

Plains zebras maintain their family grouping, even when fleeing from potential danger. When threatened, zebras first gather together and then move off in a line, the highest ranking mare in the lead. The family stallion defends the group, at times aided by adolescent stallions, which stay behind to attack the enemy and then gallop to catch up with the group. When zebras meet, they greet each other by stretching out their necks and touching noses.

At sunrise, zebras head out in single file to graze; they have no specific territories of their own. They feed on grasses, leaves, and bark and also enjoy eating mineralized earth. They can go no longer than three days without drinking. Because zebras eat tall grasses, these equines open up grazing land for other species, thus playing an important role in the savanna ecosystem.

30.

TARANGIRE NATIONAL PARK, TANZANIA, 1976

30.: During one of my best trips to Tarangire National Park, the animals were abundant and the grazing areas rich. The herd fled at my approach, under the watchful eye of the dominant male.

Plains zebras travel in herds of tens of thousands across the open savannas of Africa. Within the herds, family units, which may include as many as twenty individuals, are preserved. The family typically consists of several mares and foals and one stallion. Mares devote their energies to their foals, while stallions work to keep the group together. Other groups consist purely of stallions.

31.

ANTELOPE AND GAZELLES

RUAHA NATIONAL PARK, TANZANIA, 1990

31.: The extreme wildness of the oryx makes getting close to this animal difficult. This time, I was fortunate. The oryx were in the right light at the right moment and gave me the opportunity to make this series of photos. The long, straight horns of these great antelope gave birth to the legend of the unicorn.

These oryx are of the fringe-eared variety, also called Kilimanjaro oryx. Nomadic animals that inhabit the steppe and savanna, oryx move about in pairs or small groups of six to several dozen individuals. Predators include hunting dogs, leopards, and lions, but the most serious threat comes from humans.

32.

33.

TARANGIRE NATIONAL PARK, TANZANIA, 1990

32. and 33.: It took the engine breaking down for us to discover this herd of female impalas in a clearing. The animals did not flee. I have to admit, I was initially preoccupied with fixing the motor. I didn't like the idea of spending the night out there on the side of the road. I didn't take the photos until later on that afternoon.

Sociable animals, impalas live in troops and herds that roam freely through established territories. In the mornings and late afternoons, impalas graze on short grasses, flowers, fruit, and foliage. Midday is reserved for resting. The females here may be members of a male's harem. Unlike the male of the species, female impalas have no horns.

34.

35.

SERENGETI NATIONAL PARK, TANZANIA, 1976

34. and 35.: The thickness of the waterbuck's fur makes this animal look soft in the light. In this photo, one sees the precise moment when, surprised, waterbucks act with perfect prudence. Whenever I come across them, there is always one brief moment before they decide to flee in terror or wait, frozen, for danger to pass. This is one of those moments.

The habitat of the common waterbuck, or defassa, consists of grassy savannas, gallery forests, and woodland patches. Nearby water is a requirement. The male's territory is localized, with individuals defending specific areas for as long as a year.

36.

37.

38.

40.

41.

TANA RIVER DELTA, NGAO, KENYA, 1973

36.: At the marshes of the Tana River, I came across this reedbuck, which was as surprised as I was. This is the only successful photo I have taken of this animal in twenty years. Reedbucks are fearful and have been extensively hunted.

This female reedbuck is probably of the mountain or the Bohor variety, both of which live in eastern Africa. Both species frequent open grassy areas, stony hills, mountains, and outcroppings. The mountain reedbuck can go without water for a long time, while the Bohor must find a water source frequently. When hunted, both lie flat on the ground and then leap up at the last moment.

RUAHA NATIONAL PARK, TANZANIA, 1990

37.: This female gerenuk, alerted to an alien presence, attempted to find out where the danger was coming from. Also known as the giraffe gazelle, the animal maintains a highly stylized stance no matter what it is doing—even as it stretches its neck to tear off some acacia thorns.

The gerenuk, or Waller's gazelle, is an elegant animal with graceful, long legs and neck and a slender head. Its long legs allow it to stand erect and browse on the foliage of bushes and trees. This animal meets most of its water requirements with food. Chief predators are cheetahs, leopards, lions, servals, hunting dogs, caracals, and hyenas.

39.

CATS

SAMBURU DISTRICT, KENYA, 1977

38. and 39.: This was the second time I'd visited Samburu. With its soft light and charming chiaroscuro, Samburu exudes a feeling of well-being that enhances the sensuality and indolence—rather than the aggressiveness—of these felines.

Once common throughout Africa, the Near East, and India, the cheetah may be found today only in the steppes and semiarid regions south of the Sahara. In the Serengeti area, only about 150 cheetahs remain. The feline's predators include lions, leopards, hyenas, African hunting dogs, jackals, large birds of prey, and humans.

MASAI MARA GAME RESERVE, KENYA, 1990

40.: Even though the cheetah is able to run 72 miles per hour for 20 to 30 seconds, this one had just failed to catch a little antelope. Worn-out, panting for breath, sitting under the beating rain, it impressed on me a sense of terrible isolation.

Along with its extraordinary running ability, the cheetah has outstanding eyesight and good senses of hearing and smell. Its legs are long and slender, its body long, narrow, and greyhound shaped. Surprisingly, this cat has no roar, though it can growl, purr, hiss, and chirp.

Although the cheetah is the world's fastest mammal, it can only maintain its remarkable speed for about 960 to 1,300 feet. If it hasn't caught its prey by then, it must give up the chase. If it has been successful in its conquest, it must usually rest for twenty to thirty minutes before beginning its meal. Gazelles, hare, porcupines, oribis, dik-diks, impalas, and young warthogs are among the cheetah's prey. The cat needs little water and will drink a prey animal's urine in an emergency. The cheetah usually hunts by day.

41.: This photo challenges the reputation that lions are "king of the beasts." This lion was so out of breath from overeating that it was unable to walk. An excess of food is one reason for the lion's short life span, an average of only twenty years.

Lions may justifiably be called lazy animals; they rest twenty hours out of every twenty-four. They require shady areas (beneath or in trees and thickets) for their repose, and lion cubs can die of heat prostration if left exposed too long in the sun. But lions eschew dense forests, needing open country ranging from semiarid desert to moist savanna.

42.

43.

44.

45.

46.

47.

48.

49.

SERENGETI NATIONAL PARK, TANZANIA, 1985

42.: For an hour, these two young lionesses played as if I weren't there. Entranced, I didn't move a muscle. I took these photos without any particular aesthetic intention—just for the pleasure of it.

Female lions, renowned as huntresses, often form groups and alliances with other females to share a territory. Extremely social animals, lions are most often seen in large family groups consisting of a few males and up to fifteen females with young of various ages.

SERENGETI NATIONAL PARK, TANZANIA, 1974

43.: This was one of eight lions that came to investigate us at our campsite. The first time, at sunset, they seated themselves not far from us, and we had to start the car to scare them off. For their second visit the following night, we built a fire to keep them at bay. The third visit was the most startling. We were sound asleep when we heard a scratching noise around the tent, which began to move. Furious at being disturbed, half asleep, and heedless of the potential danger, André Martin emerged from the tent. The animal was busy pulling out the tent pegs. I watched as my friend picked up a piece of wood and began yelling at the lion. Subjugated, tail between its legs, it took off to find the rest of the pride.

With exceptional hearing, sight, and smell, lions are fearsome hunters of gazelles, antelope, zebras, and other midsized to large mammals. Lurking through the brush, the lion first stalks its prey to as short a distance as possible. In the ensuing attack, the lion tries to kill its prey with a bite to the neck or throat. The cat rarely attacks humans, and then only when old or wounded and unable to hunt normally.

SERENGETI NATIONAL PARK, TANZANIA, 1985

44.: At first, this lion watched me in a blasé manner. Although I was behind the wheel of the car, I felt completely unprotected, the bone and flesh object of the lion's attention. I was the only thing around to interest the lion. I took the picture and quickly left.

The "king of the beasts" produces its impressive roar to announce its dominance over a particular territory. Lions also send throaty calls across the terrain to guide one another back to home turf. When mating, the male lion moans, and the female purrs, groans, and growls; she roars when the male withdraws.

GORILLAS

VIRUNGA VOLCANO, RWANDA, 1987

45. and 46.: This volcanic zone in the center of Africa shelters tropical forests unique in the world. To arrive at Rwanda's gorilla reserve, one walks along branches 6 or 7 feet above the ground and is continually threatened by the leaves of giant nettles. This park was under the administration of Jean Pierre Van der Becke, who was responsible for the African Wildlife Foundation's Mountain Gorilla Project.

Gorillas awaken between six and eight o'clock in the morning and then spend roughly two hours at their first feeding. Preferred foraging grounds are at the edges of dense forests, where the apes find ample offerings of leaves, buds, stalks, roots, fruits, ferns, and fungi. A favorite food is wild celery. Gorillas are strictly vegetarian and eat meat only when trained to do so in captivity.

VIRUNGA VOLCANO, RWANDA, 1987

47., 48., and 49.: Gorillas live in families, or clans. Each group is given its own name by the park-keepers. If one personality dominates, the whole group is given that individual's name. Otherwise, the group simply receives a number. These apes are members of Group No. 6.

Wild gorillas are peaceful creatures whose only enemies are leopards and humans. Their behavior is not territorial or defensive: When gorilla troops cross paths in the rainforest, they may ignore each other or socialize briefly, but they do not fight. Older male gorillas may fight to win dominance over a female, but even this is rare. Gorillas are found only in the rainforests of Africa, with their range concentrated in two areas—in the west near the Gulf of Guinea and in the east from eastern Zaire to western Uganda and western Rwanda. Gorillas fall into three species: the western lowland gorilla, the eastern lowland gorilla, and the mountain gorilla. These species look alike, but close observation reveals distinctions in the length of hair (pelage), shape of the nostrils, length of the arms and legs, and other features.

50.

51.

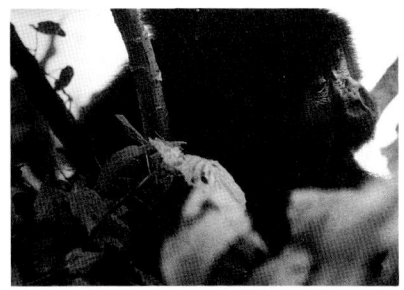

52.

50., 51., and 52.: As I approached this little ape, my arm brushed against the tree branches and created quite a commotion. The reaction of the Suza group of gorillas was instantaneous and violent. Then, as abruptly as it had begun, the deafening uproar stopped. Once again, the silence of the plant world reigned.

"Gorilla feeding habits go hand in hand with the politics of plant conservation," Jean Pierre Van der Becke explained. Each family consumes a small part of its territory, leaving intact three-quarters of the vegetation. The family will then repeat the pattern in an adjacent territory.

Gorillas are highly intelligent animals that have been trained to converse with humans using sign language. Among themselves, gorillas communicate using their throats and bellies. Rumbling sounds emerge from the primate as it eats, indicating pleasure. The gorilla uses sharp barking sounds to make its young behave and produces whooping barks when alarmed or frightened. Chest beating, roaring, hooting, screaming, and ground thumping are all behaviors that suggest a male gorilla's ferocious nature. The male also dashes from side to side and tears up vegetation. These displays are intended to intimidate the gorilla's male competitors and impress any females in the vicinity.

Gorillas, particularly the mountain gorillas of East Africa, face extinction due to the destruction of their habitat, the rainforest. Though outlawed, poaching still poses a threat. Only one hundred years ago, when Germany began colonizing East Africa, the mountain gorilla population numbered in the several thousands. Today, only four hundred individuals are believed to remain.

53.

Buffalo and Wildebeests

Amboseli National Park, Kenya, 1980

53.: I was on slightly higher ground than these buffalo when I took this picture, which allowed me to create a truly horizontal composition. The photo does not convey the clamorous noise the herd makes en masse.

Cape buffalo live in open terrain in eastern, southern, and central Africa. Frequently cattle egrets settle in large numbers on a buffalo's back. There the birds feast on horseflies, ticks, stable flies, and other insects that swarm around the buffalo's hide. While this occurs, the buffalo ceases its usual tail swishing and leg stamping to keep the insects at bay, allowing the birds to perform their task.

54.

Tarangire National Park, Tanzania, 1990

54.: Buffalo are dangerous animals, but it's quite possible to walk up to them. Gifted with keen hearing and sense of smell, the buffalo is extraordinarily mobile. Over a period of twenty years, I have been charged by buffalo many times. Along with the elephant, this is the animal that scares me most.

Cape buffalo can be identified by their powerful horns, which curve down and around to point up and in at the ends. In the center, the horns are fused together in a massive helmet shape.

55.

56.

57.

58.

59.

60.

61.

MASAI MARA GAME RESERVE, KENYA, 1986

55. and 56.: Here, at the end of their journey, the wildebeests were visibly tired. The thousands of beasts desired only to cross the river and carry on their migration, yet none seemed willing to take the risk.

Vast herds of blue wildebeest—sometimes as many as 400,000 individuals—migrate across the Serengeti-Mara plains after the rains.

57. and 58.: To me, the crossing seemed to last almost an hour. In reality, the wildebeests had forded the river in ten minutes, struggling against the flowing water, losing their footing in the effort. Not all of them made it: Several animals floated down the river bellies up. A little one got stuck between two boulders, not quite in the water but not yet on the shore. When I tried to move it, the jaws of a crocodile yawned open just behind it, then arched violently away, disappearing without touching the wildebeest.

Generally nomadic, Serengeti gnus settle in certain areas during mating season. Young wildebeests, usually born in February or March, are especially vulnerable, because the herd undertakes its migration in the rainy month of April. When the herd's route traverses a river, crocodiles take the opportunity to prey on the small and less sure-footed.

59.: These wildebeests, in an aura of light, illustrate perfectly what I've always loved about animals: a certain feeling of wandering. The richest possible tonal range—from black to white, passing through all shades of gray—adds to the aesthetic quality of this photo.

The gnus of the Serengeti wander the plain in herds searching out short grasses and other forage plants. Their migrations occur biannually, taking them to the southeast in the rainy season and the northwest in the dry season. Though gnus navigate water with some awkwardness, they are undeterred by rivers and other waterways in their migrations.

60.: While waiting on high ground, the leaders of the pack went back and forth endlessly on reconnaissance missions. In fording the river, they run the risk of encounters with crocodiles. Several times we thought they were going to cross, but they would always balk at the last minute.

We left for a while. When we returned the clamor had grown louder. Along the steep banks of the river, the dust began to rise, blocking out part of the sky: The wildebeests had begun their crossing.

Blue wildebeests, also known as blue gnus, fall prey to a range of predator species, including lions, spotted hyenas, Cape hunting dogs, leopards, cheetahs, and crocodiles. Young wildebeests are especially vulnerable to attacks by jackals and spotted hyenas, which are numerous in East Africa. Newborns are initially safe from these predators, because gnus give birth to their calves surrounded by other members of the herd.

BIRDS

TARANGIRE NATIONAL PARK, TANZANIA, 1976

61.: It took two days to get from Nairobi to Tarangire National Park by car. I don't think I've ever had so many flat tires and engine problems as during those forty-eight hours. One must keep in mind that as many as 620 miles can separate one park from another. The car had to hold its own, and we did too. I saw this plover near the car.

Plovers are rather forward, noisy, and restless birds that inhabit marshes, shores, and open country. Their favorite foods include mollusks, worms, various insects, and the larvae of water-breeding insects.

62.

63.

64.

65.

66.

AMBOSELI NATIONAL PARK, KENYA, 1973

62.: My first pelicans. Tired after a day of driving and lying in wait for animals, I had decided to head back to camp when I saw these birds alight on a pond. I waited until they had gathered together for the night ahead, then got out the tripod and started walking toward them. What followed reminded me of a comic ballet. Every time I advanced, the pelicans retreated, always keeping the same distance between us.

On the ground, the white pelican has an awkward and slow gait, but when airborne, this huge bird flies with powerful and majestic wingbeats. When migrating, pelicans fly in straight lines or in V-formation.

VIRUNGA NATIONAL PARK, ZAIRE, 1987

63.: The fishing grounds of Vitshumbi are a dream location for a photographer. One never has to wait for the birds to come; they're always there first, patiently awaiting the return of the fishers from Lake Edward. One only has to see the pelicans strolling around the fish market to understand their extreme familiarity with humans.

Essentially gregarious birds, pelicans often fish cooperatively in groups. They catch medium-sized fish by scooping their bills rapidly into the water; fish are held in their neck pouches, called gular sacs.

VITSHUMBI FISHING GROUNDS, VIRUNGA NATIONAL PARK, ZAIRE, 1987

64. and 65.: The fishers had just come in from Lake Edward when the huge bird arrived. I wasn't shooting anything in particular at the time. I heard the sound of wings beating behind me and had the feeling that I would do best not to turn around. I simply raised the camera above my head and aimed. The bird crossed into range. It was only later that I realized I had photographed a marabou.

If ever there were a bird put to advantage by flying, it's the marabou. Though clumsy and ugly on the ground, with a fleshy gular sac hanging from its neck and a bald head, the marabou is graceful in the air. It is sought for the feathers found under its wings, which are used to make feather boas.

The marabou is an enormous, hulking stork easily identified in flight by its massive bill. Its eating habits resemble those of a vulture: It locates carrion from on high and swoops down. The marabou also feeds on frogs, other birds, and locusts. It walks with its head lowered between its shoulders and its gular sac swollen up.

Marabous live in tropical climates along broad, shallow rivers. They frequent lakeshores and sandy riverbanks but are also able to live in drier areas such as savannas. The marabou is fond of perching in treetops.

RUAHA NATIONAL PARK, TANZANIA, 1990

66.: These birds, francolins, don't like to fly. Their plumage blends into the high grasses and acts as a good camouflage. The francolin likes to walk along roads and can sometimes be seen near the tires of a car.

The yellow-necked spur fowl is the most common of all francolins in Kenya and northern Tanzania. Its habitat includes open bush country, the peripheries of forests, and dry country. In the early morning and at dusk, the yellow-necked spur fowl calls out with a *graark, grak, grak.*

67.

68.

69.

70.

71.

67.: I sometimes saw this bird from the car walking alone or in pairs. It can also be seen by herds of wildebeests.

In one of a few different displays intended to intimidate or impress, the male kori bustard—inflates its neck, raises its crest, and ruffles its feathers. This is the fighting stance. Kori bustards inhabit open grassland plains and open thornbush.

MASAI MARA GAME RESERVE, KENYA, 1990

68.: The spoils of a zebra are evidence of a cruel cycle. The animal was killed and devoured by lions, the remains polished off by hyenas before vultures moved in to take their share—but not without first engaging in a beak-and-claw tussle to get at the booty.

The vulture is primarily a scavenger feeder and rarely attacks or kills prey itself. It feeds mainly on the soft tissues of medium-sized to large animals. Individual birds search singly for food but will congregate with others around a carcass. Both parents feed nestlings by regurgitation. Vultures are silent birds except when they spot a kill or are hissing and bickering over it.

ARUBA TSAVO, KENYA, 1973

69: I discovered my first secretary bird near the dam on the Aruba River. This bird has an eighteenth-century demeanor: mannered and precise. It is both seductive, with its red and yellow markings around the eye, and fearsome as a snake hunter.

The secretary bird is a conspicuous, large, long-legged, and long-tailed bird that frequents open plains, bush country, and farmlands. It is a formidable predator of snakes and rodents, particularly rats. The bird kills its prey with a strong, downward stamping of its foot. It gets its name from its crest, which reminds one of the quill pens that office clerks once kept behind their ears.

ARUBA TSAVO, KENYA, 1973

70.: The hammerkop is the bird that most inspires sympathy in me. Its vocation is as a great builder of nests. These nests can be gigantic, and the female hammerkop, when dissatisfied, will insist that it be built all over again.

The hammerkop has spawned more legends in Africa than any other bird. Many tribes believe that it is bad luck to disturb or injure a hammerkop in any way. These birds build huge nests high in trees, sometimes taking six months to assemble them. They construct the nests primarily with sticks but decorate the outsides with all sorts of materials.

AMBOSELI NATIONAL PARK, KENYA, 1972–1973

71.: I was driving across the Amboseli plain when I saw this heron walking in the grass, probably out hunting. By the time I stopped, it was in the process of swallowing a snake, still pursuing its route, unperturbed.

The black-headed heron is a tropical African species that breeds in dry and damp open areas. When on the ground, this solitary bird walks with careful steps; in the air, it flies slowly. Hunting behavior is also slow, patient, and deliberate. The heron spears fish, amphibians, and small mammals with its bill.

72.

GREAT RUAHA RIVER, TANZANIA, 1990

72.: This goliath heron is a giant, nearly 5 feet tall. I see these birds every time I come to Africa and have always been impressed by their fragile elegance. My greatest regret is that I've never been able to get really close to one—they're so shy, always keeping their distance.

Standing almost as high as man, the goliath heron is a gigantic and heavy bird. It inhabits both coastal and inland waterways and especially likes the shores of large rivers and lakes. Goliath herons sometimes feed in pairs, but they are usually solitary. They are rarely seen in the vicinity of humans.

73.

LANGUE DE BARBARIE, SENEGAL, 1991

73.: I had often heard about the terns and sea swallows on the Senegal River estuary in western Africa. My work would have been incomplete without these birds from the Langue de Barbarie and the Djoudj Reserve, important nesting grounds. This day, I had taken a boat to get to the island in the middle of the river. As I approached, the birds took off, hanging stationary in the air above their nests. Some did not hesitate to attack me.

Included in this mass of gulls are the black-headed and sooty varieties. Some may be winter visitors from Europe; others, like gray-headed gulls, commonly breed by African lakes.

74.

RUAHA NATIONAL PARK, TANZANIA, 1990

74.: Far from Dar es Salaam and Nairobi, Ruaha National Park is neglected by tourists: It's a solitude that suits me perfectly. The animals are not overly shy, which makes for excellent working conditions. This ostrich was strutting about as calmly as could be.

The ostrich is the largest living bird, taller than man and one-and-a-half to two times heavier. The ostrich cannot fly but flees from danger by running at speeds of up to 43 miles per hour. Its diet consists of seeds, roots, fruits, leaves, and flowers. The ostrich is well known for its habit of swallowing small, bright objects, such as coins, nails, keys, and the like.

75.

VARIOUS OTHER BEASTS

RUAHA NATIONAL PARK, TANZANIA, 1980

75.: In this area of the park, the grass had been burned, and these warthogs rolled happily in the ashes. They seemed unperturbed by the presence of the lion family sleeping in the shade of the nearby brush. I waited in vain for something to happen.

Warthogs, members of the pig family, camouflage themselves by wallowing in dirt, which adheres to their fur and skin. The skin itself is thin, and since warthogs have no subcutaneous fat, they can freeze at 32 degrees Fahrenheit. For this reason, these animals are often seen lying heaped together in cold weather.

76.

77.

MASAI MARA GAME RESERVE, KENYA, 1990

76. and 77.: Rain, gusts of wind, a glowering sky... the giraffes met all this head on. This series of photos is the most despairing of all that I took. Lake Victoria, nearby, generates storms of incredible violence.

At times reaching a height of 19 feet, giraffes are the tallest of all mammals. Their long necks consist of seven vertebrae, as in other mammals, but these vertebrae are very elongated. Though it is hard to miss a giraffe ambling across the open African savanna, the animal finds good camouflage within stands of trees. There, too, it can satisfy its considerable appetite, especially in stands of acacia. Despite its many thorns, the acacia's young leaves and shoots are the giraffe's favorite food. A large male can consume 75 pounds of food every 24 hours.

78.

SERENGETI, TANZANIA, 1972

78.: The world in reverse: This solitary jackal had been chased by a young antelope, which succeeded in wounding the jackal with its horns. More skittish than hyenas, jackals are usually the ones to yield when the two animals compete for a carcass.

The black-backed jackal, like other jackals, has a reputation for slyness and cowardice. It is thought to eat only the remains of carrion killed by larger mammals such as the lion. While the jackal will partake of a freshly killed carcass once the lions have had their fill, it will also kill for food itself. The jackal prefers a varied diet and may eat small mammals, insects, such as flying ants, reptiles, and fruit. The black-backed jackal is a denizen of the savanna.

79.

CAGUERA PARK, SOURCE OF THE NILE, RWANDA, 1987

79.: Blond grass covers the low hills surrounding the Caguera Park basin. This small mongoose emerged each morning and night from its burrow. I took this photograph near our tent before one of our daily excursions.

Banded mongeese inhabit dry and moist savannas south of the Sahara Desert. Unless the weather is excessively hot, mongeese spend most of the day hunting down their favorite foods: insects, spiders, centipedes, scorpions, small mammals, birds, eggs, fruit, roots, shoots, lizards, amphibians, and snakes. Prior to eating a frog or other amphibians, the mongoose will roll it in the sand to remove the slime from its skin. While hunting, mongeese keep in contact with each other by issuing a continual twittering call.

80.

MASAI MARA GAME RESERVE, KENYA, 1972

80.: When fleeing, little black rhino follow their mother. With white rhinoceroses, the opposite is true. Today, only a few white rhino remain in Kenya. Though more numerous, the black rhino population is seriously diminished.

The bond between a rhinoceros mother and its offspring is extremely powerful. It is, in fact, the only stable relationship that exists between these otherwise solitary animals. Baby rhino can stand on their feet within an hour of birth and begin to nurse within three hours. Only one baby rhino is born at a time; the mother is devoted to this offspring until shortly before giving birth again.

81.

81.: Wallowing in the dust, this rhino fell asleep in the sun. I was able to get close without its hearing me. Little soft-beaked birds picked bugs off its skin. There was a rare tranquility in the scene.

Rhinoceroses spend a fair amount of time sleeping. They doze in the shade at midday and sleep as long as eight or nine hours at night. Three or four times a night, they may wake to eat, urinate, or defecate. Rhino habitats are varied and include open savanna, thick brush, or open forest. The animal is unable to live in hot, wet regions. Unlike elephants, rhinoceroses do not roam over large expanses of territory but confine themselves to a small home range.

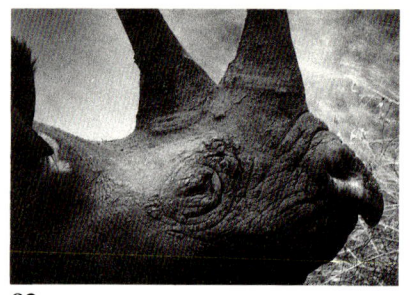

82.

NGORONGORO CRATER, TANZANIA, 1978

82.: To arrive at this crater, one follows a long road that rises from the Serengeti. On the lip of the volcano, you can see the impressive spectacle of hundreds of animals below. Guards protect the rhino from poachers.

A black rhino is no blacker than a white rhino. The two species are distinct chiefly in the shapes of their lips and bodies. The black rhino is a wandering animal, especially partial to twigs. Its large, pointed upper lip is well adapted for grasping leaves and shoots off trees. Compared to the white rhino, it is smaller but has longer legs. The lips of the white rhinoceros fit neatly together, allowing for efficient grazing; this species eats mostly grasses. While lions can endanger a stray young rhino, humans are the adult rhino's only enemy.

Bibliography

Arnold, Caroline, photographs by Richard Hewett. *Hippo.* Morrow Junior Books, New York, 1989.

Broadley, Donald G. *Fitz Simons' Snakes of Southern Africa.* Delta Books, New York, 1983.

Chivers, David. *Gorillas and Chimpanzees.* Gloucester Press, New York, 1987.

Cramp, Stanley. *Handbook of the Birds of Europe, the Middle East and North Africa—The Birds of the Western Palearctic.* Oxford University Press, Oxford, 1980.

Douglas-Hamilton, Oria. *The Elephant Family Book.* Picture Book Studio, Saxonville, 1990.

Grzimek, Bernard. *Encyclopedia of Animals.* Van Nostrand Reinhold Company, New York, 1968.

Haltenorth, Theodor and Helmut Diller. *A Fieldguide to the Mammals of Africa.* Collins, London, 1977.

Johnsgard, Paul A. *Bustards, Hemipodes and Sandgrouse—Birds of Dry Places.* Oxford University Press, Oxford, 1991.

Kevles, Bettyann. *Thinking Gorillas, Testing and Teaching the Greatest Ape.* E.P. Dutton, New York, 1980.

Kingdon, Jonathan. *East African Mammals.* 3 vols. Academic Press, London and New York, 1974.

Mackworth-Praed, C.W. *Birds of West Central and Western Africa.* Longman, White Plains, 1970.

Mattison, Chris. *Snakes of the World.* Facts on File, Inc. New York, 1986.

Overbeck, Cynthia. *Elephants.* Lerner Publications Company, Minneapolis, 1981.

Pitman, Charles R.S. *A Guide to the Snakes of Uganda.* Codicote Wheldon & Wesley, Ltd., London, 1974.

Sattler, Helen Roney. *Giraffes: The Sentinels of the Savannas.* Lothrop, Lee & Shepard Books, New York, 1989.

Schlein, Miriam. *Jane Goodall's Animal World.* Atheneum, New York, 1990.

Schmidt, Karl P. and Roger F. Inger. *Living Reptiles of the World.* Doubleday & Co., New York, 1957.

Smithers, Reay H.N. *The Mammals of the Southern African Subregion.* University of Pretoria Press, Pretoria, 1983.

Williams, John G. *A Field Guide to the Birds of East and Central Africa.* Houghton Mifflin, Boston, and The Riverside Press, Cambridge, 1964.

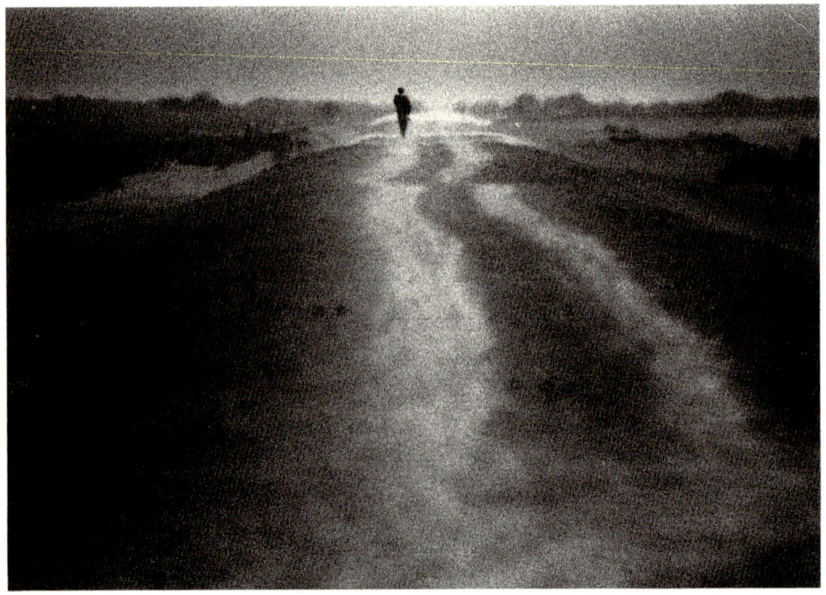

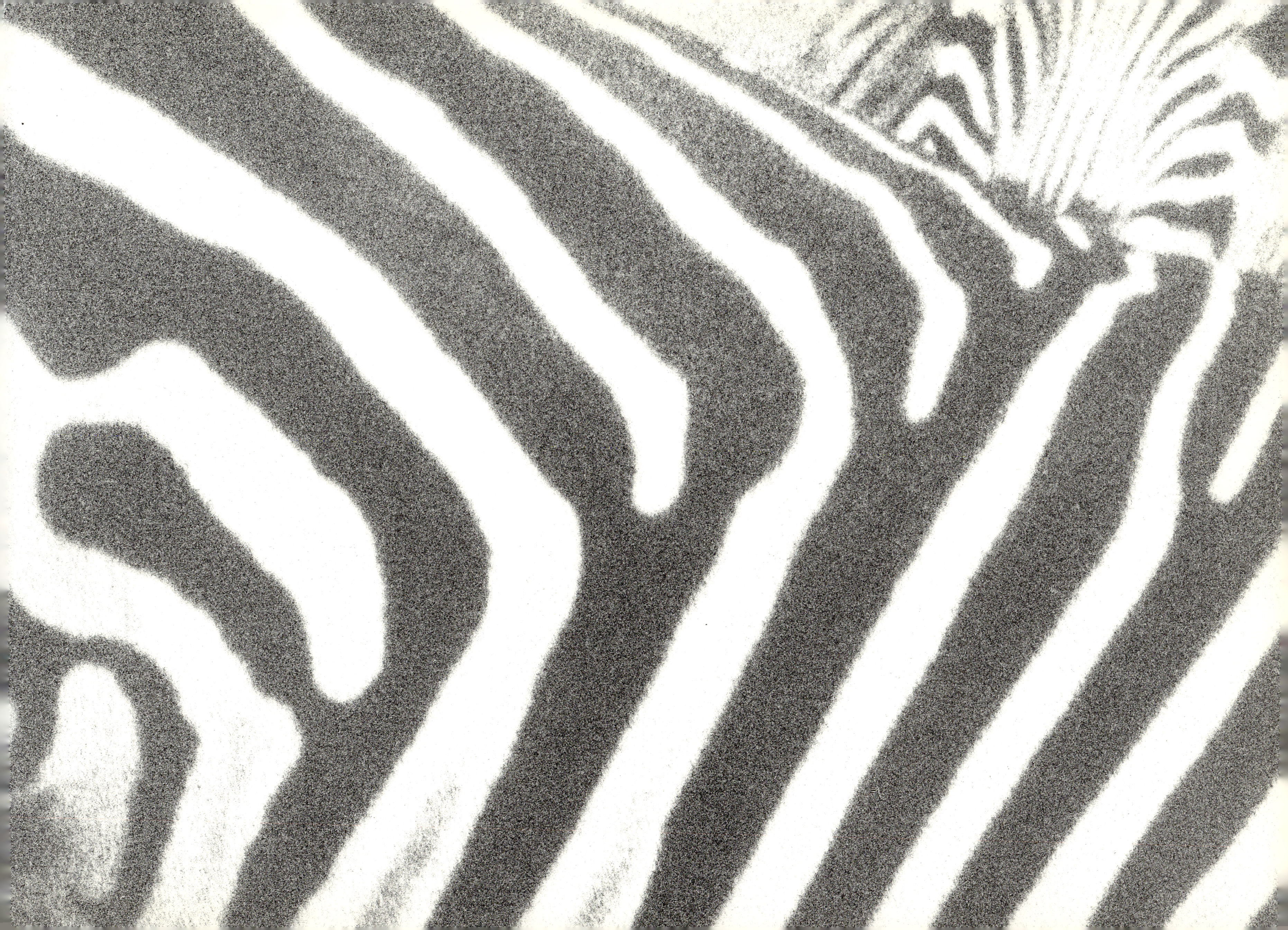

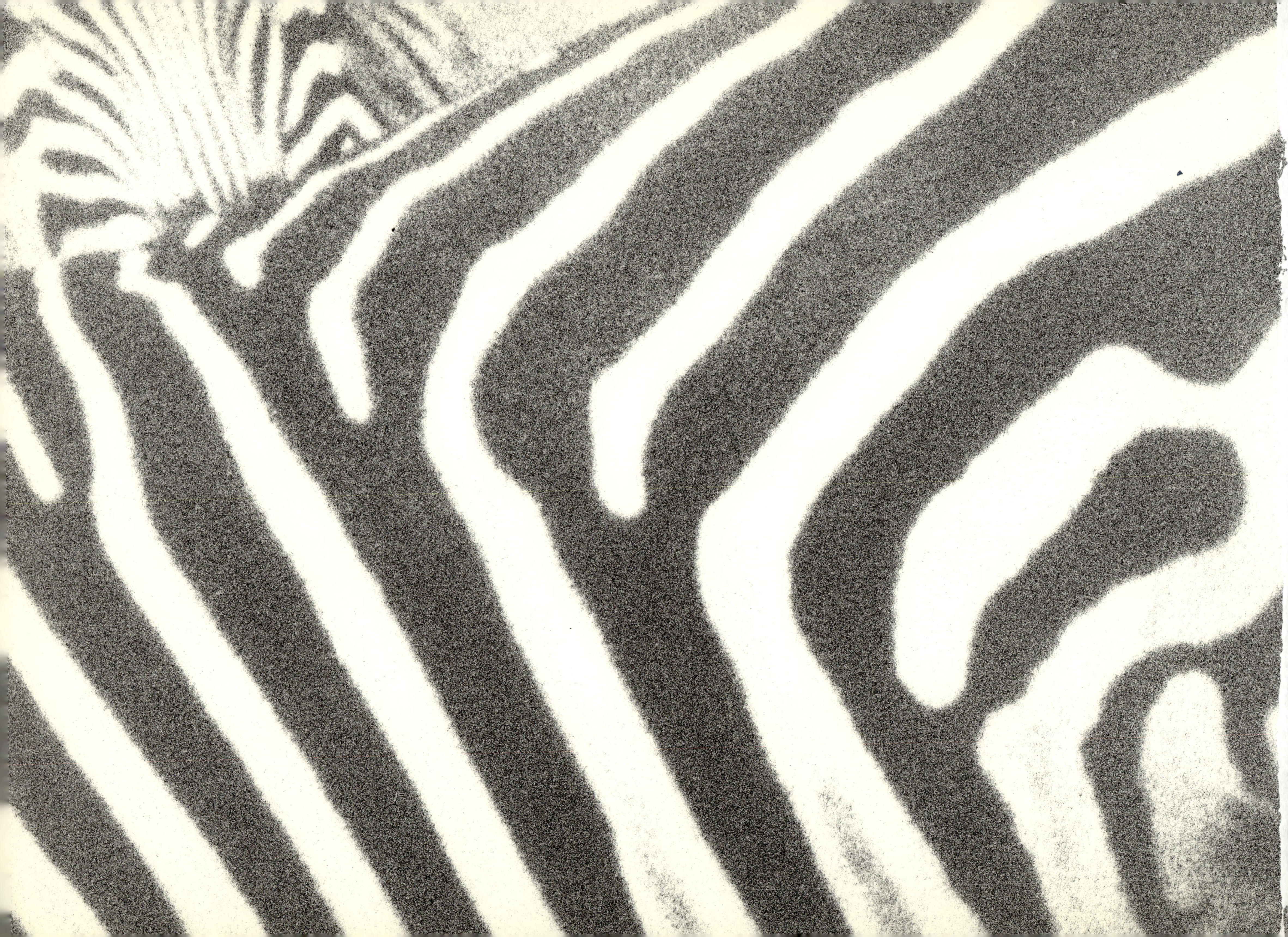

416